PENGUIN BOOKS
ONCE WAS BOMBAY

Bombay-born Pinki Virani, 42, a journalist for nineteen years, has risen from correspondent to editor. She has reported extensively on race relations from Britain and the politics of communalism from all over India. Pinki Virani holds a Masters in Journalism.

Pinki Virani's other best-selling books are *Aruna's Story* and *Bitter Chocolate: Child Sexual Abuse in India*, both firsts of their kind in the country.

W0232759

PINKI VIRANI

Once Was Bombay

PENGUIN BOOKS

An imprint of Penguin Random House

PENGUIN BOOKS

USA | Canada | UK | Ireland | Australia
New Zealand | India | South Africa | China | Singapore

Penguin Books is part of the Penguin Random House group of companies
whose addresses can be found at global.penguinrandomhouse.com

Published by Penguin Random House India Pvt. Ltd
4th Floor, Capital Tower 1, MG Road,
Gurugram 122 002, Haryana, India

First published in Viking by Penguin Books India 2000
Published in Penguin Books 2001

10 9 8 7 6 5 4 3 2

ISBN 9780140287912

Typeset in Garamond by SÜRYA, New Delhi

Printed at Repro India Limited

For the Journalists of Bombay who fight to preserve the sanity of this city under siege; and without whom it would have long since succumbed.

'We must become the change we seek in this world.'
Mahatma Gandhi

'Tis not the dying for a faith that's so hard—every man of every nation has done that; 'tis the living up to it which is difficult.'
William Thackeray

CONTENTS

ACKNOWLEDGEMENT

A work of non-fiction is impossible without qualitative inputs from professional people who take the time off to contribute in generous measure.

For this, and thus for ever, I am grateful to each and every person named—otherwise, too—in this book; as I am to Nurudin Virani and his daughters Numaish, Scherezade and Rozina. Plus, the Bombay Police; Somshekar and Varma Corporation for the usage of their song from *Satya*; scribes Nishi Prem, Dhananjay Karnik, S. Husain Zaidi and Gary Smith whose brilliantly conceived article in *Sports Illustrated* has influenced a section of this book.

No professional work is possible without personal support. For which I am relieved to have my friends Sandhya and Amitabh Pandey. And my landlord who gave me a flat to write in—unconditional shelter in a city such as this, it takes a good man to allow it.

I stand equally indebted to my editor Raj Kamini Mahadevan; and my two abiding pillars without whom I would quietly crumble, V. Shankar Aiyar and David Davidar. Romba kashtam kuduthen, romba tanx.

Thank you, all.

Who killed Bombay?
We did. Each of us who thought ourselves to be an island; and took positions to maintain personal privileges, purses and prejudices.

Who turned a shahar into a shamshaan ghat, our city into a crematorium, the fires of which keep burning as the corpses keep getting heaped on, in a city of gold now filled with ash?

Our politicians did. Every single one who has passed through the sewers *of* contemporary political history.

Beginning with Mohammad Ali Jinnah whom his doctors had informed that he had but a brief while to live, and yet he insisted on partition; heroism at any cost, uncaring of what would undoubtedly happen to those who preferred not to pack up and leave with him. They are still paying the price, the brave ones who believe this to be their only home; the sins of the fathers—even ostensible ones—always visit the children. This is God's way of ensuring that families learn.

And yet, karmically, we condemn ourselves to repeat history. That partition again in Bombay when Bal Thackeray chose to launch his movement which summarily excluded meritocracy. And then, once again—this time the final apocalyptic partition—when Lal Kishan Advani set out on his yatra of malevolence on a mechanized rath. Have they ever really cared about us, these men in Jinnah mould? Or our children—the traumatized survivors of riots and bomb blasts—whom they now insist must carry on, holding aloft their flaming torches of hate? Will they let our successors live out their dreams in the city of their birth; or must they be forced to leave their mothers and motherland so as to shut out the vituperation of their political successors?

We always liked to believe that Bombay was an island, unaffected by matters elsewhere in the state or the country. What a genuine shock it was to see for ourselves that something happening so far away to an old building should change our lives forever. As Justice B.N. Srikrishna puts it in his commission's report of the riots which followed the structure's demolition, 'The rath yatra clashes were thunderclaps portending the storm.' Now we have moderation as the BJP's mask-of-the-day and its family doing the rest, that jumble of alphabets in capital letters which indulges in low-intensity, localised communal sniping, carried out in relative quiet, while the state government looks away discreetly. Analyse Abheek Barman points out: As long as the head count is below some horrendous threshold, sniper fire does not penetrate upper-class consciousness, brutalized by caste violence, political killings and the daily din of religious fanaticism.'

But what about us, the middle class?

The workers, the taxpayers, the salaried, the ones forever condemned to remain anonymous and yet suffer the most because every government has claimed to be for the poor and been by the rich? Us, who have converted the mechanics of a civilized life in Bombay into its centrality? We, who have brought to this city with our behaviour the inherent decency of a Madras and the day-to-day intellectualism of a Calcutta? Yes, we came into our own after liberalization when we became a cynical campaign cool of a marketing strategy for filling glossy publications with advertisements—the great gullible middle class, buyers of anything sub-standard and over-priced but with a foreign label. We did not bite, we are habitually circumspect; we were promptly forgotten. The middle class rules in the West, but middle class India has always been ignored by even the supposedly socialistic politicians. Thus *our* own history never champions our cause; and because we do not champion our own—instead we make deals to survive—history never feels sorry for our exclusion.

We are led to believe that events outside our homes should never touch us. 'Go to office, open your shop, keep working,' they exhort, 'don't chink about it, just manage, adjust, we will take care of everything.' And we go, lambs to an everyday slaughterhouse, proud to be Bombay's backbone even if we never receive anything concrete in return for it. And now see how foolish we are, how trusting, because as we look at past newspapers and police records—the two tellers of Bombay's greatest truths—we find that *we have* been had. To use apun ka Bombay ka language, 'Solid chutya banaaya.'

When the British had to be sent back home we were out on the streets, shoulder-to-shoulder; during the Indo-China war we took off our bangles for our jawans; 'Aye mere watan ke logon, jo shaheed huye hain unki zara yaad karo kurbani.' Dying every day cannot constitute a shaheed, and thus there can be no 'aankh mein paani' for us the middle class. And we must also remain dry-eyed; what else can we be.

We can only avert our eyes and try and hold our breaths as we journey through the corridors of our city every morning, every night in return direction, aching but without fail. Trying not to look into those miles upon mile of slums, on the one hand; ugly but expensive buildings on the other. They say the slums first came up because of floods and droughts elsewhere in the country, records suggest that latter-day migration has been from Maharashtra's small towns and villages because there is not enough to keep them there. But isn't our state supposed to be the most progressive and where is all that money going when Bombay is paying through its nose to support several states as the country's commercial capital? They say the buildings are expensive because they came up hurriedly to house this flood of rich people who came from Karachi and Sind during partition; the structures are ugly for the same reason, no time to design them. Therefore the only architecturally interesting buildings of Bombay are the ones put up by the British and the art deco ones on Marine Drive and Shivaji Park which came up a little later.

So, here we are caught between what is always called the 'filthy' rich but never the 'stinking' poor. Well, we must just return to our one-bedroom flats to convert some space into a toilet-cum-bathroom so that the bathroom can become the kitchen and so that the kitchen can become the second bedroom and the child's study table can go to the living-room balcony and the balcony can be enclosed to make place for it; the grills can go up on the balcony and right around the house because bullets ricochet these days; and on these grills can be stored all that for which there is no place any more in the tiny house, the tricycle, the big cooking pot, that trussed-up bundle of clothes to be ironed, whenever there is time, on the pressing-table folded up behind the bedroom door.

The politicians said Bombay must be with Maharashtra and when their clamour peaked in the late fifties we looked away as they beat up the Gujaratis who wanted the city for their state; not that being in Gujarat would have been any different as is now being proved. They said everyone must speak Marathi and we set up expensive tuitions for our children; now their children go to English schools and their families produce Hindi pictures. For a brief moment there, a very small while, we wondered aloud if Bombay could simply be a city-state, that would have been splendid, but we were shouted down, by the industrialists who saw this as a curtailment of their business interests, by the politicians who looked at it that way too. No chance of it happening still, even though the industrialists might well agree today, and Bombay certainly generates enough money to take care of itself; it would be wonderful though, a sustainable solution to most of Bombay's current problems.

Bombay as a city-state: just think about it; most of the politicians leaving the city and taking their nurtured voters with them, the unclogging of state government as we now see it, a chief and his management-experts—chosen by us, paid by us, answerable to us—from the best of our bureaucrats, to run our city's corporation. Bombay the city-state: a model for the rest of the country and internationally.

Ah, this couching naïvete. If wishes were horses would not the middle class be cantering by now?

In the meanwhile we must keep swiveling our chins. As when we looked away when they beat up the South Indians and burnt their shops because they spoke better English and were good at accounts. We averted our eyes when the goons went to where the Sikhs live in the city and demanded protection money while other goons beat up their brethren in Delhi after her guards shot Indira Gandhi. After that we never sat in a sardarji's taxi even if the man's cab was the only one available; earlier our fathers would make sure that we flagged down only such taxis to take us back home after the night-show pictures. How must they have felt, those sardarjis when we just went away from them; and those sardarni widows who waited, and waited, for justice and fought for it for so many years to indict that black-spectacle wearing politician in Delhi? Is this how the Muslim widows must feel, after the Srikrishna Commission report which indicts similar spectacle-wearers and justice is not seen to be done?

We look away, anyway, when they keep terrorizing people from communities, religions, castes and sub-castes not our own. Muslims, turned into the M-word. Now Christians, a C-word. Ayodhya, so far away and yet each brick they tore down there added one more in our neighbourhood.

What should we do now? Vote with our feet when the elections come, kick them all out, this time forever, and induct fresh politicians? But lots of very rich people are not going to let this happen because once again, Bombay is not an island and that which happens elsewhere has to affect us. Yet again. The big shots will keep both fronts fed and funded—the Congress and BJP—as one will always be in power with the other one waiting. Besides, what worth are middle class votes in what the politicians have twisted into a virtuous hoax which we call democracy?

But vote we will have to, in full strength this time. To understand what this can mean, look at the last election's scenario: fifty-five crore voters were on the poll list, a 60 per cent turn-out means that thirty-three crore voted, 30 per cent of this went to the BJP, that is 9.9 crore people. Ergo, 9.9 crore decided for 98.9 crore people who their leader should be, a little over 10 per cent of the population sealed the fate of an entire country. No choice this time but to vote for MPs and MLAs who will truly represent us; only then can Bombay finally get a set of politicians who will be city-born and middle class. Not small-town hicks who go berserk at the first sight of power and glamour, not feudalists and rapists, murderers, rioteers, extortionists and chain-snatchers; not henchmen of politicians who are puppets of gangsters in Dubai and Malaysia.

How to manage this? Ignore everything that they tell us about supposed stability and fractured mandates; they are the liars and the hypocrites who have been exhorting us all along to 'live with India's differences'. Why can't they make equally honest attempts within coalitions when we throw up these differences in our mandate? Why should we deny our desires to give them 'stability to govern'? A few facts here, courtesy *India Today*, on Italy in the context of how coalition governments do not necessarily have to ruin a country. Number of governments since 1948—in India, fourteen; in Italy, forty-plus. Number of political parties—India, thirty-one; Italy, twenty-five. The GDP ($ billion, 1997)—India, 347; Italy, 1,155. Per capita income (in dollars, 1997 figures)—India, 390; Italy—20, 120. The lesson: coalitions did not derail the Italian economy, rather it has played an enabling role, because it is rooted in the principle of a free and open market. Government, anyway, has no business being in business. But are Indian politicians willing to release the country's economy from their tight leashes when they can so easily control it in name of neo-swadeshi and pseudo-socialism?

And so let us—for the first time in our lives since our country's independence—not pay attention to these political parties. And let us, instead, vote for the most able candidate. Ignore the candidate's party; look, instead, for education, a progressive background, lack of criminal record, that much-maligned word secularism, genuine sincerity, real passion for change and the capacity to make that difference for us. Or else, we, the middle class will once again condemn ourselves to catatonia, functioning in a swarming inchoate mass with merely fixed points on any given day in our lives: the office, temple-church-mosque, home, the kitchen. Worse then, for the middle-class woman who cannot explore her potential or further her talents in a structure determined to categorize women strictly between the have and the have-nots; the chiffon and the chulha; and damn the woman in between. She cannot find herself? She can keep railing against fate and descend deeper into madness.

The political parties will increase their din, suggesting that we are responsible for their mistakes. They—who cannot deal with each other—promise us stability. But what are they actually feeding us while frightening us into submission? Herd poison. When we finally looked in that direction during the riots we saw the cumulative effect of this herd poison. We saw what happens to crowd behaviour—inclusive of the police in the crowd. Psychiatrists say that when fed herd poison over years people lose their power of reasoning and their capacity for moral choice; their suggestibility is increased to the point where they cease to have any judgement or will of their own. They are subject to sudden excesses of rage, enthusiasm and panic. Every man, and woman, in that crowd, then, is one who has swallowed a large dose of that painful intoxicant called herd poison. It is an active, extravagant drug; the politicians who dispense it know this well.

There are politicians and there are politicians who change things for the better. We live in the world of the former, the politicians. But Bombay—and, indeed, the rest of India—is too dangerous a place now for its problems to be dealt with successfully by today's mediocre and parochial politicians. We must vote for leaders who will shape our future, not those who want to survive the present at any cost.

But let us, also, be brutally honest with ourselves. Will a new government really change anything? Will the courts function faster, will the police stop being communal, will the municipal corporation be less corrupt, will gangsters simply go away, will government actually function?

No, of course not to that immediate degree; but we know that new brooms are supposed to sweep clean and only we can make this happen. We will have to, nobody else has ever done it for us anyway. We cannot wander like this between two worlds: one dead, the other powerless to be born. Where nothing feels real and nobody really feels. No, we cannot continue living in this wasteland of crooked deals and listless souls.

So let us not underestimate our own strength. The West was won by its middle class, it made its presence soundly felt, unitedly, over an extended length of time till the present. Today the western middle class has its own culture—that of contentment—and no politician dares to use fear as the key to sabotage it. No inner-city dweller uses his poverty as a justifiable excuse to be bestial towards the middle class, breaking the windscreens of its cars bought on instalments, burning its buses, stopping its trains. And yet it is not a world that has been won without difficulty—for men have had to listen to their daughters, women have had to tell their sons how to behave. Everyone has had to confine religion strictly to their homes and rein in their prejudices. Self-discipline in most middle-class localities in the West has swept away garbage, including that from the past which destroys the present; or else the future can get lost in this conflict.

Yes, it is time to do our real dharma, and God knows there are as yet tough times ahead. But we will be sending out a message—which we will have to ensure we sustain—to the politicians that it's over boys, it is time to behave.

If we do not, then it is truly all over for our country and for our cities. For Bombay, for us and for our children. There will be no new millennium for the middle class, because the politicians will have strolled away taking our future with them. Khel khatam, paisa hajam.

July 1999   **Pinki Virani**

CRIME & PUNISHMENT

Manish Shah is not a bastard-builder. He is forty, married to Sarita, they have a boy and a girl, ages eleven and eight; the flat they live in is not in the spiffiest of buildings but it is family-owned and on Malabar Hill, the highest point of Bombay and thought, by some, to be an island unto itself.

Sarita and Manish Shah moved to America, to live very happily; but then they came back because his family in India said matters were improving after liberalization and Bombay, too, as a consequence would change for the better. Manish Shah returned, assisted his brother in their family construction business and then set up his own, Dhruva Builders, named after his son. When he thought of doing this he consulted his childhood friend and good pal since twenty years, Yogesh Shah, and together they set up this new venture less than five years back.

It is 9 a.m. and Manish Shah is getting ready to leave for the office of Dhruva Builders, on the main island, in the once-walled area called Fort. On his way down Malabar Hill, at the curving sea-hugging sweep which leads to Chowpatty, he will pass the site on which he hopes to build a penthouse for himself. The plot is a hundred and fifty thousand square feet, Dhruva Builders is to develop only a part of it. On this part he will build Sahnidhya, meaning togetherness; they have thought up the name jointly, Sarita and he, Yogesh and his wife Malvika. Sahnidhya will have only six floors plus the penthouse and it will be a fine building, with good construction material and aesthetic detailing, not some new-money architectural horror.

There have been the typical problems, by-now standard in Bombay for any builder, in the land's initial development. Plus one killing. The man shot dead is Vallabh Thakkar, known to appease all kinds of gangsters as long as he could continue putting up his buildings. Manish Shah is aware of this, so when Vallabh Thakkar suggests he develop a portion of the land, Manish is hesitant. He discusses it with Yogesh, their behind-the-scenes strategist.

'What do you think?'

'You first tell me why you are so uncomfortable about it.'

2

'Builders are supposed to be outright bastards or else they can never manage to put up even one structure in Bombay. We don't know how to be bastards.'

'True, but we are managing with our other projects, perhaps not the way we would like to, but we are being as decent as possible under the circumstances. There are no laws in this city which allow for happy housing, not for the buyers or the sellers.'

'I keep thinking that we are not cut out for this line.'

'May be we are not, but this is where we have earned our money and where is the alternative just now? We are committed to our current projects and we have to finish them, a lot of our money is tied up in them.'

'So what do you want to do about Vallabhbhai's offer?'

'Can we be absolutely clear-cut—one hundred per cent certain—that the part of the land we develop will have no encumbrance?'

'I honestly don't know.'

'Then let us talk to him and if we are satisfied, we will do a small bit of the land, perhaps just one good building.'

Manish Shah laughs, 'Yeah, I will put my penthouse on top, a good home for my kids, and then we will get out of this line.'

He visits the site. On Vallabh Thakkar's side of the land, he notices an encroachment, a cult has put up its board overnight, sent some people to occupy the dilapidated building which is to be pulled down; one of the squatters approaches him. 'This is our land, our swamiji meditates on it when he comes to Bombay.'

Manish tells the man this does not concern him as he has nothing to do with that part of the land.

'The whole thing is ours, this is the highest point of land in all of Bombay, and swamiji needs open land to meditate, you cannot construct anywhere on it.'

Manish patiently tells the man that he should take up issue with Vallabh Thakkar, as far as he is concerned his side of the land has an absolutely clear title.

'You are denying a Hindu the right to practise his religion properly? Be careful, you can get into trouble, swamiji has many followers among corporators and ministers.'

Manish Shah shortly tells the squatter he can go and complain to the police, he will prove his credentials to the law and order network of the city and not to some goon. Manish leaves and when he speaks to Vallabh Thakkar about the incident, he is assured that all is being taken care of.

Vallabh Thakkar is shot dead. Appeasement is actually an alligator. That carnivore which you feed thinking that at least it will not eat you until the last.

Dhruva Builders decides, given the situation, to defer construction for a while.

Morning, nine o'clock, and Manish Shah will drive past the land looking at it with some longing, a feeling not any different from the kind which smites anyone who—some day—wants their own home. He will drive himself, the driver has been absent since a few days. The cleaner has just finished washing the car and moves with his bucket when Manish Shah walks towards it.

Santosh Adivalekar, alias Bandya, is standing at the bus stop across the road, waiting in the balmy, February-morning sun. With him are three men, and the squatter. The squatter points towards Manish Shah and walks away. Bandya crosses the road, enters the building's compound with his men and shoots Manish Shah dead in the front seat of his car.

Manish Shah was not a bastard-builder.

B ut how is inspector Vilas Nimbalkar to know this when the phone rings at Malabar Hill police station? It's a fine bungalow, the old Wireless House, which the Malabar Hill police uses until they shift to their own place closer to the foot of the hill. Inspector Nimbalkar likes the building and its high ceilings, he is not looking forward to shifting to what is bound to be kachra construction, builders and their contractors cheat too much these days.

Nimbalkar has come to Malabar Hill only recently, his first case was that of builder Dilip Walecha being shot by Dawood Ibrahim's men. After that most complaints from Malabar Hill have been servants doing in their employers, the memsaabs getting stabbed in the afternoons. These are educated people who have travelled the world, why don't they check out their servants and building's watchmen before employing them, photograph them, have them registered with the police? Nimbalkar shakes his head and picks up his extension when it rings. Another builder shot dead, some Manish Shah.

He takes constables and leaves for the spot; the victim has been rushed to the hospital. He leaves some constables there to speak to the car's cleaner, start with the preliminaries and drives to the hospital; the victim has been declared dead on admission. Inspector Nimbalkar opens a file and meticulously begins work on the investigation, every detail is recorded between those two pieces of cardboard; the file become thick, and thicker as the Bombay police chips in.

Manish Shah has been shot with two kinds of guns, a .455 revolver and a 7.65 pistol. They fired nine rounds on him, one live cartridge fell to the car's floor, nine bullets embedded themselves in different parts of the car, some after travelling through him, and five in Manish Shah. There are fifteen injuries on his body, one bullet has gone in clean through his cheek and come out from the other side, some have riddled his back with little holes as he fell sideways in the front seat and they continued killing a dead man.

Bits of the car are removed, stuffing from seats, leather, scrapings from the door, shards of blood-stained glass, drops from the pools of blood, pieces of flesh from them, the bullets: these are securely bagged and sent to the laboratory; the car is sealed until it can be returned to the family. Manish Shah is examined, his is described as a 'well-nourished, cold body'; he is de-bulleted, post-mortemed, stitched-up and sent back to Sarita Shah.

A ll over the city builders, middle-level businessmen, producers and more receive the intended message through Manish Shah's death, those resisting till then immediately pay up; some to small-time extortionists taking advantage in a why-not-me-too manner. The phone also rings in the office of Dhruva Builders. A man asks to be put through to Yogesh Shah, the telephone operator says he is in an emergency meeting, the man aks, 'Pooncho, Manish Shah key paas jaane ka hain kya?' Does he want to join Manish? Yogesh takes the line.

'You saw, what we did to him?'

'Who are you?'

'Dekha key nahin, tumhara dost ko?'

'How do you know I am his friend?'

'We know everything. You saw his body? You counted the bullets?'

'Who are you? What do you want now?'

'Dagdi chaal se bolta hain, Sharad.'

'What do you want?'

'Maanga jabhi nahin diya, dekha na, kya hua?'

'What are you talking, you have never asked us for anything. We don't even know who you are, why are you calling me, why did you shoot him?'

'Chutya bananeka koshish nahi karneka, samjhaa kya? Waapas phone karenga.' Don't try to act smart, wait for the next call.

The line clicks into a long tone. Yogesh Shah puts down the receiver, picks it up again and in a daze dials home. Is everyone okay, Malvika, the kids, his mother who slowly walks to the nearby temple at this time of the day? Everything is fine at home. For now. For ever? Yogesh walks into the cloakroom and splashes cold water on his face, he finds himself sweating inspite of the office being centrally air-conditioned, he leans against the cold wash basin and tries to collect his thoughts. The police? He should inform the police!

No, wait, that man said they know everything about him, what if they turn vicious when he calls the police?

He goes back to his cabin and tries, as calmly as possible, to go through the day; there is no other call and by the evening Yogesh Shah is convinced that someone has pulled a nasty prank. He replies to some more letters, speaks to some more people—the investors are still phoning, families who have booked flats with them are frantic with fear that the buildings may not be completed now that one builder-partner has been shot. Yogesh Shah realizes they feel he is going to be shot too, he is drained as he reaches home.

Somewhat relaxed after dinner, he resolves not to tell his family anything. The phone rings, he absently answers.

'Khana khaaya? Theek hai na, biwi bachaa? Maaji mandir se aa gaya?'

Yogesh Shah does not reply, he silently disconnects, and decides to ask for police protection for his family. It will be in place by the morning. It is a dark night, every sound and sensation is magnified; a car back-firing on the street, his heart beating . . .

Police inspector Vilas Nimbalkar is informed of this development and given instructions, re-arrest Arun Gawli.

Gawli is his caste, he comes from the milkmen community. Arun Gulab Ahir, whose father came to Bombay from Madhya Pradesh as a mill worker, settled in the Dagdi chawl of Byculla, a warren of rooms like the thousand others in an area filled with out-of-work men as the mills began closing down. Powerlooms located out of the city were more economically viable and producing cheaper and better cloth, unionism was acquiring militancy in the Bombay mills, the five-year strike in the early eighties sounded the death-knell for these mills and their workers. The young sons of these mill workers took to the streets, not willing to go back to their villages in Maharashtra, Madhya or Uttar Pradesh, uneducated and filled with resentment; a fertile breeding ground for crime and future footmen for unscrupulous politicians.

Arun Gawli, though, became a don by default. He hung around in the hooch dens and matka addas and played carrom in an atmosphere surcharged with the idea of finding a hero—any legitimate hero, and if he could not be found he must be invented—for the masses who saw themselves as deprived. Names like Rama Nayak and Babu Reshim were big then, underworld men, as was Parasnath Pandey, the matka king who was stabbed to death. Arun Ahir was picked up by the police in this connection but released. Thus was born the fame of Arun Gawli.

Dawood Ibrahim made the next move in adding to Gawli's aura, he invited him to join in the gold smuggling, Gawli declined, he preferred bootlegging. With the odd killing and assault thrown in, knives, bottles and swords flying thick and fast. Fate inadvertently assisted Gawli again, some men went into the Saat Rasta lock-up and finished Babu Reshim; Rama Nayak later got shot in an encounter. And while Dawood and the Pathans slugged it out among themselves for supremacy, Gawli moved in on Dawood's brother-in-law Ibrahim Parkar. He set out to be the head of the Byculla Company, getting an enormous push in this direction by the mouthpiece paper of a communal party which went to town on police inspector Madhukar Zende trying to scale down the size of a Ganapati idol.

Dons understand that religion is the opiate of the masses as much as politicians do. They set up huge idols in lavish pandals for the Ganapati festival. Varadarajan Mudaliar, Matunga's godfather-gangster, put up such a big idol each year and its cult spread so far and wide as the granter of wishes that someone as educated and worldly as Jaya Bachchan visited it when her husband was very sick. The size of his ego is directly proportionate to the size of his Ganapati idol during the festival. The then deputy commissioner of police Yadavrao Chinda Pawar understood this well and began systematically ensuring that Varadabhai's idol and pandal size be decreased. Finally, the Bombay police was able to build their own chowky in the centre with the complete cooperation of all the residents of the area, and Varadabhai's pandal was shifted to a corner of the road, thus scaling down its size.

The Bombay police is working on similar lines for Chota Rajan's Ganapati in Chembur, the gangster lives in Malaysia but ensures that a huge idol is installed during festival time in this Bombay suburb where his family resides. But during the late eighties, Madhukar Zende's crackdown on Gawli's Ganapati was rewarded with vitriolic editorials in the afore-mentioned mouthpiece the gist of which was: 'During Muharram the taziyaas of the Muslims get bigger and bigger, why does the police do nothing about it? Why should they think of reducing only the size of the Ganapati idols of aamchi muley?' Aamchi muley, our boys; taziyaas, the flower-bedecked religious symbols a section of Shia Muslims carry on themselves as they wind their way in an annual mourning procession.

The mouthpiece then declared, 'If the Muslims have Dawood, we have these boys.' This was just what Arun Gawli needed to turn into the answer for Dawood Ibrahim; B(yculla) Company would wipe out D(awood) Company. Gawli remained in favour of the communal party until he started his own in 1996, the Akhil Bharatiya Sena. A buoyant Bombay Stock Exchange, the city's building boom—gangsters in the underworld and other parties moved from demanding protection money to outright extortion—this being a democracy, one communal party already minting money in this pseudo-legitimate fashion fuelled Gawli's desire. Besides, Dawood was in Karachi, Abu Salem and Chota Shakeel in Dubai, Rajan in Malaysia with his aides Guru Satam and Rohit Verma in Kathmandu, Ashwin Naik in London. Ashwin's brother Amar Naik was killed in an encounter by the police's ace marksman Vijay Salaskar in 1996. The stage was clear for Gawli to go legit.

Arun Gawli's Akhil Bharatiya Sena showed its strength with a massive rally in early 1997, which people were paid handsomely to attend; however Gawli, by now called Daddy, was conspicuous by his absence because he was expecting to be shot dead. Twenty sharp-shooters sent by

Chota Shakeel, a Dawood aide, were lined up on the top of several buildings in the Kala Ghoda area to gun him down. Mummy, Gawli's wife Asha, a devout Muslim turned equally devout Hindu, addressed the mammoth rally.

With Mummy taking care of the administration, Daddy turned to gathering resources for the assembly elections due before March 2000. He was sent to jail, he operated through cell phones and chits sent to his wife with instructions scribbled on them. Under each set of instructions written in Marathi he signed in English. One crore rupees was taken from Vallabh Thakkar and thirty lakhs 're-invested' with him on the condition that he return double the amount in one year. Vallabh Thakkar agreed, but was shot dead. By Gawli? By Dawood? By either of the Chotas, Shakeel or Rajan? Appeasement is an alligator.

Gawli felt that Vallabh Thakkar's son, Manish Thakkar, should pay up. Following Vallabh Thakkar's murder, the squatter on the Malabar Hill land approached Gawli's boys to lean on Manish Shah. Gawli was informed that Manish Shah could be the key to the money as he could speak to Manish Thakkar. Gawli then decided that his trusted lieutenant, Bandya, could get the money from Manish Shah since he was a partner in the land's development; Bandya could also shoot dead Manish Thakkar to frighten Manish Shah into submission. He sent his wife a note in Marathi: 'Asha, tell Raja to get Bandya to deal with the Manish Shah matter immediately.'

Bandya contacted the squatter and asked him to identify Manish Thakkar for them. The squatter—sensing this as an opportunity to settle that small score, seeing this as the best way to claim the land for ever—deliberately led the shooter to Manish Shah.

Santosh Adivalekar alias Bandya is declared absconding, as is one man with him, another is let of for lack of evidence by the courts, the fourth is out on bail, as is the squatter. Asha Gawli is arrested and released on bail, she is also given permission by the court to leave the city and go on a 'pilgrimage to Pandharpur'.

Arun Gawli is re-arrested by Vilas Nimbalkar and gets bail yet again.

He is on the line again, Sharad from Dagdi chawl. Yogesh Shah tells him that he has one request, Sharad should not call him at home again, he is leaving for the office now.

The small building in the middle of two prestigious colleges near Chowpatty resembles a fortification, tightly shut windows, grills, a wide cover for the main door. Security guards the entrance, a policeman in mufti cradles his AK-47, the people in the lane are pleased with him, that night he apprehended a robber for them. His driver takes the car closest to the entrance, keeps the engine running as Yogesh Shah quickly enters it, the policeman in mufti with his AK-47 gets into the front. They speed down Marine Drive, idle at lights and not one driver idling alongside raises an eyebrow at the sight of a gun in a car; the city is used by now to seeing people of all kinds with protection, especially its own politicians who appear to need the maximum of it.

Yogesh Shah reaches his cabin, slips off his shoes and prays. He settles into work, there is a bill on his desk, from the government for Rs 50,000 for the protection it has given him. He is looking at it in complete amazement when the phone rings.

'Dagdi chawl sey.'

'What do you want?'

'Kya, you are very angry today?'

'No I am not, I am just wondering what price my life has.'

'You want to know if we want a khokhaa from you? Chalo theek hain, we know you now, you can give us ten-twelve petis to start with.'

'That is all my life is worth, to start with ten-twelve lakhs? I will tell you what and you listen to me, I am not giving you a paisa, not a paisa, forget about khokhaas and crores later. You do what you want, understand?'

Yogesh Shah bangs down the phone, it rings again.

'You are really very angry today.'

'Listen to me, listen good, I don't care any more, I am telling you to please kill me. Do me a favour and let us finish this once and for all.'

He hangs up, takes a deep breath and laughs hysterically. He wonders who he can write a letter to; it would be amusing, if nothing else, to find out if politicians with protection get bills too and if they ever pay them.

The politicians are leaning on their police. 'The people want to know,' they piously proclaim, 'what the law and order is doing about Arun Gawli.' They are informed that the police is doing what it can within its legal framework.

Not enough, ordain the politicians.

Arun Gawli is served an externment notice in November 1998, his battery of lawyers force its temporary suspension notice by moving the High Court seeking quashing of the notice. Externment is an obsolete weapon in today's scenario; in Hindi film lingo it is called tadipaar. In legalese it is part of section 56 A of the Bombay Police Act, written during the nineteenth century, under which any person dangerous to the city's peace can be externed beyond two city limits for a maximum period of two years. This has to be done at the discretion of an officer ranking at deputy commissioner of police (DCP) level.

DCP Dr K. Venkatesham serves the externment notice to Gawli, he moves the court, an enquiry is instituted by asistant commissioner of police L.M. Dutraj who submits his report on 30 December in which he is classified as 'fit for externment'. High Court judge Vishnu Sahai rejects Gawli's petition on 4 February 1999, Venkatesham invites Gawli's lawyers to his office, an ivy-clad, quaintly British building at Byculla, on 8 February to argue against the externment order. Gawli's lawyer Prakash Shetty insists that the police is externing his client with 'malafide intentions' and 'this is being done at the behest of Shiv Sena chief Bal Thackeray' because Gawli's Akhil Bharatiya Sena is being perceived as a political rival to the Shiv Sena.

Gawli—who once refused to leave jail because he feared for his life, now flushed out of the security of his maze of rooms—poses in white khadi complete with Gandhi cap for the battery of press and television cameras at Dagdi chawl; he bows low in front of the temple below the chawl as the cameras click and whirr furiously and gives a sound byte, 'They are scared of my political clout and they want to send me away so that Dawood can finish me off.' He is put into a bus and packed off to Pune, his city of preference. He chooses the village where his in-laws live, near Pune.

Does anything change? 'It helps,' says the joint commissioner of police for crime D. Sivanandhan. 'He has twenty cases of murder, attempt to murder and extortion against him; now he cannot keep filing court cases and people need not go to Dadgi chawl where he used to summon them.' People will have to go Pune while Gawli, in this age of communications will simply keep operating by cell phone, the way all his colleagues in Dubai, London, Karachi and Malaysia do. There is also an army of trusted aides, some of whom figure high on the list of most wanted, who can take charge in his absence as they have done in the past—there are instances of him having spoken to them through a cell phone from his cell in Amravati jail.

There are follower-leaders in Pune too, in the approximately 200 Akhil Bharatiya Sena shakhas in and around Pune. Arun Gawli has patterned his Sena exactly like the other one, complete with shakhas, branches. There are 4,600 shakhas in Maharashtra, Rajasthan, Madhya Pradesh, Delhi, Uttar Pradesh, Gujarat and Haryana with approximately 5,50,000 members all over India. In the Pune-Lonavala region he has associates like Babloo Makwana and Sharad Barte who actively train new recruits. There are around 600 gangsters in the entire area who, divided into five groups headed by Gawli associates, swear complete allegiance to him. They are paid a salary per month, there is also a kitty of Rs 30 lakh which senior gang members can use during emergencies. Gawli's physical presence in what once competed with Bangalore as the pensioner's paradise may actually revitalize his forces. It has certainly revitalized the economy on the highway on Pune's outskirts leading to Gawli's current lair: the shopkeepers and hoteliers in the vicinity are delighted with the surge in their business because of the people who come to meet him.

This changes a lot for Pune; it does nothing for Bombay, he is remote but still in control. And he is not Bombay's only abiding nightmare.

Police officer Vijay Salaskar gets up with a start, the zeroing has begun. Salaskar never sleeps well before an encounter, he has nightmares, concentric circles close in on him in three dimension.

His wife, Smita, lays a soothing hand on his brow and gives him a cup of tea before she leaves for her job with a bank. Their eleven-year-old daughter Divya has already left for school. Often times he comes back home after Divya has gone to bed, no wonder she clings to him on Sundays, specially when he goes for a walk with them during which Smita does her marketing, then they take her to the temple. The forty-year-old Bombay-born Salaskar is not particularly religious but he believes in God and does not smoke, drink or chew paan; self-discipline imbibed in his teenage years when he went to listen to Sane Guruji's kathas and be a part of the Rashtriya Swayam Sevak drills. He was the shakha pramukh, branch head, for the Shiv Sena in Goregaon when he saw the advertisement for police officers and applied. An M Com., he joined the police force as sub-inspector.

The first shoot-out came in 1985, Raju Shahabuddin, an absconding rapist, robber, attempt to murderer and hafta khor, had to be apprehended from a Malad slum. As Vijay Salaskar entered the little room, he fired, there was retaliatory fire, that was that. 'I did not think anything of it,' says he. 'One of us had to die, he did. Each encounter drains me, but this is not because I think of who has been shot as a human being. He is not, but I do wish people would not call me an encounter specialist because the human rights activists now have the impression that I am a bloodthirsty, trigger-happy man. This is simply not true, just because I have a gun—two guns—in my hand does not mean I feel the need to keep pulling a trigger. It is not like, okay here is my gun and there is a crow and bang!'

He runs his long, curving thumbnail against his cell phone thoughtfully, there is another one by his side—two hot lines for his informants, this kind of information cannot wait. He has dealt with Amar Naik, Sada Pawle, Vijay Tandel and Sharad Bandwe with this information. These are predominantly Gawli men, or ex-men as is now the case, perhaps this is Salaskar's earlier Shiv Sena conditioning surfacing? He laughs, easily and naturally, 'This charge can be then levelled even when there are encounters with Dawood's people or Chota Shakeel's. No, it is just that I spend a lot of time and energy on my informants and so far they have told me about Gawli's men, it does not mean I would disconnect if there was information on Chota Rajan's men. All ruthless criminals, especially those misusing the judiciary, should be dealt with so that the people stop going to them. But how does one blame the people. The traditional ways of getting justice are failing or getting compromised. The courts are taking too long, and the police has no jurisdiction in civil matters. If someone is cheated of five lakh rupees where will he go? To the don who will take half but get him back half immediately.'

Because speed is of no essence in getting him the commendations or cash rewards due after dealing with gangsters, Salaskar has simply stopped filling in papers for them. 'The red-tapism and the bureaucracy drives me mad,' says he quietly, without even the slightest inflection of frustration in his voice, 'and, anyway, I have received the highest honour which can be bestowed on a policeman, the President's Medal, in 1988 itself; the rest can come if and when it wants to.' In 1990 he shifted to the Narcotics Bureau where he saw how international criminals operated and when he was transferred to the Crime Branch, he decided that he wanted to go where the action was.

And so he watches his target for six months, he studies movements, he keeps his informants happy and tapped in, he looks for his target's weakest link, then he moves in. Another one bites the dust. Except that for every one shot, another five hatch and become big in no time. 'Very young people are entering crime today, they are anonymous people, the kind you cannot trace back. Some come from the state's interior, but mostly these Maharashtrian boys are from the city itself.'

The mobile under his thumbnail rings. Tonight, in

another hour, on Sewree Road. Vijay Salaskar checks his AK-56, he double checks his .38; the AK-56 is what he carries to feel good, the .38 is what he uses, a Titan Tiger made in Miami, Florida, with a Red Indian big chief's profile on the side with six chambers in which he fills dreamily-golden, deceptively-small bullets. He gets into the jeep, he drives himself, 'I believe in myself.' His policemen get in too. The circle is closing, to zero in.

He is on Sewree Road, focussed, driving his jeep, his revolver to his right on the dashboard. It is night, 10.40 p.m., his headlights pick out Santosh Adivalekar alias Bandya, builder Manish Shah's murderer. For a split-second Bandya is frozen in Vijay Salaskar's headlights, like a startled rabbit with red eyes on a highway; he whips out a gun and fires; in one swift, unbroken motion Salaskar picks up his Titan Tiger with its big chief on the side, and returns fire. Three rounds, the first so that he should collapse, the second to make him unable to keep firing and the third to prevent him running away.

As Bandya turns into a darkly spreading stain on a broken pavement, Sarita Manish Shah puts her children to bed. Tomorrow is going to be another difficult day, she has to help Yogesh Shah close down Dhruva Builders.

Babliseth takes a deep drag on his cigarette and studiously does not look at his daughter haranguing him, he wonders if he can throttle her. He is mildly taken aback by his own thought; but now that it has risen, he follows through. Perhaps he could just chuck his cigarette butt down her always open mouth, into her throat, and she will simply choke; ah, the instantaneous relief.

'And you do not even look at me when I am talking! Goddammit! Why are you always looking at someone who is never there in the room!'

So many exclamation marks, and always shouting so loudly, on the phone also yelling away at her beleaguered friends. Shit, she screams at them, and oh fuck; always fuck. Faack, when she feels particularly expressive which is all the bloody time, faack, faack, faack. Sometimes, on Sundays when he is home since the shop is closed and her friends call, he slyly picks up the phone's extension from the kitchen to listen to what her friends have to say to all her fucks and shits. They sound patient with her, her friends; calmly resisting her attempts to steamroll them into the ground as well.

Briefly Babliseth feels bad for her, his first child born in a Dongri chawl. Everyone talks in higher volumes in chawls and so abusive, it stays with them for the rest of their lives even when they move out of the chawls. His other three daughters are born in Mazagon, see the difference in their demeanour; he feels kindly towards them as they help themselves to dinner quietly.

'I am here, across the dining table from you, talking to you! Hello! Daddy! Are you there?'

She is trying sarcasm now to rile him, Babliseth is not going to fall for this, oh no, he is not. After Rozena went he has become adept at tip-toeing across the minefields their first-born keeps laying for him all over the house. Rozena who died at forty-nine, leaving behind this, this . . . this mess.

26 April 1989, it would have been their thirty-first wedding anniversary today. They had left for their honeymoon in Bangalore immediately after their wedding at Dongri's open-air Noor Baug; how beautiful Rozena had

looked with her lace sari and a pearl choker wrapped stylishly around her forehead instead of her neck, how rakish he had felt in his two-toned spats and karakul cap at an angle. This one was born about nine months and two minutes after they got to Bangalore.

And how proud he had felt when he held her as a little bundle, ignoring his mother's plaintive thought about no son. He had also ignored his mother's suggestion about naming her Nafisa Begum; Babliseth was feeling particularly lucky and had gone straight from the hospital to the Mahalaxmi Race Course to bet on a mare that had never won before. It won that day, he named his first-born after the mare, another matter that the horse never competed again. He knows he had been stunningly individualistic in doing so, his damn daughter keeps reminding him of it as spectacular irresponsibility on his part.

'Daddy! Why aren't you paying attention? You have to stop giving them money!'

Oh Rozena, Rozena, it is three hours, twenty-nine days and twenty-six months since you went away.

'Daddy, listen to me, please.'

Babliseth blinks, she is saying please. He focuses on his first-born who is looking frazzled, her small eyes behind her thick glasses are boring into him, her short hair is awry in exasperation, the hundreds of pimples on her face are spot-red in anger, her fat and hairy arms are on the table with her fat fingers feeding her big mouth as she eats-talks-splutters through her food; when she gets up from the table she will heave herself out of her chair, she has huge hips. My God, what a horrendous child he has fathered;

23

but how is a man ever to know how his seed will sprout?

His second daughter releases a short sentence in the lull. She is his pride, born a full five years after the first, the son he never had, he would have liked her to sit at his shop, at the galla, the cash box of his kingdom. Rozena wanted her to become a doctor, she never got enough marks and Babliseth never had all that money for the enormous donation required to make doctors, they had admitted her in a pharmaceutical college; doctors, medicine and tablets, not too much difference there, and at one-fourth the cost. He truly likes her, he has named her unusually too, but she never complains, she is nice, his Achchiwali. His third, Teesriwali, has got a smart job with an airline; his fourth, born eight years after Teesriwali, is his Chhotiwali.

Achchiwali quietly says, 'Daddy, your cigarette.'

Babliseth grinds his cigarette with its long tail of ash into his dinner plate, between the mutton bones and the cooked cabbage, he hates cabbage. Teesriwali sighs and looks away, Chhotiwali giggles.

The Loud One is in full throttle again, 'Daddy, you have to stop giving them money. You have to stop getting scared, don't you see that fear is the key for them? Your fear pumped them up and they started with wanting token amounts for their festivals, you gave it knowing fully well that they spend it on alcohol. Now they are at everyone's door demanding money for bricks.'

Babliseth gives money to whomsoever comes to his door because he has daughters whom he must protect. Old man Victor next door gives money because he has grandsons who must not be attacked. Laljibhai, the bania downstairs, gives money because he does not want his grocery shop damaged. Parvez, the pavwala down the lane, gives money because he does not want his eggs smashed. You give the money not only because you are frightened they will hurt your family and property but because they come in the name of religion backed by local parties comprising drunks and drug addicts, history-sheeters and racketeers, and unemployed youth who stand below buildings and smoke, refusing to make way for your women until they are spoken to.

For as long as Babliseth can remember, the people of Mazagon have been giving money. The sardarjis in the building down the road gave money when goons showed up at their doors to 'protect' them as their brethren in Delhi were being killed after Indira Gandhi's assassination, the families gave and gave, and finally moved away from Mazagon to the suburbs to reside in a locality predominantly their own. The Jews gave money, as did the Chinese dentist at the corner, the Christians gave and the Parsis gave and then they too began leaving Mazagon when the pressure became too much. The by-product of communalism is the loss of gentile neighbourhoods. The Muslims gave, and they keep giving; and the Hindus gave; and they keep giving money too; because how many tight knots of menacing youth can you keep summoning the strength to turn away, even when you know full well that they will use this 'festival money' to set up loudspeakers at full volume on pavements blaring film music and drunkenly dance the night away?

Still, he supposes, he must as a father try and keep this conversation going with at least a question.

What bricks?
How is daddy to know about bricks?
He doesn't read about Ayodhya?
Aapa leave him alone, what's the point?
What bricks?

A sound at the entrance, his son-in-law to-be is at the door, Babliseth believes in always leaving the front door open because Rozena believed that this is how Lakshmi comes. Lately there are only big bandicoots gaining entrance, they have become quite bold in their hunger, scampering around Mazagon's lanes after sunset and up the wooden stairs of Bottlewala Mansion, right through any open door including Babliseth's. Achchiwali, on holiday from pharmaceutical studies in Belgaum, is in the process of devising a method of keeping out the bandicoots since Babliseth refuses to close the front door. Good with her hands, she is attaching a paatya, a flat wooden slat, to the bottom of the entrance; the kind put up to prevent infants from crawling out of front doors.

Babliseth's son-in-law to-be trips over the paatya and lands inelegantly straight into the hall. Teesriwali glares at Achchiwali as she jumps from the table to rush to her fiancé's aid, Chhotiwali giggles, the Loud One goes faaaaack.

Babliseth rises from the table and gravely greets his son-in-law to-be. He comes from a very well-known, respected Ismaili family, also from Dongri but shifting to a fancy flat in Bandra. His father does a lot of work in the jamaat, their community. His daughter and his jamaai-to-be have known each other seven years, since their college days; everybody has told Babliseth that he is lucky to have his daughter marry into such a fine family. All that apart, jamaais should be treated with respect, and Babliseth apologizes about the paatya by offering him dinner. He gestures vaguely towards his dinner plate, the young man looks at the butt among the bones and smiles weakly. Teesriwali brings a warning note into her voice, 'Daddy, he has had his dinner.'

Well, best to leave them to it, although he wishes the fellow had showed up earlier in the day, after all he has a bike and his petrol pump is just down the road near the Lakdaa Bazaar at Byculla. Now he will have to miss the news followed by twenty minutes of channel surfing before he has his splashy wash and goes to bed. Babliseth starts clearing the dinner table while his daughters crowd around their brother-in-law to-be. He potters and bangs about the kitchen, cracking a glass there and breaking a plate here although how does it matter, he can always get a hundred more from his shop, and if crockery did not break in people's homes how would glasswarewalas like him bring up their daughters? Tomorrow morning he will get up and quickly cook doodhiwala dal, before the Loud One can get up and fix another of her goulashes. Teesriwali had learned how to cook delicious food from her mother, Achchiwali is also not bad, but the Loud One, baap rey! Babliseth opens big glass bottles and flings several dals from them into a pan for overnight soaking.

Chhotiwali comes into the kitchen and hovers

tentatively around the gas stove, 'Daddy, I think there is a problem.'

Babliseth already knows there is going to be a problem, his astrologer has told him so, the next one week is not good, but the stars will change on the seventh day for the better. He smiles at Chhotiwali reassuringly, she appears uncertain, then she slips away into the darkness of the bachchey-log ka bedroom. He goes for his wash, lathering the Pears oval on his handkerchief, rubbing in some more till a mound of fragile soap bubbles pop up between his thumb and dialling finger. He likes washing his own rumaals and with Pears, they smell nice when he holds them to his nose when his nostrils are tickled by the hay-wrapped bundles of crockery in his dukaan. He sets the somewhat diminished Pears back on the soap dish and wishes he could point out to the Loud One that the Mad Dog can be right. But she will scoff, that too loudly, as she did when she refused to allow Mad Dog to come home.

How much she had yelled. 'I don't want him here in our house to harass my sisters, you understand? I don't care if mummy cooked chicken for him, she had to tolerate him because of you and your idiotic beliefs in half-arsed astrologers. Did this arsehole ever tell you that your wife was going to die so suddenly? Why can't you at least go to a good astrologer instead of these cheap charlatans? You want money, I will give it to you, but don't allow yourself to be set up by such haraamis! Look at the way he used to eat when mummy cooked all that food for him, like a hungry, mad dog.'

Mad Dog said he understood the Loud One's bachpanaa,

her childish outburst was because her stars were bad right now, he suggested Babliseth take him to Delhi Darbar for a dabba-ghosht and biryani instead. Yesterday also, at an equally convivial lunch at Delhi Darbar, Mad Dog had warned him about the tough week ahead. Babliseth had pressed some money into his hand, but Mad Dog chose to be circumspect, he refused to divulge what the problem would be. Babliseth had also asked about the Loud One, Mad Dog had shaken his head sadly, lost cause, she can only marry a widower and that too only when she turns forty-five. Her stars are like that.

Babliseth stretches out on his bed and lights his last cigarette for the day. He can hear them talking in the hall, and here is the Loud One, as always, holding forth.

'But how can you do this? Why should you just run away from your own country?'

Jamaai-to-be, 'Aapa, lots of Muslims are leaving, they don't like what is happening.'

'Of course nobody likes it, and I like it even less that I am being forced to take a position. Please understand this, there are very many Hindus who are equally concerned but there are others who feel compelled to take an anti-Muslim stand because it feels pro-Hindu.'

'That makes it worse, then, doesn't it, for us Muslims? Aapa, we have been handling all the problems thrown up by this city and country just like the Hindus. But then when they turn against us, what are we to do? There is contempt in their eyes when they look at us.'

'Oh, come on!'

'How many examples do you want me to give you of

decent Muslim families whose neighbours see them with hostility and suspicion. Sweeping statements are made. "Tum Mussalman log, you can marry four times, you have too many children, go to Pakistan." How dare they tar us all with one brush? Can't they see that there are castes, sub-castes and communities among Muslims just like among Hindus?'

'No, they can't. We Indians are experts at side-stepping the problems in our own homes while commenting loudly on what we consider anti-social behaviour in the homes of our neighbours. And, anyway, why care if all they say is untrue for you.'

'But they are forcing their views upon me, they want to isolate me.'

'Don't be silly. But when you say this I realize the real tragedy of this whole Hindutva-business. We—the Hindus, the Muslims, everyone—will have imprisoned ourselves into water-tight compartments along with our inherent imbalances. So every damn thing will remain a niggling nightmare because to air it openly, try and start a dialogue, will first be incendiary and then politically-incorrect.'

'Aapa, what are you saying? Are we to keep getting brutalized and feel noble that we are doing this for India? Let me tell you what happened yesterday in a posh Bandra society. This man came down from the seventh floor to the first floor flat and started abusing the family, "You Muslims, you are filthy, eating all that mutton and throwing the bones on my car parked below your balcony. I am going to complain to the police, they will teach you a lesson in the lock-up." Naturally the first floor flat-owner fought back and this went on and on until the secretary of the society intervened and called an emergency meeting. Turned out the rubbish was being thrown from the second floor flat which did not belong to a Muslim.'

'I hate myself for asking this, was the secretary a Muslim?'

'No.'

'Well then, there is hope for our country yet. Look, everything can become a reason to want to go the West where the life is undoubtedly better but not without outbursts of racism. And God knows there are enough rich Hindu families flying there to deliver their babies because of the citizenship which automatically follows. But I think what Muslims must realize is this; the more Muslims leave, the greater will be the persecution of those left behind. When the British ruled Bombay, the ratio of minority communities to the Hindus was relatively high, that is why riots were comparitively sporadic, the British could not succeed in divide-and-rule through religious strife in Bombay. Muslims have been leaving steadily beginning with partition, Christians are quietly leaving as are the Parsis, the Jews are almost gone as are the Anglo-Indians and the East-Indians.'

Achchiwali, 'Maybe this is what they want, that we should all leave.'

'Aapa, I understand what you are saying but what else can one do? They came to our petrol pump this afternoon and demanded a lot of money from my bada baappa, my father's elder brother. He remembers what they did to the Muslims during partition and they threatened him saying

31

we will put you through another partition very soon, we are going to set fire to your pump. My father is very shaken and feeling terribly insecure.'

'Oh don't be silly, they can't do that. You have a hospital on one side of your pump and a Parsi colony on the other.'

'Do they care? They specially pointed out to the Lakdaa Bazaar near the Parsi colony, you know the entire wood market is owned by Muslims. Bada baappa got too frightened to think rationally, he has told my father to find a buyer immediately for the pump while Muslims can still get good prices and insists that the young ones should start migrating, settle in the West and call their elders.'

Babliseth hears a sound of deep distress, his heart goes out to his third daughter. This makes him even more irritated with the Loud One, he itches to slap her, hard. She has no bloody sense, this is no way to talk to a future son-in-law, he will run away. This is all her bloody garam hawa talking, literally. He had told Rozena that he did not want her to go to Regal cinema when *Garam Hawa* was being released. As it is there were problems then, people felt the Muslims would get upset and they kicked up a big fuss without even seeing the stupid picture. Then Indira Gandhi saw it and ordered it to be released, the Muslims loved *Garam Hawa*, they went and saw it again and again. Rozena took a half day off from the school she was teaching in and took the Loud One with her to see it.

Babliseth was so worried about a riot being caused by someone else just for the fun of it and all that glass being broken at the theatre, that he left his shop and stood outside Regal till the picture got over. Rozena came out with her nose all red, weeping away over Balraj Sahni and his suffering daughter, this had prompted the Loud One to also burst into, what else, loud crying. He had bundled them into a taxi, imagine spending on a taxi because of a bloody picture, dropped them home and taken a bus back to his dukaan.

They had even had a little fight in the taxi when he told Rozena she had no business taking their daughter for such an adult picture, she could have always gone with her teacher-friends.

'But Babli,' Rozena had protested, 'she has a right to see life as it is, you cannot keep taking her to Taraporevala Aquarium to see the fish swimming in their tanks all her life.' Rozena had turned pert, 'She sees more than enough about how adults actually behave in the family. And besides, you do not seem to have noticed that she is no longer a child.'

Babliseth had been short with his wife from the front seat of the taxi, he did not want his daughter's head to be filled with valiant nonsense. Rozena had replied, equally shortly, from the back seat; back, front, back, front, back, angry sentences bounced about with the taxiwala driving silently; until the Loud One set up a fresh wail, 'But I went with mummy to see my kabuliwala!' So much for not being a child!

Bloody kabuliwala, another Rozena-created problem. When *Kabuliwallah* was released with Balraj Sahni as the Pathan from Kabul who comes to sell dry fruit in India, Rozena took this one, she was a child then, to Dongri's

33

Derby Talkies to see the film. This one began screaming and shouting and beating her little hands against the wooden seat, 'I want my kabuliwala, bring back kabuliwala.' Something to do with Balraj Sahni being falsely accused in the film, arrested and thrown into jail.

They lived in Dongri—a mountain flattened out of recognition—in those days, in a room on the third floor of a chawl opposite the Children's Jail at Umarkhadi. His eldest brother had turned drunkard and was stealing things from the house to buy booze, when he could not find anything to steal which was fairly quickly since they were poor, he began running up huge bills at the hooch joint on Jail Road South. It was a matter of time for gangster Karim Lala to show up and demand the dues. And what does this one do? She sidles up to the gangster, tugs at his salwaar because he is a tall, strapping Pathan and looks up to his great height with a trusting question, 'Aap kabuliwala hai na?' Babliseth had to drag his daughter in as she kicked and screamed and even bit him while Rozena paid up from the money she made by giving tuitions to the chawl children.

She's still at it, doing her damndest to break her sister's engagement.

'When do you have to leave for the States?'

'In two weeks.'

'So soon! But how can we organize the wedding in two weeks?'

'Uh, no. Aapa, I cannot get married to her until I settle there and call for her.'

'Why not?'

'Uh, the thing is they have an amnesty scheme going

on in the States right now, they are granting resident status to the Mexican farmers who have been working on their side of the border on the farms since several years. The American lawyers there are organizing fake documents and farmer identities for anyone who wants to avail of the scheme.'

'But you are an Indian, and your country's passport affirms your true identity.'

'I guess once I get there I'll have to get a dog to chew it up.'

Saala gaandu is already sounding like an American; Babliseth flops over on his tummy and falls into a dreamless sleep.

If Babliseth's life were to be visualized, it would be like a twelve-inch pizza with two of its slices eaten. Except that he hates pizzas because they are not wholewheat which is why he likes rotis and chapatis, Rozena made mounds of them for him.

So, imagine a huge chapati with two pizza-type slices missing from it, Babliseth's life rotates and revolves along the circumference of, and among, the uneaten part. In geographical terms this would mean the slightly-awry semi-circular shape of Byculla to Mazagon to Bhendi Bazaar with Dongri along the way. Byculla, at the Masina Hospital, where most of his children were born and his wife died, once the palace of the Sassoon family who donated its chandeliers to the Royal Opera House. Where are those grand chandeliers now that the Royal Opera House has been shut down? From Masina Hospital, a right at Lakdaa

Bazaar, past where tragedy queen Meena Kumari is buried. When she died of drink and unhappiness and they all came to Mazagon to lay her to rest, Dilip Kumar's shoes were promptly stolen outside the cemetery. Do the local boys still play cards on her grave, 'Ek patta Meena Kumari key naam sey'? Past Hasanabad with Mazagon's answer to the Taj Mahal, a mausoleum with cool and wide marble steps, comfortingly fluttering doves inside its dome and elegant minarets. On to Bottlewala Mansion down the road from Hasanabad, into the Number Three bus, final destination the dukaan.

The two eaten slices of this chapati-pizza are the rest of Bombay to which Babliseth wholesales, retails and rents his cups, glasses, plates, chunky beer mugs, gaily hand-painted lemon sets, bone-china tea sets with elegant spouts and those aachaar barnees: large ceramic jars gentle-brown and off-white on the outside, comfortingly cool to the cheek on touch, holding within the fiery secrets of a thousand grandmothers. And their collective sadness, bequeathed to their daughters.

Babliseth's great-grandfather was Rawjibhai, a Hindu in the Jamnagar region of Gujarat who converted to the Shia Imami Ismaili faith, simply put he became a follower of the Aga Khan, an Ismaili Muslim. The altered circumstances certainly seemed to help Rawjibhai who made enough money, or so he thought, to last several generations. His son Peermohamad married into equal wealth but that did nothing to keep his wife who, utterly sick of his feudalism, chauvinism and compulsively gambling ways, dumped their son Mohamadali at the village mela, and ran off with another man to live, hopefully, happily ever after. Peermohamad married again and moved with his son to Bombay. He took a bungalow at Chowpatty where they had carriages drawn by six horses each and the multitudes of servants were gifted thick gold chains at every Id. He once took a ship to Egypt to bring back a massively blue diamond for his current mistress, la dolce vita at its dolcest, the good life at its best. Mohamadali grew up with a never-empty glass in one hand and a racing book in the other.

Babliseth's mother, though, came from good stock. The Padamsees of Waghnagar near Bhavnagar in Gujarat were grain merchants who sent their sons to Bombay, one-by-one, when successive droughts tore open the heart of their village's earth. They set up Salehmohammed Padamsee & Sons, a trading company at Chakala, close enough to the docks. They taught themselves English, opened several trading accounts with assorted countries and even cracked through the lantern market to Germany. They bought the fanoos in wholesale and sold them at wholesale for quite some time, making their little profit on re-selling the strong wooden packing in which the lanterns came. When the brothers Padamsee were convinced they had wiped out the competition in the fanoos market, they began thinking of actual profit.

They made enough money to construct a physically en famille environment as well, Padamsee Wadi at Mazagon, although the brothers also maintained separate establishments all over the city. Babliseth's mother Noorbanoo Padamsee was born at one establishment while her sister Sherbanoo was born at quite another as were their brothers Badrudin, Sadrudin, Nurudin, Amirali and Akbar Padamsee. Noorbanoo's marriage to Mohamadali was celebrated with due enthusiasm, recalls her internationally renowned artist brother Akbar Padamsee, with carriages filled with dry fruit and gifts dashing around on deliveries. He remembers what followed, 'Disaster. Mohamadali frittered away all his wealth on wine, women and gambling; we even started a separate trading company for him at Salehmohammed & Sons, Indo-Japan Trading, but he just would not show up at work and if he did, it would be so grudgingly as to further demoralize the office workers.'

And so, named after one of his illustrious mamas and nicknamed otherwise, Babliseth was born in this chawl in Dongri, three steep flights up, with its toilet outside where he joined a very long line every morning, his water-can in his hand, to hurry up and finish so that he could reach work at the printing press across the road. Matric fail, he had started working at the press while his father was still drinking himself into a stupor with his elder brother now joining in. And then he met Rozena, the Madhubala-like Rozena whose hand he was scared to touch for fear that the black ink of the hot-type left on his hand from the press would stain her fairness, like daag on the chand.

Thus it was a great source of joy to him when Sherbanoo spoke to her brothers and said that Rs 60,000 be given to Noorbanoo so that her second son Babli could start a proper shop, and finally a proper life which could also benefit his younger brothers and only sister, the beautous Shah Sultan with long, lustrous, jet black hair till the back of her knees. A glassware shop was purchased on good will—that is, lock and stock and name board outside— in the middle of Bhendi Bazaar which by then had turned into a booming business district, the classical musicians of the Bhendi Bazaar gharana had physically moved out of the area much earlier.

Bhendi Bazaar, so named because of the bhendi, okra or the Indianized ladies finger vegetable, planted row upon row in the entire vicinity during the thirteenth century rule of the Solanki ruler from Gujarat, Raja Bhimdev. The raja brought with him several useful fruits and vegetables as also trees, and had them planted all over, from them the names of localities evolved. Parel, from Paral or Padel, the trumpet flower tree; Wadala, wad, the banyan grove; Chinchpokli, the tamarind dell, Cumballa Hill the lotus grove, Byculla from bhaya or cassia fistula and Umarkhadi, the fig tree creek opposite Babliseth's Dongri chawl which was filled in and a children's remand home put on top of it.

The creek was completely filled in and around Umarkhadi too, and bridged by a road all the way to Bombay's middle island, Mazagon. From down-market Dongri Babliseth worked, and worked so hard in his dukaan that he could make that leap of faith to middle-market Mazagon. With vastly-improved family circumstances, Shah Sultan was married into the well-known Jamal family of Bangalore, his intelligent brother Salim could go to London courtesy a scholarship of the Fondation Aga Khan to study textile engineering. Now

Babliseth could take his Rozena back to Mazagon, Rozena who was so pretty that she used to get called the Madhubala of Mazagon while she grew up there. He was taking his Madhubala home.

Though, strictly speaking, Rozena's ancestorial home was another country, then called Persia, subsequently Iran. Rozena's ancestors were the Persian Parsis who fled Iran for India around a century after the fall of the Sassanian empire in 651 AD to escape religious persecution. They sailed to India in the late eighth century, first landing at Diu and living there for nineteen years after establishing the highest of sacred fires which burns to this day in the south Gujarat village of Udwada. They moved to Sanjan, where the local ruler Jadi Rana looked at their tall, fair men with hostility. Dastur Naryosang Dhaval, their priest-astrologer, asked for shelter from Jadi Rana who directed that a bowl of milk be brought to him filled to the brim. The king told the dastur that the bowl would spill over if any more milk were added to it, as would his kingdom. Dastur Dhaval removed his gold ring and slid into the bowl of milk, 'We will settle in your kingdom without displacing anybody, but just as the ring does not dissolve in the milk we shall maintain our separate identity, and like this gold ring we will prove ourselves to be worthy and precious to those among whom we live.' The Hindu king relented and told the Persians they could settle in his kingdom provided they adopted Gujarati as their language, their women dressed in the Hindu manner and their marriage processions held only after sunset.

When Rozena told this story the gold ring became

sugar mixed in the bowl; which is exactly what her ancestors had done, approximately a thousand years after they arrived in India. This section of the Parsis married Hindu men and women, and they in turn intermarried and became Hindu, and some of them by now in Kutch, awed by the Aga Khan's Persian background, became Ismaili. And some of these families came to Bombay for a job. Their women worked as hard as the man, like the widowed Khadijeh Mody with her young son Ismail, her daughter Roshanara whom Babliseth could only think of as Rozena and her livewire sister Sakkarkhanum. They settled in Mazagon, with its strong Parsi and Persian settlements, in the lane called Hathi Baug, where the royal elephants were once garaged; abutting Love Lane, a dell once tree-lined and shady where the British boys and girls furtively met to hold hands.

Sakkarkhanum Mody took to Ismaili activities most determinedly, she emerged as the captain of their Girl Guides, here she met Ghulamhussein Damanwala, equally conscientious about community affairs, whose forefathers, as his name suggests, came from Daman and who was an enthusiastic member of the Boy Scouts. Girl Guide meets Boy Scout, Cupid strikes, Ghulamhussein introduces his fiancée to his childhood friend who promptly falls in love with her sister. Who refuses to acknowledge his ardour, there being several suitors for the Madhubala of Mazagon. Babliseth wears down her resistance by standing under the lamp post at Love Lane, from where he can see her window in Hathi Baug, every single evening. Ghulamhussein and he take the girls out by taxi, bring them back by taxi and then walk home because there is no money left. They pretend they have been invited to the grandest of weddings in the city but are not taking their girlfriends because it will bore them to tears, let's go for a walk at Chowpatty and eat chana instead.

So much, how many more, shared trials and tribulations and laughter and tears. And at last he has bridged the gap to the point where he has got his own home, away from his joint family which had traumatized her into illnesses like the weeping eczema on her fingers and led to their son being still-born because she had to stand in the hot sun while his drunken brother flung food in the house.

Babliseth, Rozena and the girls at Bottlewala Mansion bang opposite Padamsee Wadi in Mazagon; their daughters are growing up nicely and the building has just been repaired and the house re-painted with fresh tiles in the bathroom, and there is a fridge and a phone and a big colour television and just when begins the time to start growing old together she dies at forty-nine, oh Rozena, Rozena.

Well now, it is 6.40 a.m. and time for Babliseth to rise, which he does with his in-built alarm clock. He stumbles to the kitchen and bangs about, pulling out a largish steel tope, the tea-making vessel which his daughters always put back into the shelf in the night, settling the smaller vessels into the larger ones in spite of him having taken it out and kept it on the gas rink for the morning. He fills it to the brim with water and carefully, in an exaggerated stagger, goes to the big agaasi, the balcony adjoining his bedroom facing the main road, and pours the water on the tree-sapling the municipality has planted on the pavement below. Then he fills the tope to the brim once again and sets it on the gas, he lights a match and introduces it to the burner. His daughters have often told him to please use the gas lighter because the match flare invariably leaves a smudge of black on the vessel, he ignores his daughters because he lights his first cigarette of the day with the same lit matchstick.

Cigarette in hand he repairs to the balcony where his shaving mirror is nailed to the wooden vertical beam supporting the upstairs balcony. A new couple has moved in upstairs; they have made drastic renovations using the balcony for dish washing and storing their heavy gas cylinders. There is leakage now in Babliseth's balcony and he also notices that both his and the upstairswala balcony have begun tilting a bit. Bloody upstairswala gaandu, Babliseth spoke to him soon after the leakage began and the young man shrugged in a burdened way, he had a very pregnant wife to deal with and they tended to scream at each other a lot.

Buses begin trundling past behind Babliseth's shaving mirror as he gets started. He uses sinister-tipped tapering scissors and expertly wields this kattar to shape his vanishing pencil-slim moustache, he also deals with the odd growth from his ears and nose. The water has boiled, Babliseth dunks some into his chunky, large white breakfast cup and flings fistful of tea powder into the boiling water. Lowering the gas's flame he takes his cup back to the balcony to use the hot water to shave the sprinkling of salt and pepper on

43

his chin. Babliseth finishes his cigarette, the tea boils and boils and boils, turns turgid with strength.

Babliseth empties his shaving water, rinses the cup and pours his tea into it. He sips, kadak and perfect. He starts cooking the doodhiwala dal; chop tomatoes, splash some oil, toss in onions, some ready-made ginger-garlic paste he brings from Dongri and stocks up in the fridge, some dhania-jeera powder hand-pounded by the poor ladies of Madanpura. Now light the second cigarette and place it between lips because the hand is needed to stir around the masala, chop up the doodhi, stick it into the masala, stir, some cigarette ash falls in, never mind, put in the soaked dals which look a bit fermenty but never mind that too, stir, pour water, one boil, the phone rings startling him slightly: so early?

He answers it from the kitchen, 'Hul-low.'

'Daddy!'

Baap rey, the Loud One, she is not sleeping at home?

'Daddy, are you there?'

Babliseth grunts, what now, first thing in the morning.

'Daddy, I am just filing a story about a building collapse for our front page, it is the one behind the dukaan.'

He speaks, a small note of alarm in his voice, is this what Mad Dog meant, 'What about my shop's building.'

'No, this is the one behind it. But it might be a good idea for you all to get together and get an engineer to examine your building.'

He thinks; not possible, there are shops and shops and shops and above there are over one hundred small flats and the whole building belongs to some landlord so no one is going to bother. Besides, the place is likely to catch fire with all its illegal and cross-electrical connections before it simply falls down.

'Daddy! Are you listening to me?'

He grunts again.

'Daddy, we, I, want to come to the dukaan at around six in the evening.'

Oh no, not at his shop too.

'Daddy! Will you be there?'

He is tempted to say he will be out on ugraani, collection of dues from the suburban crockery shops and restaurants who buy his glassware. But the Loud One knows today is not his ugraani day.

'Daddy, we will be there at 6 p.m.'

We? Babliseth turns the gas on simmer, looks for his burning cigarette, cannot find it, goes in for his bath and is out on the main road bus stop at 8.24 a.m., four minutes late because of that one's phone call. The Number Three bus is about to change gears and charge away when the conductor spots him sprinting, he yanks on the bell's chord, the bus judders to a halt, Babliseth jumps on board, hanging on to the rail and the conductor pulls on the bell again with a reprimand, 'Kya seth, aaj late ho gaya?' The double-decker Number Three takes off down Dr Mascarenhas Road, curves at the Sales Tax office, halts at Mazagon Court, halts again at Aga Hall, sails quite majestically over the elevated Nesbit Road bridge and dips to enter the hurly-burly of Mohammedali Road.

Babliseth waggles his fingers at the conductor who

45

waggles a few back, he alights at the Char Nal junction, to his right is his shop, to his left is Rozena, he heads left from Char Nal, four taps, so named when the area came into its own selling sanitation, plumbing and hardware. Babliseth starts walking towards Rozena, he is also walking towards the actual four taps which were set up by the British as a water trough for their horses when they came to one end of their stronghold island. Beyond the char nals, was the boundary of their fort-like island up until Umarkhadi, fig tree creek.

The attar shops are just opening, Ishallah Mashallah Perfumers, Rizwan Aromatics. Movable glass counters are being placed into position at the shop's entrance with their packets of agarbattis and dulhan-red mehndi which the elderly miyaabhais use to dye their waving-in-the-wind beards. Babliseth walks past them and the ghoda ghadis, their seats covered in rich-coloured rexin, their backs cased in shiny-goldy metal reflected in the solid brass of the victoria's lamp near the driver's raised seat. The horses have been unfettered for the night from their ghadis, they are being washed and soothed at the char nal, a day's rest before trotting all evening and night up and down Chowpatty, Marine Drive and Apollo Bunder, the Gateway of India.

Babliseth enters the dargah, the final resting place for South Bombay Ismailis. Pigeons takes flight in a remonstrative flutter of wings as he walks through their wide, flagstoned courtyard. He has given his wife khandaa here, the final round of the janaazaah, borne on the shoulders of the men before it can be taken to its final resting place, dust thou art, dust thou descendeth. Babliseth refused to let anyone take his side of the four khandaas, he held her up, his Rozena, in her wooden palanquin in which she lay, dressed in only kora kapda, handwoven off white yardage, but draped over with satin green and the crescent moon and stars stitched into it in gold. Round the courtyard, giving her khandaa, and around again, 'Allah huma saleh Allah Mohamad in wa aley Mohamad, Allah huma saleh Allah . . .'

They could not take her immediately in to the burial site though, the people kept coming for Rozena's funeral, they wanted to see her face before she went. Ghulamhussein had told Babliseth that there were at least two thousand at Rozena's funeral; it was a blur to him, men coming up and saying she had got them jobs, women weeping near her because she had given them a bottle of milk every day and their daughters' wedding clothes and utensils. But when the Girls Guides draped her uniform's scarf over Rozena and gave her the salute, Babliseth had noticed a small trickle of blood, like a teardrop floating out of her right stitched eyelid and he had walked up to Ghulamhussein's doctor-son to indicate it. Rozena had died during yesterday's dusk and her eyes had been donated to the Lady Duggan Eye Bank, she had always said she wanted this.

Babliseth had refused with a broken no, he would not have his wife touched, she had suffered enough while alive. His first daughter had been livid, she had shouted, shattering the silence of Masina Hospital with its twin curved, stone staircases which met above the words Sans Souci, without worry, 'Damn you, at least let her have this peace.'

Babliseth had disappeared into the gardens of Masina Hospital, untraceable until relatives had found him to convince him of the eye donation. The Lady Duggan Eye Bank people had arrived instantaneously, they were kind, sympathetic and very caring with Rozena whose eyes they had put in a little black box, packed in her hollows with cotton and gently closed her lids with one stitch each. The funeral was the next day, Rozena had been kept on a bed of block-ice all night, they had refused to let Babliseth sit by her.

She had been out in the sun too long, the blood-tear near her eye was discreetly wiped away and now had to be the time for Rozena to leave. The fateha was read, Rozena was lowered into her grave, near her mother Khadijeh and her son whom there had been no point in naming. Babliseth's hand was held to pick up the first earth and his numb fingers shaken to let the gravel fall on her. He had waited for a year after the funeral to plant a rose bush on her grave, he had also put a specially designed marble plaque on her head-side which simply stated: Rozena.

Babliseth checks the plaque, he waters the rose bush, his brown eyes turn luminous as he tells his wife silently about his thoughts and feelings and then he makes his way to his kingdom, his dukaan, where his bhaiyyaas are waiting for him, the strong workers who help unload his trucks which come from Faridabad and Agra in Uttar Pradesh and Surendranagar in Gujarat bearing hay-lined boxes of lustre-lined cups and thick-china soup plates with scalloped circumferences. Babliseth opens his galla, the wooden cash box with its brass lid and several compartments inside divided into two sections, the top to keep immediate cash and change, paper clips, visiting cards and pens; the bottom revealed by removing this to hide the big notes in. He picks up his pichchi, the cloth duster wrapped around a long stick, and flicks at the crockery. He then settles into the chair which his chief bhaiyya, his manager Baba Deen, has set on Bhendi Bazaar's pavement for him. The chair is a high one, it reaches the shop level which is raised from the ground because water floods Bhendi Bazaar during the heavy monsoon, oftentimes even seeping inside to give the displayed cups and glasses a completely unnecessary rinsing.

The high chair was devised when it was realized that Babliseth's advancing age needed him to have a more comfortable seating space when compared with the baakdaas, those hard wooden slabs he usually sat on. A design was worked out where Babliseth would not have to keep jumping up and down from the shop's level: a wooden chair with a longer back and firm armrests the height of which was on par with the shop's entrance. Such a rage the chair turned out to be, soon every shop in Bhendi Bazaar was copying it and Bombay Furniture inside Chor Bazaar at Mutton Street across the road was churning them out by the dozen.

Babliseth turns around on his throne and asks the next door shopwala, 'Chaay peyengaa?' Kaniza Chickens says yes, and Babliseth addresses his youngest bhaiyya, But-turr, so named because after coming from his native place the first thing he broke in the dukaan was an expensive cut-glass butter pot. 'Aye But-turr do chaay lekey aa jaldi, paani cum, adrak maarkay.' Two strong teas laced with freshly crushed ginger. The other bhaiyya, also new, is about to drop a bundle of glasses inside the back of the shop, their godown. The phone rings, he answers, 'Aye ghelchhodya, sambhaal! Saala dhayus!' Careful, you doer-to-a-donkey—done-by-a-donkey?—imbecile.

'Daddy, why are abusing me?'

Babliseth brightens, it is Achchiwali. 'No maa, I was talking to this gaandu bhaiyya of mine.'

'If you abuse even I can abuse.'

'I will not appreciate it because it does not look nice. Women don't abuse, maa.' Except . . .

'Aapa abuses all the time, how come you don't shout at her?'

Babliseth grunts.

'Well?'

'So many questions in the morning, you sound just like her. Tell me why you phoned.'

'Cracko has not come again. I will fill your dabba when the dabbawala comes. But what to do about your chapatis? Will you buy naans from Bohri Mohalla?'

Cracko is their perenially absent maid Shakuntalabai, Rozena had hired her and she had grown old with them, so old that she was sick half the time and incredibly batty when she was in the house. She cracked all the crockery she washed, two reasons for her christening by his daughters who refused to sack her.

Babliseth lets loose a string of abuses, again he is not getting his chapatis in his dabba! No matter what, Rozena sent his tiffin carrier properly arranged, the colours of the dishes nicely matched; lemon yellow dahi ka kadi and green bhendi ka bhaji, golden yellow dal and baingan stuffed with tomatoes black-dotted with rai ka baghaar, rogan josh with dahi ka raita; and all this hot-hot with equally hot, soft chapatis. Even when she was working and they lived as a joint family in the Aga Hall flat, she gave instructions to Yaseen the cook. Rozena had to leave her job as a teacher when the cooking load fell on her, three meals a day for a family of too many, since one day old Yaseen keeled over and died in the small kitchen itself. The Loud One had come back from school and wept quietly, crouched near Yaseen's toppled-over red fez cap with its black tassel which he had always worn while cooking.

'Daddy, since you have made doodhiwali dal you can buy some tandoor ka rotis for your lunch and bring some home for dinner. Bring extra for breakfast too, I will re-crisp them in butter.'

Babliseth is still abusing.

'Daddy, please stop it. As it is all the abuses are so anti-women. Why are there no abuses against men?'

Baap rey, she is sounding just like her elder sister. That one is corrupting every one in the house, Babliseth makes a mental note to protect his Chhotiwali.

'May be I can also start saying gaandu, in Marathi it means maazi gaand dhoo, or come and wash my bum, you have to say it derogatorily, not in a friendly manner the way you men do.'

Babliseth cannot believe she is saying all this, 'Who taught you all this, maa?'

'Aapa did, why?'

Babliseth is angry, 'Tell her she does not know

everything in this world.' He bangs the phone down on his favourite daughter.

He sips his tea, the day has begun badly this he already knows, and Mad Dog had warned him anyway, and it is long since opening time and there is no bonee as yet, no giraak, no first customer. Kaniza Chickens points out that this might be because of the building collapse behind, business should pick up by noon.

Oh no, here is business he definitely does not need, this is really a bad week, Salim Sandaasiya is walking up to the shop.

'Salaam allaikum, Babliseth.'

'Wa allaikum salaam. Aao baitho.'

Babliseth vacates his throne for Salim Sandaasiya, better there than inside the shop, after all he is a gangster. Salim Sandaasiya has started a conversation with Kaniza Chickens, '. . . usko kal raat ko ek tamaacha maara na, saala ekdum sey sudhar gaya'.

Babliseth thinks that the Salims of this world are, by-and-large, doomed; starting with Salim who loved Anarkali and ending with this insane Salim who was inadvertently delivered by his hapless mother in a Bhendi Bazaar toilet, hence the nickname. Even if you are a good Salim, you get harassed, like Salim on the ground floor of a building in Dawood Ibrahim's lane whom the police kept picking up and regularly smacking, confusing him with the Salim on the third floor whom they actually wanted. Finally Salim on the third floor sorted it out with the police by suggesting that when they wanted him they could send the constables for Salim Tempo, since he ran a fleet of them; the man on the ground floor was Salim Accountant, he worked in a bank.

The police liked the idea and began sorting out all the Salims. Salim Kurla—he lived there, Salim Haddi—he had a prominent Adam's apple, Salim Passport—he could get any one fake documents, Salim Chikna—he was good looking, Salim Kutta—his nose made him look like a dog and not to be confused with Hanif Kutta who had once bitten a constable on his arm, Salim Gadha—who botched up every single job the underworld gave him, Salim Ketley—he began his life as a tea seller, Salim Talwar—he used swords for booth-capturing during elections and was not be mixed up with Salim Rampuri who wielded a mean knife all the time, Salim Topi—he always wore a cap and was not to be confused with Munna Topi who also wore one and who in turn was not be mixed up with Munna Dadi who had a long, flowing beard. Salim Falooda was the one who had mistakenly killed a falooda-seller on the road. Falooda— brought by the Persian-Parsis to India—is a milk drink mixed with rose and other syrups, garnished with cooling grey-black takmariya seeds and other noodle-like slippery-slidies to be served with a blob of ice cream on top. A combination merry to the tongue and throat if made well, unfortunately acquiring notoriety after Salim Falooda's mistake with the Bombay phrase: 'Mere ijjat ka falooda nahi karneka.' Do not kill my respect, self or otherwise.

Babliseth sighs, they had a Salim too, he was his favourite brother, their Salim. By the time he came back from London and started working in the textile mills, something was going wrong but who would have the knowledge to notice in those days. They were on the ground floor at Aga Hall and they got him married to the charming Mehrunnissa from the fifth floor but she did not know how to cope either with Salim's emerging schizophrenia. And then one night Salim walked from Aga Hall to Mazagon Dockyard station and jumped under an oncoming local train.

That day had started simply enough. Rozena had decided to send Maalya to Pune with some money and tuck for the Loud One who had been admitted to a boarding school there, it had been hoped that time away from home would straighten her out some. Maalya, whom Rozena and Sakkarkhanum were taking care of ever since his father had died, took the afternoon train back, from Victoria Terminus he took a local train to the Dockyard station and got caught up in the commotion of a man having jumped under the train, his head had been completely severed from his body and the constables were now looking for it on the tracks. When the constable found the head, and came holding it partly by the hair and partly by the severed neck valiantly trying to hold in the head's innards with cloth and paper, Maalya took one look and ran all the way yelling, 'Babliseth, Babliseth, Babliseth jaldi chalo.'

Babliseth sighs again, in great sadness. He suddenly remembers that their Salim had madh-chataaoed the Loud One, an Ismaili tradition where a favourite elder puts a small drop of honey on the tongue of the family's newly-born child. Rozena had insisted Salim do it because he was the most intelligent in the family.

Babliseth does not know what to do with this thought,

nor the one which follows, that the Loud One has, in turn, madh-chataaoed his third daughter.

Salim Sandaasiya is looking at him, he is concentrating so hard that he is almost squinting, 'Babliseth, kuch takleef hai kya? Kuch mere laayak kaam?'

Inspite of himself Babliseth laughs, can't have your eldest daughter knocked off by a gangster even if he is offering help.

'Babliseth, thodey glass dey do, ghar mein shaadi hai.' Give some glasses, there is a marriage in the house.

'Dhanda-paani nahi hai, kaayku peyt pey laat maarta hai bhai?' No business, why are you making it worse.

'Kya Babliseth, sab ko Yeda Yakub samjhaa hai kya?' You think every gangster is like Yeda Yakub, dubbed so by the Bombay police for his psychic ways.

'Dey nahi sakta hoon, tu hire kar dal, sastey mei deytaa hoon.' Cannot give, you can hire, cheaply.

'Ley kay jaata hoon, waapas ley kay aaoonga toh damage ley lo.' Am taking, you charge on return for those which broke.

Salim Sandaasiya chooses six dozen bara ka bamboo paliwala, twelve ounce, bamboo patterned, thick bottomed glasses used for tea by all the chaiwalas over the city which comes from the Paliwala factory near Meerut. He intends putting these glasses to all-purpose use. 'Chaay, paani, falooda, sab is mech pat jaayenga,' he explains to Babliseth with what he assumes is a winning smile.

Babliseth wishes his shop was on the other side of the road, his side falls under Pydhonie police station, the opposite line of shops go under J.J. Hospital police station, gangsters prefer the Pydhonie police and stick to this side of the road. Sometime back one set of gangsters had started patrolling the area in a jeep exactly like that of the police, except where it says Police on the police jeeps, this jeep had Polite in identical lettering. This went on for a while and one day an inspector finally got fed up and gave hot chase down the crowded Bhendi Bazaar road, one of the gangsters fell out from his jeep and fell on the median between the road; the inspector decided which police station could have the pleasure on the basis of which side the gangster's head was facing, J.J.Hospital police station it was.

A Bohri Muslim lady comes in her ridaah, their community's colourful lace-edged burqa, to buy a feeding cup. If he does not consider Salim Sandaasiya this is his first customer of the day, his bonee. Babliseth doesn't consider Salim Sandaasiya and does not bargain too much with the Bohri lady who leaves, smiling, with the feeding cup for her old and ailing father-in-law. The day has begun at Bhendi Bazaar for Babliseth, the hawkers obliterating his shop's frontage with their cheap plastic sandals and shoes for children which intentionally go squeak-squeak, the noise from the traffic, the rising smell of onions and potatoes from the nearby wholesale Mirza Ghalib Market, the loud film music blaring from the bangle stalls towards the junction where there are red and green running lights on tape-decks which do their own disco to the bass which is further deepened. 'Jhoom barabar jhoom sharaabi, jhoom barabar jhoom', twing-twing-twing streak the red lights; 'Kaali ghataayen, aaha' the green lights go haywire; 'Mast fizaayen, aahaha', all the lights turn insane; 'Kali ghataayen, mast fizaayen, jaam utha kar jhoom, jhoom jhoom', the red lights and the green lights run away with each other as the bass celebrates their union. 'Jhoom barabar jhoom sharaabi jhoom barabar jhoom' dhadaam-dhadhar dhak-dhak. Bhendi Bazaar has its own beat, a separate heart with its own veins and arteries and pulses.

The azaan and there is a lull, Babliseth orders tandoor ka rotis, has his lunch with his bhaiyyas at the back of the shop and gets back to work. At six sharp she arrives, she keeps the taxi waiting, a very presentable, well-dressed man is with her. He looks like a Madrasi.

'Daddy, this is Shankar, this is my dad.'

Now what. Why is she doing this, this man is marrying her?

Babliseth feels very bad for the man, he shakes his hand, 'Come son, come into my shop, I will order you some chana batata with tilli. You like liver? It will only take two minutes.'

'Daddy! Shankar is vegetarian.'

'Okay, I will order you some ghanney ka ras, adrak maarkay. You will have?'

The man smiles, 'No thank you, some other time. But I am not completely vegetarian anyway, I like fish.'

'Ah very good, you come home, my third daughter makes fish just like her mother used to, pomfret fried in green masala. You will eat?'

The man says he can always try it. Babliseth is beginning to feel pleased. 'Come home, come home any time, baba, we will talk there, I am home every day after 8.35 p.m.

Otherwise you come on Sunday, I will cook for you.'

'Thank you.'

They leave. Soon enough it is time for Babliseth to shut shop and catch the 8.04 p.m. Number Three back home.

At the dinner table he starts the conversation, in itself a feat.

'Aapa had come to the shop today.'

The upstairs couple is fighting, something is thrown, a table, a chair? Babliseth looks up at his high ceilings, if they were lower those two would be on his dining table slugging away at each other. 'Getting upset is not good for babies-in-stomachs,' declares Babliseth.

'Well then, he should also not piss her off the way he intentionally does.'

Babliseth grunts. Achchiwali speaks again, 'Daddy, I really think we should move from here. Mrs D'Mello's chain got snatched this morning when she was on her way to church for early Mass. And now your bedroom has also begun dripping because they have ripped out the red-oxide flooring on top, to put marble strips.'

Babliseth is surprised to discover that he has not noticed the leaks in his ceiling for himself, that man upstairs is deranged, bhenajadinaa! Born of his sister.

Babliseth notices now that his Teesriwali is all dressed for her night shift, looking attractive in her uniform of blue silk sari, the pleats all professionally pinned up at her shoulder. She is poking her spoon into her plate with its doodhiwali dal, turning something around on it. Babliseth pokes his finger into his plate to see what the problem is, it is just the squishy doodhi.

Teesriwali speaks in a resigned tone, 'Daddy, you must also let us cook.'

'Haan, but you are all busy and I do not mind.'

'Well, you work too, and we mind. Let us atleast do it on some days.'

Achchiwali is also peering into Teesriwali's plate, she gets her a fresh plate and fishes out from the earlier one, between the doodhi and the dal, what looks like a well-cooked cigarette butt. Chhotiwali giggles.

So that is where it disappeared in the morning. Babliseth re-starts the conversation.

'Aapa came to the shop today. With a boy.'

'Boy?'

'Man.'

'Then?'

'I think he is marrying her.'

'Really? What a bitch, she did not tell us anything! Do we know him, what is his name?'

'Shiva.'

'Shiva? Daddy, are you sure?'

'Kya main sarkeylaa dikhta hoon, do I look crazy? Of course I am sure, he is Shiva and he is a Madrasi.'

'Daddy, Shiva is her friend from her journalism college days, he used to come home, remember?'

Babliseth does not. 'Was he Madrasi?'

'No, he was Telugu, obviously he still is. And you are supposed to say Tamilian if he is from Tamil Nadu.'

'Was she, was she, you know, what was she with him? Sexy or steady?'

'Oh God, daddy! From where do you pick up such strange words? No, no, they were all a big group of friends from her evening journalism course and they would all come home to meet mummy.'

Teesriwali has a thought, 'But didn't that Shiva get married? Aapa and mummy even went for his reception.'

Married? She is going to marry an already married man? A question bubbles up to the surface.

Can South Indian men keep marrying?
Daddy, your query should be about Hindu men.
Ismaili men can marry four times?
Women should also marry again.
Can South Indian men keep marrying?

Babliseth channel surfs after dinner, he smokes a cigarette, he smokes another, flicking the ash into his cupped other hand. He waits till the Loud One comes home. She is surprised to see him up until so late.

'Daddy! Why are you not in bed, is anything wrong?'

'That boy who came to the shop, what is his name?'

'He is not a boy, he's a man.'

'That Madrasi . . .'

'Daddy, you better not say that in front of any South Indian! He is Tamilian.'

'That man is marrying you?'

'Why do you persist in being so sexist?'

Babliseth grunts.

'You are supposed to ask me if we are marrying each other.'

Babliseth waits, he thinks he can outwait her any time.

'Well? Are you going to rephrase your question?'

Babliseth waits.

'I'm going to bed if you have finished irritating me.'

Oh-ho, look who is talking!

'Good night daddy.'

'That South Indian who is not Telugu, his name is Shiva?'

'It's Shankar.'

Babliseth goes to bed, takes a last drag of his cigarette and thinks, two down, only two to go, the relief of it. He flicks his cigarette expertly across the floor, it will burn itself out there and stain the floor a bit but that does not matter because Cracko can always swab it off. Better than burning a big hole in the the mattress, Rozena had to shake him awake when she smelt singeing cotton. He flops on his tummy and falls into a dreamless sleep.

At the beginning of time Mazagon, too, slumbered peacefully. Surfacing like Bombay's six other islands as a dense combination of fish shit and rotting palms, was Machcha grama or the village of fish, Mastyagram in Sanskrit, Maazghar, the central portion of the house, the centre of the seven islands. The British anglicized it to Mazgon, the Parsis called it Mazagon, the Gujaratis and Ismailis named it Majgaum and the Marathis, Maazagaon, their village. When the natives left the predominantly British high-walled fort area to settle on the outskirts, in adjoining islands, the Christians build a little village within Mazagon for their parents, they called it simply that, The Village; the rest of Mazagon referred to it as Mhatarpacady,

61

the quarter of the elderlies.

As the original island of the seven isles, Mazagon went under siege by a group of negroid-like people from beyond the islands, the Sidis, who in 1690-91 seized the island. Rustomji Dorabji, a Parsi, organized a militia of local fishermen, the then aboriginal kolis, and helped drive out the invaders, in gratitude his family was granted the hereditary surname of Patel, protector-lord. Mazagon forgot the story but retained its respect for its Parsi-Irani settlers, thus when the biggest riots flared up elsewhere in Dhobi Talao, the Muslims of Mazagon remained cordial with their neighbours. The Dhobi Talao district had been damaged in 1874 during the Parsi-Muslim riots, when the Parsis living there had become alarmed at the size of a Muslim funeral procession wending its way to the cemetery at nearby Sonapur and had begun throwing stones, one of which killed an old man. About this opined J.M. Maclean, editor of the *Bombay Gazette* who lived for many years at the Byculla Club in Love Lane, 'There would have been no disturbance at all if the government had taken proper precautions to keep the peace. Unfortunately, governor Sir Philip Wodehouse left the people to protect themselves; forgetting that, if the people in India could protect themselves from violence and rapine, they would not want the English to rule them.'

Maclean was also sniffing at the Portuguese who had wed their princess, Catherine of Braganza, to King Charles II and had gifted A Ilha Da Boa Vida, the island of good life in dowry, except Mazagon which they refused to deliver. This was theirs, Bom Bahia, the good bay. The

British persisted, and took over Mazagon in 1665, England's crown leased this island with its 'excellent harbour and its natural isolation from land attacks' to the East India Company at a 'farm rent of ten pounds payable in September 30 of each year'. Novelist Thomas Moore sailed into Mazagon and lived here to draw inspiration for his celebrated *Lallah Rookh* written in 1817 where he weaved instances around Mazagon's famous mango trees which fruited twice a year, in May and during Christmas.

Quickly, and elegantly, the beautiful town houses came up in Mazagon, also among Bombay's first respectable hotels, the Hope Hall Family Hotel, and on the slopes of Mazagon Hill was built the Belvedere House, also called Mark House because it was white-washed regularly so as to be a landmark for the vessels sailing into Mazagon's harbour. The pensive ghost of one Eliza Draper is said to haunt Mazagon Hill, blessing the students who study under the lights of the hill's lamps and warning the lovers behind the bushes of their folly. Poor Eliza eloped on the night of 14 January 1773, down a rope ladder from Belvedere House. She was trying to run away from herself. Of mixed race and parentage, she was born in Anjengo, 600 miles south of Bombay, and had been sent off to England to learn enough crafts and wiles to attract a husband who could 'provide her an Establishment'. She returned at fourteen and married Mazagon resident Daniel Draper, twenty years her senior, an employee of the East India Company, from whom she had two children in 1759 and 1761.

Eliza went to England to leave her children there in 1765, she came back to Mazagon but docility did not suit her neither did her husband who rose to become accountant-general. Eliza and Daniel Draper had nothing in common, as she complained to a friend, 'Our minds are not pair'd.' While in England, society flattered her with terms like 'the Brahmine' and 'la belle Indienne' but when back, she found Bombay provincial to the point of brutality, 'a Dearth of everything which could charm the Heart—please the Fancy, or speak to Judgement'. She decided to elope when Daniel Draper started an open affair with their maid. She left two notes. To a friend she wrote, 'My heart is full. The next twenty-four hours will either destine me to the grave or to a life of reproach. I deserved better, if chance had not counteracted the good propensities assigned to me by nature.' To her husband she wrote, 'I go, I know not whither, but I will never be a tax on you Draper. I am not a hardened or depraved creature, I will never be so.'

Elizabeth's Sir Galahad was Sir John Clark of the Navy, himself the father of many children of mixed stock and in command of a frigate in Bombay, thus perfect for carrying her off by water. She boldly went down the side of Mazagon Hill on the rope ladder into his waiting arms and ship, but the union did not last long; she sought refuge with an uncle in Rajahmundry before leaving for England where she further declined through relationships with the writer Abbe Raynal and political pamphleteer John Wilkes. She died in poverty at Bristol, all of thirty-five. The spot from where the doomed-from-birth Elizabeth Draper went down Mazagon Hill has long since been scooped out and tossed into the bay, along with Belvedere House, to reclaim land for the harbour line suburban system, the Dockyard

Road Station, and the Mazagon Docks.

Part of the other side of the hill was flattened out for the Polson's butter-making factory. Diagonally opposite it came up Gunpowder Lane with its gunpowder manufacturing unit. And at the naaka, the junction, tram tracks were laid; the line A1 went all over all the islands and came back to Mazagon TT, tram terminus, every night. On the other side of the naaka sprang up Bombay's first ice factory. The very first consignment of ice to the seven islands was ordered by Sir Jamsetjee Jeejeebhoy I in September 1834 for one of his sumptuous dinners. The ice was brought in by ship, some say from all the way from America, ceremoniously chipped and served in water glasses. The *Bombay Samachar* a few days after the dinner reported that 'the host and the guests have fallen ill with a cold'. This did not stop the ice-making plant from coming up in Mazagon which, it seemed, could not make the ice fast enough for Bombay.

Then came the first of the floods of migrants, because of the famines and the droughts and the deprivation in their villages; 1881 saw an influx of 1,26,000 destitutes from Ratnagiri alone, later in 1921 Ratnagiri sent 2,36,000 into the city. They came to Bombay to survive, crowding Mazagon, sleeping on its pavements in desolately covered huddles, in what Mark Twain describes as an 'attitude of rigidity counterfeiting death'. Not all these pavement-dwellers were fortunate to find themselves kholi-tenements, some turned the open spaces on Mazagon's outskirts into slums and those who did slightly better encroached upon other open spaces to build kutcha housing which turned

65

pucca over time, and to which a floor was added. And then there were more migrants from other parts of the country, new neighbourhoods—walls supporting each other—sprang up near the old ones, ghettos within ghettos with open drains and garbage spilling out on to the streets. At the turn of the century Bombay's people, too, had taken their city for granted, homes turned into hovels with neglect. Death had to follow. September 1896 saw the dreaded bubonic plague, on an average 1,900 people died per week, at its height in 1899 over 2,800. Large crosses went up all over Mazagon and its Mhatarpacady. As did the sign by the undertaker who had to ship out the dead British: 'We can send dead body any where any how any time'. A sign of the times in the 1990s when undertakers have changed their message to 'When you drop dead drop in here'.

Dr W.M. Haffkine set to work on finding vaccines against snake and rat bites and rabies. The then Aga Khan, Sir Sultan Mohammed Shah, grandfather to the present His Highness Prince Karim Aga Khan, gave Dr Haffkine his palace to live in at Mazagon's Aga Hall, Sir Sultan Mohammed Shah also paid for all the facilities for his research and laboratory experiments. Here Dr Haffkine worked for two years until the government, convinced of the success of his methods, decided to give him official support. When Dr Haffkine's first batch of vaccines were ready not one among the thousands gathered would come forward to be inoculated, they were fearful and suspicious. Sir Sultan Mohammed Shah stood in the centre of Aga Hall, rolled up his sleeve and asked Dr Haffkine to do the needful; the crowd followed. Aga Hall was to re-convert itself into a block of flats for the Ismailis, and a school in which Rozena taught for a while and the Prince Aly Khan Hospital. Babliseth went to live there until he moved to Bottlewala Mansion in another part of what was once the jewel among the seven islands, Mazagon, Bombay-10.

And this is its history, slowly seeping out of the place and disappearing with more being lost even as Babliseth sleeps. Because there is no vaccine to eradicate the politics of communalism.

Today is Sunday, Babliseth's in-built alarm clock tells him so because it wakes him up at 8.30 a.m. He opens his eyes and feels a slight sense of panic, what will he do today, his dukaan is shut. Then he smiles, today is the last day, from tomorrow Mad Dog has said everything will be on the up, there will be no looking back.

Babliseth gets out of bed and goes through his hot water and tea and shaving routine. When he is in the balcony in front of his little shaving mirror, twisting his face this way and that, to snip off a particularly stubborn hair from his ear, he notices a lot of movement across the road. He stops to look, that Shiv Sena fellow, Chhagan Bhujbal, is coming out of Padamsee Wadi with a big group of boys. Last night there had been a fight, a big drunken one, among the new Padamsee Wadi residents, the old ones have all but left, Babliseth supposes Chhagan Bhujbal has woken up on a Sunday morning to come back and check on the peace. Babliseth does not like Chhagan Bhujbal because he lives in one of those several blocks of flats that have come up in Mhatarpacady, pulling down old houses like that! But Rozena said he was alright, 'Babli, even though he is a Shiv Sena fellow he is not like them, aamptya-bhaamptya, he actually helps people.' Rozena went to him every now and then for a bottle of blood for this one and a loan-sanction for that one; she had discovered that he adopted his brother's two children when he had died young. As if sensing Babliseth glaring-staring at him, Chhagan Bhujbal looks up at the Bottlewala Mansion balcony and raises his hand in a your-leader-wishes-you wave. Babliseth does not know what to do with this politician waving madly at him, he cannot smirk because of Rozena, he cannot smile because this man is Shiv Sena, he goes away inside.

Tea, bath, leisurely cooking, chicken boneless because Shankar is coming for dinner and he gets a bit distressed when he sees bones, the Loud One can cut salad for herself since she has turned vegetarian. Babliseth also makes dal-fry for lunch. Then he picks up the pichchi, he keeps two in the house, and gets on with the dusting before Cracko can arrive, flick, flick, flick, the last strong flick dislodges a single-stem rose holder from on top of the fridge, it falls and breaks into three pieces, ah well.

Which reminds him, he goes into the kitchen and begins checking on the crockery to see how many Cracko has cracked beyond redemption. He pulls them out one-by-one and neatly splits them into two over his doubled knee and tosses them into the bin. He examines the quarter plates, some more go into the bin via his knee-treatment. He looks at the bowls and the cups and their handles, he raps them—one sharp tap—against the basin and they crack open. Into the bin.

'Daddy! What are we going to eat on if you break everything?'

Oh no, today is a Sunday and she is at home too. Why don't evening papers come out on Sunday, that way she would be at work.

'Daddy, now look what you have gone and done! There is not one cup to have chaay in.'

Babliseth grunts, he hands his eldest-born a glass.

'Please bring some cups and plates from the dukaan tomorrow, matching ones, okay?'

Babliseth grunts, how can he bring matching ones, he has to sell those. He can only bring those pieces which are remaining from the sets which have arrived partially broken in their boxes and therefore cannot be sold. But why is she saying please. He looks cautiously at her, stiffening for the blow which she will definitely deliver.

'I quit my job yesterday.'

Babliseth relaxes, that's all right, she can now get married to Shankar, settle down and have children. He knows she and Shankar have been saving money since the time they got engaged, he knows they still don't have enough money to buy a flat, how can they, both are journalists and what do journalists earn. Anyway that is all right, they can stay with him until they save enough money. The girls won't mind giving up their bedroom and sleeping in the hall for them.

'Daddy! Did you hear what I said? Don't you have anything to say?'

'What does Shankar say?'

'Daddy don't you have anything to say?'

'No.'

'How can you not have anything to say? You can at least give me some advice, tell me what to do next!'

'Shankar will give you advice. I cannot say anything because it is in your kismet to suffer.'

'My kismet? To suffer? I can't believe this. Daddy you are so unbelievably unreal at times.'

Babliseth is stubborn is his beliefs only because he believes in them, really and truly. He repeats, 'It is in your kismet. Your stars are like that.'

'I suppose that gaandu Mad Dog told you that when you were having one of your buddy-buddy lunches at Delhi Darbar. And both of you enjoyed it, didn't you, the thought there was at least something to whip me into place? My stars, oh fuck, my stars! You really get a kick out of watching me hurt, don't you?'

How does she know that he takes Mad Dog to Delhi Darbar?

Chhotiwali wanders into the kitchen, rubbing sleep out of her eyes. 'Good morning daddy.'

'Good morning, maa. I will make you an omelette?'

'Yes please.'

Babliseth chops up the onions zig-zag on the kitchen counter's cuddapah slab itself, disregarding the Loud One giving him the chopping board. He smashes a few eggs into a tope, since there are no bowls and plates left, fishing out as much egg shell as he can from it. Some salt, some pepper, some dhania-jeera powder, some lal mirchi powder, tilt the tope at an angle and beat it all up with a spoon.

Teesriwali walks in from her night shift, she looks drained.

'I will make you omelette, maa?' He carefully breaks two more eggs into the tope because his Teesriwali is watching.

'Yes thanks, but I hope you have used the chopping board for the onions. Rats roam all over the kitchen in the night. That night when I came back from afternoon duty there was one tiny one sitting on the gas and one roaming around on the kitchen counter. I couldn't even eat my khaana.'

Babliseth has the answers, 'We will start keeping the khaney ka bartans with your plate on the dining table itself. And I will get chuha maarne ka dawa tomorrow.'

'Daddy we keep putting chuha dawa to poison the rats and they keep coming back; this building is infested with rats, the bandicoots climb up from the pipes. I came late from work that night and there was a huge one near the water pump in the bathroom and at least one more on top of the water tank in the bathroom. We should just sell the house and go away to a decent flat.'

Babliseth ignores the Loud One and sets the tawa on the gas, slices a huge cake of butter which sizzles in the pan, he slips in the egg mix and disintegrates the few bits of egg shell into the cooking omelette with the help of the tawita, flips over the omelette with the same ladle and a golden, buttery, thick omelette is ready to be cut into two with the tawita in the pan itself and served to his two daughters.

Mission accomplished, Babliseth leaves for the dukaan. He does not have to go, he has already given Baba Deen instructions for the afternoon. But this is better, given the fact that she will want to talk to him. Besides, he can phone Achchiwali in Belgaum from the shop, there being no STD-ISD at home. Babliseth is at the bus stop, cigarette in hand, and the corner of his eye catches a shoal of flying rubbish; a woman from the third floor of that building has just emptied her kitchen-waste on to the road. Babliseth takes a drag from his cigarette and walks over to inspect the waste matter, the baleful eye of a fish stares back at him among its bones and other scrapes and peels. Babliseth looks up at the third floor, ascertains the flat, stubs his cigarette and slowly begins ascending the stairs wishing he did not have to do this, Babliseth tries to talk as less as is humanly possible when away from his dukaan, his own neighbours in Bottlewala Mansion have yet to elicit more than a dozen complete sentences from him. Babliseth reaches the third floor and rings the bell, a middle-aged woman opens the door and looks at him enquiringly.

'That kachra . . .?'

'It fell on you?'

'No, no, nothing like that.'

'Then why are you so bothered?'

'The road gets dirty.'

'The municipality is paid to clean roads.'

'See, this is leading to too many bandicoots and rats in Mazagon. Can I request you to please keep the kachra in your rubbish-bin till the jhadoowali comes to collect it every morning?'

'No, my kachrey-ka-dabba will get dirty.'

Babliseth turns around and swiftly descends the stairs.

By the time Babliseth gets the Number Three and reaches the shop Baba Deen has sorted out the crockery which has to go on rent for the navjyote lunch. He is waiting for the haath-gaadiwala to cart the bundles of glasses and plates and spoons-and-things to the Parsi agiary where the lunch is being held. Baba Deen has packed in more plates than necessary.

'Arrey dhayus, itney jaasti plate kaayku pack kiya?'

'Woh Neville Godiwala ney bola hai, Babliseth.'

'Kaayku?'

Baba Deen shrugs. Babliseth gives him the day off after he loads the hand-cart and takes a bus to the agiary where the brother-sister catering team of Tanaaz and Neville Godiwala are busy with the preparations. It is a very busy time for them, Parsi children from all over the world come in this season for their own weddings and the navjyotes, religious ceremonies, of their children; not to mention the continuous weddings-navjyotes taking place on double shifts among the Bombay Parsis themselves. It isn't that there are so many Parsis left overall, it is just that their functions tend to take place in short, sharp bursts of enormous gaiety during season.

'Sahebji, Neville.'

'Sahebji, Babliseth, aao, aao. Taste the machchi-saas and tell me if it is okay.'

Babliseth discovers that the reason why Neville Godiwala wants more plates is because the quality of banana leaves has greatly declined. The banana plantations of Vasai and Virar, where the leaves mostly come from, are being ruthlessly chopped down to make way for construction; what is left is not too much you can happily eat off from even if thoroughly cleaned; one of the reasons why the Parsi and Irani children—specially those of the NRPs and NRZs, non-resident Parsis and Zoroastrian-Iranis—prefer plates. Babliseth wonders how the South Indians of Bombay, also users of banana leaves, are handling the situation. He must remember to ask Shankar tonight.

The hostess comes up to speak to the contractor and sees Babliseth. 'Tamhe ayyaa beseyla chho? Aao, aao, bhaley padhaariya.' Come, good you have arrived.

She is the Zoroastrian-Irani Parveen Shokrekhuda who has eight children and they have given her fourteeen children in turn. Most have left Mazagon to settle elsewhere in the world, her daughters Niloufer and Fareeba are Teesriwali's friends. Babliseth remembers the Shokrekhuda restaurants, and the first Irani restaurant to come up in Mazagon. It was also the first to be sold when demands for free tea and donations for festivals became larger and strident. Babliseth remembers the board right in the front of the restaurant's entrance, a long black board on which was written in firm chalking:

No Division of Beverages
    Smoking
    Fighting
    Credit
    Outside Food
    Sitting Long
    Talking Loud
    Spitting
    Bargaining

Listening to Outsiders
Change
Address Inquiry
Telephone
Matches
Discussing Gambling
Newspaper
Combing
Beef
Hard Liquors Allowed

Babliseth is halfway through his delicious lunch when Teesriwali arrives at the agiary and spots him.

'Daddy you should have waited for me. We could have come together.'

Babliseth blinks. 'But I never knew you were coming, maa.'

'Daddy, I told you two days back we were invited. I even had your shoes polished from the mochi downstairs. Are you wearing them?'

Babliseth tucks in his sandalled feet under his chair.

'And why are you wearing this old bush-shirt, daddy?'

Why are they all beginning to sound like their eldest sister?

After lunch he goes back to the shop and phones Belgaum at his daughter's hostel. He waits till she is called from the room.

'Hel-low, maa, how are you?'

'Hi daddy, tum kaisey ho?'

'Fine, very fine, tip-top. But people are throwing too much kachra on Mazagon's roads.'

75

'Daddy, why won't you accept that Mazagon is not the same any more?'

'Are you eating properly?'

'Yes daddy, and I am studying properly too.'

'Aapa has resigned from her job.'

'Really? Why?'

'Must have fought with them. It is in her stars to fight with everybody. Mad Dog said.'

'Ya? What else did he say?'

'He said the best days are beginning from tomorrow, so you will do well in your exams.'

'Did you ask him if it was okay to sell the house and move to the suburbs?'

Babliseth is silent.

'Hello daddy, are you there?'

He grunts.

'Daddy you had promised me that you would ask him.'

'Aapa has uchkaaoed you, she told you to tell me, no?'

'Daddy, it does not matter what she said. I am saying you should sell the house.'

'Okay maa, I have to put down the phone, too much money is going. Bye bye.'

Babliseth settles into the hay of his godown and takes his Sunday mid-afternoon nap.

Before catching the Number Three, Babliseth drops in to see Rozena and talk to her, he finds himself really speaking to her today, his sentences suspended over her grave in the afternoon sun. The rose bush has been watered in the morning, he gives the caretaker money for the Sunday watering. By the time he gets back home his jamaai is there. Babliseth is happy to see him, another man in the house feels nice. He shakes his hand, 'Hello Shankar, theek hai na beta, kuch khaaya?'

'Hello daddy, thanks I just had chaay.'

'Haan, you must have had it in a glass. That bloody Cracko breaks everything but they won't sack her.'

'That's all right, I did not mind the glass.'

The Loud One is on the phone in the kitchen, and her volume is rising. She has finished fighting with all of Babliseth's relatives because of Rozena and now she is fighting with Rozena's relative on the phone. 'No, you listen to me! You are supposed to be like my grandfather, you are supposed to set a good example to me and my sisters, and what are you doing? Trying to grab your landlady's room! Why must you go to the custodian and lodge a false complaint that Aunty Coomi is trying to evict you? You know very well that she cares for you. When Aunty Maisie walked out on you, she and Eileen looked after you when you were sick. How can you say that, of course it is my fucking business, Eileen is my childhood friend and you are behaving pathetically, Aunty Coomi is even willing to give it to you in writing that you can stay in her room till you bloody die, what more do you want? . . . I think this is really sick, how can you call yourself an Ismaili and go to jamaatkhana twice a day when this is how you behave? . . . So what if your lawyer is also an Ismaili, how does his encouragement of your insanity make him a better Ismaili?'

Shankar goes into the kitchen and makes her hang up.

He tries calming her down, 'Forget it janoo, he is not going to listen to you.'

'Arrey but how can he do this? It is wicked to take someone's house away from them. Do you know how long he has lived there even after Aunty Maisie left him?'

The fair and tall and attractive Aunty Maisie. Maisie Kiddenwoggen who fled religious persecution in Burma and trekked all the way to Bombay to begin life anew in Mazagon with her flesh-coloured stockings and stilettos, her cigarettes in an eighteen-inch holder, her auburn hair framing her high cheekbones and cognac-coloured eyes. She met Rozena's relative and they left Mazagon for Colaba moving into the sub-let where all the children including Coomi and Feroze Murzban's Eileen and Mozam would gather for holidays to be taken for wrestling matches at Worli for which Feroze and Rozena's relative were co-promoters. They would also get taken to Goolestan on Cuffe Parade where Aunty Maisie's sister Josephine lived. Her son Dinshaw Sanjana and all the children would be set around the huge dining table, starched dinner napkins set firmly around their collars and they were taught table manners as the butler served the courses. No fork and spoon, fork and knife; no, you do not drink your soup, you eat it; and no chewing loudly, no eating with your mouth open like a little pariah, and where is that please and thank you, please?

The children would play on Goolestan's grounds, they had formed a Famous Five Club like their Enid Blyton characters, and used the watchman's cabin as their club house. In an un-Blytonish twist, the password to their club was FO and one day, when they would not let her in, this one had run into Goolestan where Aunty Maisie and Aunty Joe sat having their customary cigarette-chat and said, 'Aunty Maisie, Aunty Maisie, what is fuck off?'

Aunty Maisie has stubbed out her cigarette, and Aunty Joe had stubbed out hers, and all the children were called up from Goolestan's garden and their mouths had been washed with soap and water. The club stood hereby disbanded, the watchman's cabin was taken down to build Sea Wind to sell it to Dhirubhai Ambani as his residence. Aunty Maisie left her man because she found him fooling around with the nurse while lying on his hospital bed of a heart attack. She moved to 4th Pasta Lane where she shared a room with three call girls, and when she died she was down to smoking beedis. All she could leave behind was her altar above her narrow bed, one picture of Mother Mary with Baby Jesus in her arms, and the other of the Aga Khan.

And this one, with her manners, please, thank you, fuck you; glaring at him when he put up his feet on the dining table and hissing sharply when he pushed the plate of oranges towards his jamaai kindly suggesting, 'Khaao, khaao, sastaa hai.' Eat freely, oranges are cheap these days.

Babliseth lights a cigarette, he asks for the name of the lawyer who is representing Rozena's relative.

'That shady piece of shit, the one who pretends to be a big shot in the community. One day I should send a long list to the Aga Khan on whom he should soundly kick on their backsides.'

The lawyer's name.

'That Merchant, Mohenjodaro and Harappa's father.'

Shankar is vastly amused, he hoots with laughter, 'Who are these poor children you are condemning as archaeological sites?'

'Arrey janoo, they are like that only, his two daughters, bloody relics. No wonder nobody wants to marry them when they have such a haraami father.'

'Chah, no need to say such things.'

'Okay baba, sorry.'

Babliseth is amazed, the Loud One is actually calming down for this man, wah! His attention goes to the yelling upstairs, he thinks she is throwing a plate, is that her husband throwing a steel glass back, their twins set up a joint wail. Poor gaandu, he cannot handle one wife and she gets pregnant and gives him two children in one shot, but sons.

'Daddy?'

He focusses, his jamaai is telling him something. 'We were thinking, we have some money collected. Would you like to sell this flat and we could get together to buy something nice in the suburbs?'

Babliseth likes the suburbs, he goes there for his ugraani. But the train rides which he will have to take every day to the dukaan? That persistent trace element of dried urine, that long and weary haul of densely packed human habitation . . .

His jamaai is explaining things logically, pointing to Teesriwali, 'She has to take the train from here everyday till the airport and back at all kinds of odd hours, when the other one comes back from Belgaum she can find a job in the suburbs and the youngest is just finishing college, so that should be no problem. We know you will have a slight hassle with the train commuting, but perhaps you could also cut down a little on your working, stagger the hours, so that you can take it easy a little as well. After all, we are all working now.'

Babliseth also gestures towards Teesriwali, 'But she will get married and go away soon.'

'Yes daddy, but the rest of your daughters are still here.'

'I will have to ask Mad Dog.'

That really sets her off. 'Mad Dog! Mad Dog! Mad Dog! He hates me for not allowing him into this house, do you think he is going to say yes the moment he knows this involves me and my happiness? Can't you see that the bastard is just a control freak, he enjoys the idea of controlling you? Or are you hiding behind him, actually?'

'Okay, I will go to another astrologer.'

'Fine, which one?'

He names him, he is famous and everyone says he is very good and she should know, he used to write for the paper she worked for.

'Him? His work is just like his name. He is a bloody charlatan. Do you know what he used to do? He would be so busy making chutya out of everyone all over the country that he would phone and say to use the matter from the year before last's file because the stars were back in identical position. Publicity ka bhooka bastard, he would come into Bombay and use the paper to let people know that he was available so that he could charge them big bucks. Serves them right, of course, for turning into suckers. Do you know, when he would insist that old matter be repeated from the files, the editor never said anything because he was his own jaatwala. Soon after the editor left the proprietor threw him out on his bloated backside.'

Babliseth nods, she had to say something like this; the lamp of truth always shines with too lurid a flame in her case. Her stars, her kismet, what to do.

He offers his jamaai a counter-proposal. 'You two get married, baba. And stay with me here, maybe you can stay with me forever if these girls get married fatafat.' He looks at Teesriwali, his eyebrows raised in enquiry.

She nods in agreement, 'You can try it, aapa and bhaijaan, see how it works. At least you will be together.' She sounds pensive, and she looks so very sad when she says this.

Babliseth tries to change the topic.

I spoke to your mother today.
Oh daddy!
Yeah? What did she say?
Shush janoo!
I spoke to your mother today.

The phone rings. Teesriwali answers it. She is overjoyed, and then she says, 'What?' She listens, she turns white as a sheet, she says, 'Okay, I will call you back, just wait there.' She picks up her purse and runs out of the house.

Babliseth lights a cigarette, he turns on the television with the remote control and rapidly changes channels.

The phone rings again, the Loud One jumps for it. 'Yes I know you have been calling me about it, yes I know I should have called you back, I am sorry. But I wish you'd be a little more sensitive. Why don't you have someone else speak to him? Your sons-in-law have refused, so now you are asking me to do this for you? No, I have not asked him as yet. Do it now? Listen, this is not a good time, I have to keep the phone free for my sister . . . oh, all right, hold on.'

She puts her hand on the mouthpiece, 'Daddy, do you remember that widow who used to come here, the one with the two daughters?'

Babliseth does not.

'The one whom mummy used to call Talwar Ki Dhaar because the woman would keep saying she had walked on a sword's edge to raise her children alone?'

Babliseth still does not remember.

'Well, she wants to talk to you. She has been phoning all the time, she had been calling me in the office too.'

'What does she want?'

'Why don't you talk to her?'

'Just tell me what she wants.'

'This is odd for me. Daddy, please take the phone.'

Babliseth changes channels.

'Daddy, she wants to marry you. She wants you to marry her.'

Shankar gasps, Chhotiwali looks fearful, Babliseth turns off the television and answers.

'Tell her I have not as yet forgotten your mother.'

The Loud One chokes as she speaks into the phone

83

and then hangs up. There is silence in the high-ceilinged house of Bottlewala Mansion, dogs yap in the darkening lane below, some neighbour's television rises and falls with anecdotes, out of sight but never out of hearing. They sit like this, Babliseth and his family, until she runs in shaking and breathing in short bursts of sharp crying.

'Aapa, aapa, I called him so many times and he would not answer, I wrote him so many letters, I told a friend of mine in California to check. Aapa, he has married an Ismaili girl there.'

Chhotiwali breaks into sobs.

'What! Are you sure?'

She tries gathering herself to speak, so low that Babliseth has to lean forward to hear, 'I just went down and spoke to him, I called him long-distance, he said his father had insisted because his father had never liked our family. Even when he was here he would keep telling me that we were not a good family, but I never told any . . .'

She sinks to the floor in a faint.

Oh Rozena, Rozena.

August 1992. Babliseth is smoking his last cigarette, he is in bed, retired for today but listening to the conversation in the hall between his jamaai and his eldest daughter, she is distraught. They are to marry in the next forty-eight hours in the house itself and they cannot find a Hindu priest to perform some religious rites in a Muslim's house. She wanted only a court marriage, he said his father would also appreciate a small ceremony. She said fine, get one of your priests, all the brahmins refused. She had thrown a fit and it had taken all her sisters to calm her down. Babliseth had been pleased that she had not simply cancelled her wedding, he had met her in-laws to-be, good people. And that nice sister of Shankar's, Rukkumani, she had mixed up the sambhaar with the ghee in the rice and served it to Babliseth because she was worried that he would not know what to do with it otherwise, there being no chapatis.

They, his daughter and his jamaai, had then gone to the Arya Samaj where their reaction had been so fanatical that it had upset the unflappable Shankar beyond measure. The Arya Samaj priests declared that because she was a Muslim they would have to do all of the following. First a small pooja, then her shuddhikaran, cleansing, then the change of her name, they suggested Parvati, which would complete her conversion to Hinduism. Shankar had fired them at the Arya Samaj head office, 'Some politicians decide to spoil the name of Hinduism and you get influenced by that?' To no avail, he had then spoken to his friends to hunt for a priest and it was a fairly wide let's-hunt-for-a-pundit circle by tonight.

Babliseth hears the scrape of a match, a cigarette is lit; and another. Bloody Aunty Maisie teaching her how to smoke!

'What is wrong with all these pious pricks. Why are Hindus so insecure about their religion?'

Shankar exhales. 'Janoo, you have to realize that the religion's followers are in utter crisis today. We are doing terrible things to ourselves.'

'So I must be terrorized into submission in the name of Hinduism?'

'Take yourself out of this, think of those being terrorized in the name of reservations. You know my friend Francis who works in that bank? Well, he sat for a banking exam. There were 500 people in the examination hall, he stood eleventh, there are twenty vacancies for that senior officer level, Francis has been denied because he is not a scheduled caste, scheduled tribe and the rest. In effect, the people who are being given the jobs are being told by the government, "We are putting you in this responsible position because you are unfit for it".'

'I am sorry for him, I really am, but what does this have to do with my current situation? We still don't have a dick-head to marry us. Why don't you phone your father and tell him to forget about it, let's just go to the court and be done with it. I hate this whole thing anyway, a wedding day is supposed to be the happiest in a bride's life but I am already deeply miserable. Just look how badly we are beginning this phase of our life together.'

'Janoo, please don't penalize my father because of the thoughtless actions of his religion. And don't get so dramatic about the rest, it will get sorted out.'

Babliseth nods in his bed.

'And me, my father, my sisters? What are we being penalized for?'

Babliseth frowns, yes, yes, say all this and he will run away, he will not marry you, then you will learn. Stupid bloody idiot! Twenty-five per cent Parsi, twenty-five per cent Kutchi, twenty-five per cent Hindu, twenty-five per cent Muslim and one hundred per cent insane, that's what she is.

The phone rings, Shankar gets it, 'Raghu, hi, bol.'

Raghu Nandan Dhar is Shankar's Kashmiri friend married to the Maratha woman Ujwala Patil who had sailed twice around the world in an open boat. Ujwala has sallied forth this time to find a priest, she has bamboozled one of their purohits into performing the ceremony at Bottlewala Mansion.

Babliseth flops on his tummy and falls into a dreamless sleep.

At the wedding of his daughter who looks downcast to his jamaai who looks nervous, not too many of the twenty invited have shown up on time because they were told that the muhurat would be at 10.21 a.m., the Ismailis understood this to be the auspicious time the ceremony would begin. The purohit ends the show at 10.21 a.m. and looks around, to find a few glazed eyes looking back, he then grandly declares, 'Zhaala!' Done!

Babliseth stands behind his jamaai, guarding him almost, who knows what might happen if she suddenly decides to lose her temper all over again. Ace newspaper photographer Mukesh Parpiani records this event, Babliseth protecting his jamai from his daughter, blows up the picture to a ten-by-ten and sends it for Babliseth who puts it into Rozena's cupboard.

January 1993. It should be dark, pitch dark with not a light on Mount Road and Dr Mascarenhas Road, but it is brightly, fiercely lit, with the fires burning everywhere. All of Mazagon appears to be in flames; and one whole line of parked taxis have been torched, the other line opposite is untouched, who told whom where to park and in which line? The sky is a blood orange, have they set fire to the Lakdaa Bazaar? There is the sound of gun fire, continuous gun fire echoing down Mazagon's deserted lanes. Chhotiwali stands by his side and her eyes are wide, she is deathly-still.

Babliseth is standing in the shadows of his balcony and thinking of Rozena singing the bhajan she sang on All India Radio, 'Raakhna ramakdaa maara ramey ramtaa raakhya re.' These dolls made of ash and dust, how my Ram makes them dance. He smiles, she sang so well.

His third daughter calls from inside, 'Daddy please, come inside, bring her with you, she should not be seeing such things.'

He comes in, the television is on, every international channel is showing Bombay burning, and its Muslims being hacked mercilessly. The phone rings. She answers, it is from Bangalore, 'Ya aapa, hi, no don't worry, we are okay, no they won't do anything to our building because there is a Hindu shop downstairs. Your father-in-law called, Rukkumani and her husband have also phoned, they want us to stay with them in Ghatkopar till it is all over. Ya, bhaijaan keeps calling, he says daddy should not go anywhere because they are taking down the trousers of men to check who is a Muslim, if he is circumcised they are knifing him to death on the spot. No, I swear I am telling the truth. Ya, he is better now, his bruises are almost gone. Here talk to him.'

Babliseth takes the phone to talk to his eldest daughter who has shifted to Bangalore, her husband has yet to shift there, she wants them all to come there immediately. He knows it is of no use, he tells her that. 'If this can happen in Bombay today, it can happen anywhere tomorrow. How much will I run with my daughters, how far can I run? When can I finally stop running?'

She cuts in, he listens, he comforts her, 'No don't worry I am okay now. The police were beating up all those protestors against the Babri demolition on the roads. Yes, I had half-way pulled down the dukaan's shutter but still the police came into the shop and beat me and my bhaiyyas badly with their lathis. They also broke some crockery, that is all.' He pauses, 'They won't do anything in the dargah, will they? They should not disturb Rozena.'

She is crying so hard that he has to hang up on her. He has not told her what happened when he went to a giraak for ugraani soon after the first phase of these riots; he thought he should quickly collect the money because he would need it to send his bhaiyyas to their native-places and fill food in the house. The giraak said, 'Kya Babli, dikhayen tum log ku barabar, hum log ne? Jaao idhar sey, saaley Babar ki aulad, Pakistan jaao, paisey-waisey ki baat bhool jaao.' The man whom he had sold crockery to for over twenty years for his shop in the suburbs and who had always called him Babliseth simply told him that they had finally taught him, and his kind, a lesson.

We showed you.

March 1993. Babliseth is at Rozena's grave, he is weeping, he is crouched near her nameplate and his shoulders are shaking, his body is heaving, she has been gone since January 1987 but he has never cried, not even at her funeral, and today is the day.

He went this morning, back to the giraak for the money because business had come to a standstill in Bhendi Bazaar from 6 December of the past year, when they pulled down the Babri Masjid. Today, after so many days since the bomb blasts, his daughters had let him go back to the dukaan. He had taken a bus to the suburbs for the ugraani, to the same giraak who had told him to get out from his shop. And the giraak had seen him and quickly said, 'Arrey Babliseth, aao, aao, baitho. You should have phoned me, I would have come with the money. Arrey Babliseth key liye ek chaay laao, garam.'

You showed us.

Oh Rozena, Rozena, Allah ka shukhar hai that you are not alive to see this.

B abliseth has long since left Mazagon. It is a coincidence that the Number Three bus tends not to be on time any more.

His eldest daughter is back in Bombay, her husband could not leave the city, it was not in her kismet to be happy in Bangalore. His second daughter is a pharmacist, with a good job in the suburbs. His third daughter has got herself a promotion, she works very hard. That twice-divorced ex-fiancé phoned her several times from America and even came to Bombay, he wanted to marry her now, as he put it in Americanese, 'Let's get together again'. She answered in matching Americanese, 'Take a hike, a long one.' Chhotiwali has gone into teaching, like her mother; she had a small breakdown after the riots, but she is a good educationist today and draws her spiritual sustenance from a Japanese movement which her sisters insist has brainwashed her. But Babliseth feels that her beliefs are not being imposed upon any one, so what is the harm, after all some dharam is better than no dharam. His son-in-law Shankar is doing very well as a journalist, touch wood, Mashallah! He and his wife have yet to buy a flat, they still cannot afford a one-bedroom in South Bombay and she is not willing to buy in an only Hindu or only Muslim building. Babliseth has shifted to the more cosmopolitan suburbs, his small flat is in a quiet, garden-filled enclave. He visits Rozena everyday, and he goes to the dukaan everyday because before he died Mad Dog has said that Babliseth will live to be eighty-nine and it is in his stars to work till then. Only three weeks and twenty years left of the new millennium before he can join Rozena.

There are new owners in his old house, lots of people who have converted part of his daughters' bedroom into a bathroom. The municipal corporation people have been paid to ignore this, just as they were paid to ignore everything upstairs. Both the balconies are tilting dangerously, the upstairs man refuses to chip in financially to fix it, his wife wants to go away to Canada to join her sister and husband who left Mazagon recently. They fight a lot over that. Their twins have grown, they keep failing in school. One of them is downstairs just now, surrounded by his friends and perched on his father's parked motorcycle, brandishing a toy gun and chanting a popular Hindi film song, 'Goli maar bhejey mein, dhichkyaon, bhejaa shor karta hain, bhejey ki sunega toh maregaa kallu, tu karega doosra bharega kallu, dhichkyaon!'

The little punk jumps up and down on the seat, he jabs the gun into the air, he keeps pulling the trigger, his voice and that of his friends rise to a near-frantic crescendo: Dhichkyaon! Dhichkyaon! Dhichkyaon!

C'MON BARBIE . . .

All the men at this party seem to have guns in their pockets, and I'm longing to use the Mae West line, 'Is that a gun in your pocket, or are you just happy to see me?' But nobody knows me. Nobody's even talking to me, I make this tentative foray into the wives' group, huddled in one corner of this darkened, airconditioning-blasted party place with an Arabian name. Some wives in long skirts and pantsuits are on the kerchief-sized dance floor jerking to 'I'm a Barbie girl, in a party world, c'mon Barbie, let's go party, aah, aah, aah, eeh.' The disc jockey switches songs and they begin bobbing to Bombay's national anthem. 'Bhejey ki sunega toh maregaa kallu, tu karega doosra bharega kallu, goli maar bhejey mein, dhichkyaon.' The sari-ed rest are in aforementioned huddle discussing Hauz Khas saris, I hover uncertainly at their fringe, they ignore me too.

I'm feeling cold, severe aircon always disconcerts me, I need to go to the loo, I try catching husband's eye; too busy to notice he is in animated conversation with the pink-and-podgy host who is sweating profusely in his designer waistcoat. I really have to go, I fight my way through the crush of bodies quaffing multi-coloured drinks, and wander out of party place to find the ladies powder room. There's a man holding a huge gun at the door, I ask him for directions. He impassively points with it to a gaggle of AK-47s, glinting in the dim light of the corridor. I thank his gun and walk down, excuse me, excuse me, do you mind moving that butt out of mine? They are guarding a politically-risen son, inside taking his leak. For his party's sake I hope he is relieving himself copiously, thunderously even; they have their sons-of-the-soil image to protect.

The ladies in our loo are tossing their expensively identically tinted hair this way and that, smoothing their short black dresses over their panty-lines. 'Oooh,' squeals one, patting a perfect curve into place, 'I think I just felt cellulite.' I feel abnormal in my salwar-kameez, I want to be like them, crackling with brittle sex, anorexic till their backs curve like crisp okra; multi-orgasmic, born-again bhendis. I go back into the party and tug at husband's arm to tell him this. 'Don't be silly,' he says before going back to his conversation, he is now talking to a heavy-duty industrialist, 'they are just automated fashion victims.' I wander off to a corner and sit down, seems to me that to get noticed at parties I have to be one of two things: under-bred and over-dressed, or over-bred and under-dressed. I'm mulling over these impossibilities when a Donald Duckie gives me a huge balloon with a pin. We are all supposed to burst our balloons with our pins at the stroke of twelve midnight, the host's birthday.

The Duckie, his backside stuffed with padding to have his tail stick out, rips off his beak-mask and takes centre-stage to jerk around a marionette, 'Nine, seven, five, four, three, two, one . . .' Pop go our balloons, pop go the champagne bottles, happy forty-third birthday whoever you think you are. Politically-risen son joins in the general singing, looking self-conscious, his arms crossed across his chest; defensive sort, all his pictures in the papers are also like that. He has been in the papers a lot, something to do with him sending some man to see a movie in a Pune theatre and the man dying in his seat. In Bombay when you now get threatened you are supposed to check on the gangster's antecedents by asking 'Poona mein picture dikhaayengaa kya?' But obviously all these industrialists and stockbrokers and assorted barons don't feel threatened by this guy, or else why would they make it a point of inviting him to all their parties? The mantra starts up again, it's back to the dance floor, 'Soch woch chhod bhejaa kaheko kharochna, apna kaam maal haath aye to dabochana, yede woh maregaa joh darega kallu, bhejey ki sunega toh maregaa kallu, goli maar bhejey mein, dhichkyaon!' Our job is to grab all that we can get, don't listen to your brain as it will kill you, the brain thinks too much, blow it out with bullets.

Husband wanders across with another heavy-duty, a stockbroker, 'Meet my wife, she has just come from Bangalore, and then he wanders away. The stockbroker smiles tentatively, 'So you like Bombay, bhabhi?' I want to tell him that I'm feeling like an immigrant in my own city, instead I brightly launch into this account of a stockbroker whose sperm count varies with the changes in the Bombay Stock Exchange index. His wife wants to get pregnant, they don't want to adopt and their highly-paid fertility expert consults an obscenely-paid shrink who co-relates the entire problem. The broker's spermies go down when the BSE index goes down, this being a bad time, his sperm count cannot be too good. The husband and wife are encouraged to take a holiday in Mauritius and she comes back pregnant.

'Uh, nice,' says the heavy-duty stockbroker edging away.

I watch a society writer memorizing the evening, her eyes dart like a lizard's all over the room, she is thin-boned and sharp, like those boys with breasts who clog the city's pubs, she has inserted a huge earring into her exposed navel. I wonder if I should get my navel pierced too, may be that would make feel like I belonged. But you need to be almost reptilian in body for that, and I have tried exercising to lose all that weight I have put on after coming back to Bombay, I even joined one of these terribly expensive aerobic places. I would come back home exhausted and sleep for several hours, waking up very hungry.

May be I should turn society columnist myself. I used to be, once upon a time, under the name of Pam Dyson, my boss chose that. I got invited to lots of parties so that I could write about them, it was fine with circulation climbing until I thought I could inject some sidelights. Like this party where the host had taped a message to his bedroom's door for all of us to see: 'I love your nutmeg nipples'; and this other Robin Hood fancy dress party where a couple came dressed as Friar Tuck and Maid Marion carrying placards around their necks 'Friar Fuck' 'Made Marion'. The boss did not let me pull all this in. This high-society woman walks around hand-in-hand with her married French diplomatic boy-friend and the journalists at the Press Club christen her 'The French Lieutenant's Diplomatic Bag', I think it's clever because Meryl Streep's *The French Lieutenant's Woman* has been all the rage and I put it into Pam Dyson but the editor knocks it off. He also edits the bit about Nutmeg Nipples being deserted by her man-friend, 'You want to get run out of town? You want our advertisements to be stopped?' he thunders. 'Why can't you write about who-all came?' But it is always the same people. 'Why can't you write about what they wore?' Always the same thing. 'What they ate?' Mushroom vol-au-vents all the time. He takes away Pam Dyson from me when I tell him I don't want my column to turn into a personal piss-pot for the celebrities and a permanent butt-nuzzling toadie like him, he also does not give me a raise of my mandatory Rs 100 a year for the next two years.

Well, nothing much seems to have changed since then.

Maybe I could just have a baby, that would make husband insanely happy, and I do have time to fill. Not the best reason for having one but I could have this cherubic, peaceful Buddha-like baby whom I could wheel around Shivaji Park, stopping to discuss nursery admission anxieties with other flustered mothers. Little Steps which interviews parents, Little Angels which wants donation; maybe I should start a nursery myself and call it Little Pricks. You can make a lot of money like that, from one small room in your house, terrorizing other people's shitty brats and their parents are so grateful to you.

It's a thought, I should consult husband.

I'm wondering if this would be a good day to broach the subject of the nursery when Ashok Row Kavi phones. Ashok, crack reporter of our time, editor of the gay magazine *Bombay Dost*, gay activist and film critic for a while; I had asked him to review a Hindi film and he filed copy declaring Indian cinema had 'come of age with the homosexual *Deedar-e-Yaar*'.

'Hello you silly cow, I heard you were back. How are you?'

'I'm an eighty-kilo chain-smoking menopausal hippopotamus. How are you?'

'Listen, do you want to come for a fancy dress party with me? I'm going as Little Beau Peep with her basket stuffed with condoms. You can come as her shepherd.'

I take up his invitation to visit his Humsafar Centre from where the city's gays do some great work in counselling, AIDS control and networking with India's homos. What he does in his personal life is, of course, a riot; suffice to say that he is not the tough, undeluded mother-fucker—father-fucker?—that he makes himself out to be. When I get there, Ashok Row Kavi is completing an interview with an American journalist, who is taping the entire conversation. The screen-saver on the Humsafar computer laterally scrolls 'I'm so gay I can't think straight'. I help myself to a tea and talk to a swishy sort who wants to know which lesbian group I belong to, I am struck dumb, the swish explains that he thinks I look like one, besides I am in drag.

I look at myself, I think I'm very cosmo in my trousers, tucked-in blouse and jacket.

'See what I mean?' he says. 'When we wear skirts the straights insist we are in drag, so when women wear men's clothing they are in drag too, right?'

Wrong, and he can kindly bugger off. He swishes away and I turn my attention to a group of eunuchs from Cheetah Camp in Chembur. They get called in by collection centres and gangsters to go and lean on a debtor, it works better than sending bouncers. One of them has beautifully shaped eyebrows, I tell the eunuch so, he preens. They have come to collect their monthly quota of condoms, Ashok Row Kavi and Humsafar are very insistent that they use them. There are 2,260 new AIDS infections every single day in the city and no less than a quarter are out of heterosexually irresponsible behaviour, meaning it has nothing to do with gays and hijdas and blood transfusions and prostitutes; just 'normal people' bonking away irresponsibly.

The eunuchs are actually men, several of them in

Bombay are, with all their appendages intact; they just dress so to make some bucks when they service the northern truckers entering the city at the check-posts. The truckers tend to be a problem, they refuse to use the condoms.

The American journalist turns to them and wants to know if they are aware that AIDS can be spread through oral sex as well. They nod, they add the truckers don't mind the use of condoms then. The journalist turns back to Ashok Row Kavi and says, 'Well this has been great. One last question. How does it feel to be called the father of the Indian homosexual movement?'

'Why not the mother?'

I ask the American journalist if the gays in America are also like the gays in India—penetration-driven, the act being more important than the entire relationship. 'Well yes,' he drawls, 'that's the man in them. But the female in them collides with this because it is like the woman anywhere in the world: in search of security and wanting to feel settled.' The journalist is bisexual. Now that's a lot of collision. 'Not really,' he smiles. 'it's by choice.' I'm confused.

Ashok pulls out a huge box of flavoured condoms to give the eunuchs, he gives me one to examine. The eunuchs talk to him, somebody has been showing up at their settlement wanting to use AIDS victims as guinea pigs for their experimental vaccine. Ashok takes down notes, he give them instructions, he says he will also help deal with this. I unroll the condom on my thumb and smell it, it is faintly raspberry-jammy.

The Humsafar phone rings, it is a call for Ashok from Delhi. He has just managed to stymie another group of hucksters trying to cash in on the sexy cause of AIDS by attempting to siphon away ten thousand dollars of foreign funding into their own pockets. The ultra-cultured voice of the lady at the other end tells him this is no way to behave. She adds, 'If you fly in this evening we could do some collective bargaining.'

'You mean, like think of ways to share the loot. Thanks, but no thanks.'

The livid lady hangs up.

I tell Ashok I like the idea of his Humsafar office. I see a lot of otherwise 9-to-5 straights bonding in the conference room. But do the upper-crust guys ever come here?

'Are you kidding? At private parties they go straight into the bedroom and flop on their stomachs wanting to get fucked till their eyeballs rattle. But they won't come out of the closet. They would much rather turn to electric shocks, aversion therapy, injections, all sorts of very expensive techniques to try and get knocked out of it. But homosexual tendencies do not just go away, you know, this has been scientifically proven now. And then they get married and make the poor woman's life absolutely rotten by furtively cruising in the evenings. Bloody Gucci gaandus.'

Ashok gives me the Sanskrit genesis on the g-word, goond maithuna, anal sensual meet. Oops, made a mistake in its meaning, didn't I?

We exchange notes, he gives me the juice on this well-attended party where an emerging captain of industry sits in the middle of a sofa with his wife on one side, and then their joint girlfriend arrives so he puts out his left hand on the sofa while everyone is watching from the corner of their eye and the girlfriend sits right on it, pretty blissful family picture that.

Our giggling comes to an abrupt halt when a shattered young boy is led in, his father's brother has violently raped him when no one else was at home. Humsafar takes care of an increasing number of such cases in the city.

Ashok Row Kavi, his Humsafar, his trained counsellors get down to work in a city being savaged.

SALVAGE, SAVAGE

It is—by any standard—a magnificient pile of architecture, the Victoria Terminus; UNESCO is looking at including it in the World Heritage list, like the Taj Mahal; the Indian railways is in correspondence with them on the subject, their people have been coming in for inspection. In the beginning it was called Bori Bunder, or the quay where the sacks were loaded in the trading town of Bombay. When the British decided to connect Bombay with the rest of the world by land, the first train in India—and the entire Indian subcontinent—was inaugurated on 16 April 1853, and it ran twenty-one miles from the make-shift wooden structure at Bori Bunder to Thane. The euphoria was enormous, bands played, there was pomp, there was pageantry, people congratulated each other and came from all over the country to purchase tickets and take train rides up and down, Bombay to Thane and back, their children waving gaily at the paddy fields and the herons on the way.

The idea of India chugging straight into the heart of a city was appealing, over one hundred acres of the Mody Bay at Bori Bunder was reclaimed to construct Victoria Terminus (VT); it took ten years to complete, and Rs 16,30,000 of which the chief architect Frederick William Stevens received Rs 5,000 as fees. Stevens put in a high-vaulted blue-starred ceiling, Italian marble and specially excavated, fine-polished blue Kurla stone along with the Porbunder variety. He believed that God lies in the details. He, therefore, drew out each and every detailing with his own hands, supervised its execution by the students of the J.J. School of Art as they filled in the ornamentations and the embellishments—the panels, the dados and friezes, the loggias, the buttresses, the arches and the superb stained glass windows. Stevens also constructed the Bombay municipal corporation's building across the road in a different style of architecture. In 1900 the architect of the city's two most impressive buildings died in his forties. Ravaged by the city's mosquitoes he succumbed to malaria and was buried at the Sewree cemetery; his grave has long since buried itself under several others.

Stevens has to simply stay forgotten as architect of Bombay's largest public building even when UNESCO finally decides on VT's worthiness as a World Heritage site, after all he was British and they were the bad 'uns. So bad that they left behind 58,000 kilometres of a railway network; to which post-1947 have been added 4,600 kilometres inclusive of the recently-laid 760 kilometre Konkan railway line. They gave their best to the railways, everything worked out to the minutest discipline, down to the station cash book, the code words to be exchanged when cash bags do, the design of the cash box. Today the hundreds of professional Indian officers who run the country's railway system commendably feel compelled to hang on to this workable tradition by the skin of their teeth, there are too many politicians about who want to change things around because the British were bad.

Bad, bad: knock off Victoria rani from her perch on the facade of VT, re-name the entire thing; and just a minute what are all those British gods and goddesses on the outside, scrape them off the stone! No, no, those are distinctive sculptures to symbolize what Bombay stands for, engineering, commerce, agriculture, like that; and that figure right on top on the dome is not a foreign goddess, it represents progress. Is progress not an Indian goddess? Theek hai, theek hai, let her be.

Let these also be, the slums that have come up alongside the railway tracks; the slum children throw stones at passing trains with unerring accuracy to blind commuters for life, but kya karen, these things happen in a democracy. In a 1998 survey there were 41,000 encroachments cheek by jowl on the tracks, most of these provided free electricity and water supply by the politicians. They live here, they marry and multiply, their progeny play on the tracks, their washing is done on it and their cooking, and their defecating. They make it impossible for daily track maintenance by the railway workers who are too scared of their stone-throwing abilities, thus they slow down trains and alter track conditions. Their dirty bath water, their leftover food and their faeces, their very lives seep in to alter track geometry: ballast bases change structure and tracks sink. Each of Bombay's suburban trains can fly at eighty-five kilometres an hour, but because of altered track geometry which can topple an entire train, speed is reduced to thirty kilometres an hour, in railway language this is called 'imposition of speed restriction'; in railway ethos this means an entire time-table calculated, agonized over, created, printed and then distributed is rendered completely useless before application.

Forty-one thousand huts can hold to ransom 59,00,000 of Bombay's commuters on the suburban lines. New local trains cannot be introduced because the old ones are choking track capacity, old ones are choking track capacity because 'poor people' cannot be moved from the tracks; to lay one kilometre of track these days costs ten crore rupees. And so commuters must risk being blinded for life with stones and water balloons filled with acid; and the women must look away from the seats in the compartments meant for them and hold their collective breath because early every morning the track-livers get on to the parked train and shit all over the women's seats, they never do it in general compartments. And this, a minor complaint in comparison: idle track-dwellers contemptuously play who-can-spit-the-farthest on passing trains, right on the trousers and saris of the commuters hanging out from the doors because there is no place inside the compartments.

And so they have to pack themselves in like sardines, these 59 lakh suburban commuters per day. Mukul Marwah, railway senior, has coined a polite term for them, after consulting his copy of the Wren & Martin: superdensecrushload. Super dense crush load. In the peak hours of 8.30 to 11.30 a.m. and 4.30 to 8.30 p.m., these commuters are to use local trains which have an installed capacity of 1,850 passengers. The superdensecrushload packs itself 5,000 to a train—twelve commuters to every available square metre—which is forced to run at fifty-five kilometres less than its speed so that they do not die and reach home, safely, a full hour later than what it would have taken if the tracks were clear of another kind of people. This is what it means during the monsoon: the railway's pipes under the tracks—meant to drain only water—is connected to the city's 130-year-old drainage system. The track-livers clog the railway's storm-water drainpipes with their refuse including plastic bags, and so when it rains flooding on the tracks is inevitable, resulting in trains drastically slowing their speed to a mere ten to fifteen kilometres an hour when not suspending services until the water subsides.

And this is what it means for the motorman driving that train. He bends down and touches the station with his fingers and then he touches the fingers to his forehead before taking on captaincy of this ship under which the tracks sink. He does not know if he will reach home safely either, the encroachers physically stop trains and savagely beat up motormen when their children are injured by passing trains while loitering on the tracks. There have been instances when they got angry because their protruding television antennae broke when whipped in impact against a speeding train. The railway authorities are now trying to guard their land which has not been encroached upon, as yet, by giving it to their own employees for growing vegetables.

The Shiv Sena-Bharatiya Janata Party government decrees that all encroachers before 1 January 1995, are being regularized. The railways points out that this cannot be applicable to them for obvious reasons. Fine, says the state government, move the encroachers at your expense; this will cost Rs 400 crore, nevertheless the railways approaches one set of encroachers, 1,561 hutments between Kurla and Bhandup, 900 of these say they will shift only if given places which will not be too much of a commute for them from their places of work. A group of legitimate commuters called Citizens for a Just Society move the Bombay High Court which decrees that the railways may be exempt from the state's slum scheme and may clear hutments within thirty feet of the tracks so that they can also start construction on the fifth and sixth much-needed corridors of railway space. Political 'workers' of a party of a certain hue stage dharnas and track rokos threatening self-immolations.

'It is nothing new any more,' says Mukul Marwah. 'The railways built a new terminus at Bandra which was of no use because there was not enough access from the road to it, encroachments on the government land were chocka-block. We tried to demolish the illegal structures with the assistance of the state government in 1991 and a member of parliament came and lay down in front of the bulldozers. Now we are trying to do something, anything, about the hawkers outside VT who block our entrance from all sides but we cannot because that land does not belong to us, it belongs to the municipal corporation; so we have them evicted, they come back within forty-eight hours, it is like emptying the sea into itself. The corporation worked out hawking zones—they should have declared blanket non-hawking zones instead—and nearly destroyed the peace of many lanes all over the city in the process. Concerned citizens took up the issue and now they are locked in a legal battle in court with the hawkers who have political backing.' He sighs. 'When I began this job with the suburban railways ten years back I was a different person, I hoped to summon the tenacity of a fox terrier at will for my job. Then I was filled with mind-blowing anger. At the end of the day I am helplessly and hopelessly intellectualizing the whole thing.'

Pakya has an answer to all this, even if he grandly mixes up all rules, regulations, tradition and laid-down norms, tosses them into the air and holds his hands out for what falls into them. 'Emergency lagao Bombay mein.'

Impose emergency on the city. Who will?

'Wohi jo Malabar Hill pe badey bangley mein baithta hai, apney president ka bhai. And we should also explain to him to make Bombay separate, like Delhi or Singaapur.'

Pakya means Singapore, either a union territory or a city-state, and he is referring to the governor. He is not authorized; besides, it is undemocratic to declare an emergency.

'Democracy, this is democracy! If I ever stand for elections I will show you what is democracy. I will win, I know that, it does not cost that much per hut in the slums. I have done enough booth-capturing to know how easy it is to swing an election in your favour.'

That sounds a little simplistic, but is he going to stand for elections ever?

'Andhey se chudwaao, phir ghar chhod ke aao?'

Pakya's language is liberally peppered with cuss words, an entire sentence can be a horrific abuse in a combination of Marathi, his mother tongue; Hindi, the Punjabi-ized version he has picked up while hanging around on several film sets; and Bambaiya. His opinion of standing for elections is that he has no wish to get buggered by voters who refuse to see the light and assist themselves and then even insist on being pampered with sops and special treatment till the end of their lives. Pakya started by being careful about his language when he first phoned, albeit briefly.

'I hear you are looking for me. Kaayku?'

For a book on Bombay.

'Apun buk-bik nahi padta.'

The book, a part of it at any rate, would be about you.

'Kaayku? Nako, faaltu mein tension nako.'

Subsequent phone calls, with him doing the telephoning as he would refuse to leave his number, finally leads to a meeting. He suggests the meeting point be the Khada Parsi, 'Tere ko, sorry, aap ko maalum hai na kidhar hai?'

The Khada Parsi is the Bombay Municipal Corporation's little in-house joke. The statue outside their building, and opposite VT, stands tall and when viewed from a certain angle, appears erect. Ergo, Standing Parsi.

'Tu, sorry, aap aao Khada Parsi pey, main pehchaanega, TV pey bhot time dekha hai. Main safed shirt pehnega, pup-peel mobile rahega haath mein. I will recognize you.'

At precisely the appointed time he swaggers up a purple-cased mobile in hand; he could be a well-to-do stockbroker on his way to work at the nearby Bombay Stock Exchange building, average height of the Indian male, clean-shaven, no distinguishing features, dressed sedately in a stark white long-sleeved shirt and neatly-tailored dark blue trousers. His shoes are trainers, though, thickly padded and securely soled, so as to not slip if the need arises to run. And his trouser's side pocket has a slight, suspicious bulge.

He suddenly turns unsure, he puts out his hand and takes it quickly back, he tries a namaste, he flicks back the collar of his shirt from behind his neck and settles for, 'Myself Pakya.'

Pakya is Prakash, he does not want his surname in print or which village he comes from in Maharashtra; he lived on the railway tracks for a brief while, he moved when he was offered more money to help encroach upon another space, then another, yet another; that money—and more he has made through other means—has enabled him to buy a three-room kholi in a pucca building in Andheri. Distant relatives and acquaintances live in other encroachments, several authorized slums and some are just starting their lives on the tracks with their children learning the fine art of flinging stones to blind passers-by. Why do they feel compelled to do this? And why don't their parents stop them? Do they feel this is their way of bridging the money divide?

'What divide do the children of pucca homes have when they throw out their old parents or beat up their own wives. Aaj kal ka bachcha log haraami hai. Hoyegaa hi na, raat ko ma-baap jaanwaar banta hai to din mein kutta hi paida hoyegaa.' When parents are the kind who behave whimsically they produce uncontrollable pariahs.

He sets the record straight on the encroachers. 'It is not like it is only a business for all of them, some come with genuine hopes in their hearts, then they realize how selfish Bombay is, and refuse to move. Then they are given water, electricity, jobs in the corporation, money to vote, toh maamla fit ho jaata hai because in their gaons they have nothing. Haan yes, some are brought in and encouraged to live where they like. But they don't care about all that, apun kay baap ka kya jaata hai?'

Whose father, what goes. Do any of his relatives live in a proper building?

'Haa hai na, bharke hai Cuffe Parade mein.' He laughs, jeering at his own joke about lots of relatives living in high-rises.

He chooses 'America ka wada pav' for the chat. McDonald's it is, at VT, where he orders a chicken burger and soft drink, breathing in the drink in sharp slurps. He looks over the rim of his straw, utterly unconcerned about the mildly annoyed glances his noise is inviting in the early-evening lull of the fast food eatery. 'Kya kaam tha bol, sorry bolo. Achcha isko pehle chhod deneka, mereku yeh aap-bip nahi jamtaa hai.'

He is getting comfortable, abandoning caution, settling into his chair and wanting to know why a book should be written on him.

No reason.

'Aisayich? Faayda kya hai phir tereko?'

No faayda, no personal gain.

'Achcha, you want to spend time with a tapori-type thinking he will be like Bhiku Mhatre?'

Aren't these types like that? He is referring to the almost endearingly dangerous character of Bhiku Mhatre played by the talented Manoj Bajpai in Ram Gopal Varma's critically-acclaimed film *Satya*.

'Even Bhiku Mhatre is not like Bhiku Mhatre, samjhi kya? Now the phillum is a big hit so sau chutye, . . . oh sorry, hundred punters are patterning themselves on him. You have interviewed him, Bhiku Mhatre?'

No. What's with the purple mobile?

He laughs, 'Mera girlfriend ney diya, mera happy budday ke liye.'

Pakya turned forty-eight recently, his girlfriend—twenty-one years younger—is a starlet, doing roles in Hindi films and on television; he has been married once, no children, his wife ran away with a Muslim neighbour from the slums to the gulf. 'Uska aadmi, her new husband, I am told she is very happy with him.' He sounds genuinely happy for both of them. It was not so easy when she upped and left, Pakya burned, he drank himself silly, he went to her

113

parents' shanty in their slum and hurled filthy abuses along with a few stones at their door. He went to the Muslim side of the slum and drunkenly hurled more stones and abuses at the door of his wife's new father-in-law. 'Landya!' The Marathi word for circumcised men used contemptuously with the non-scientific notion that the removal of a foreskin leads to less of a man.

Surprisingly no riot ensued when Pakya desperately and drunkenly tried to pick a fight with a closed door. Perhaps this was because it was in the early seventies and the slum was recovering from a terrible riot. Justice D.P. Madon's commission of enquiry, which published its report in 1974, is a preface to Justice Srikrishna's current report on the post-Ayodhya demolition riots. Justice Madon, then a judge of the Bombay High Court, gives a graphic description of what happened when Shiv Sena leader Bal Thackeray visited Bhiwandi and Mahad to whip up passions over a disputed structure claimed by one set as a masjid and by the other as a temple. The then Jan Sangh was also involved, accompanying Thackeray to Mahad in his motorcade of twenty-six cars, six trucks and three state transport buses; may be this is where L.K. Advani got his rath yatra idea from. The Congress government in power then did nothing to stop Bal Thackeray, they did nothing to stop him in the post-Ayodhya riots either. Bhiwandi burned first, Bombay burned twenty-two years later.

His runaway wife's father understood the folly of seeking revenge during that tinder-box time, he waited till Pakya could turn sober and said, 'Let her go Pakya, neither you nor I could give her a decent life here. When I came to you with my daughter's proposal I did not realize she did not want this life any more; I thought she would be happy to just look after your home, you are both so young. Tey aata geli sukhi-sukhi jaaoon dey, don't curse her for trying to find happiness. Me tujha parat lagna karun deto.'

'Buddhey ne barabar bola, the old man was right. He even said he would get me married again, the mhaataara has two more daughters. Pan kaan pakada main, no marriage-birraige.'

Kaayku?

'Doodh bajaar mein milta hai, bhains ghar me laaneka jaroorat kaayku?'

There cannot be this disgusting equation between a woman, a buffalo and milk.

He grins, slurps his drink some more, then tries to look bashful. 'Appo appolo, arrey sorry.'

Apology accepted. How much has he studied, any at all?

'Aye kya bolti hai, college finis kiyela, woh bhi Englees mein.'

Ah, he speaks English then.

'Fatafat bolta hai, poonch kuch. Okay you say something in English and I will translate it in Hindi and tell you, say something bhaari okay, don't think I am stupid and say Jack-and-Jill-went-up-hill.'

Culture commands a clear commitment to intellect and to its use for a rational, humane and politically independent criticism.

He takes a bite of his burger, chews, glares at it in his

115

hand and flings it on the table. He clears his front, top teeth with his tongue. 'Bhot bhaari hai baap, waapas bol.'

On request, since it was too heavy for him, it is repeated.

He shakes his head, 'Barabar hai, chal abhi jaane dey.' He changes his mind, 'Achcha main bolta hai, pan gussa nahi hone ka, kya?'

Okay, no taking offence.

'Gaand maraaye dhaniya boye. That is what it means.'

Pakya tends to be orifice-fixated, even when unconsciously—and retro-accurately, as in this case—summarizing things. For all that trouble, is his translation, of tolerating so much while taking on that much more, all you get back is one small spice seed. Which, he adds, is precisely what is going to happen in the upcoming elections.

'Shiv Sena will lose, BJP will gain and lose, Congress will also win and lose; but what will the public get for getting gaand maraaoed for so long? The same hulkutts, nobody new; just that satisfaction about casting a vote.'

Who does he think will be chief minister?

He thinks, then shakes his head, 'If the BJP comes in Maharashtra then it will definitely be Gopinath Munde. Hona-ich mangta, woh apne Pramod Mahajan ka saala hai; he is his brother-in-law.' Pakya stops to laugh in admiration, 'Kya shaana hai Pramod Mahajan, baap hai ekdum sabka, he loses his seat in Bombay but still becomes a minister. You see him on television, he is very shrewd, ek din apna prime minister banegaa. See how he put the Shiv Sena fully in charge in Maharashtra to create havoc? Then to soothe feelings he sends his brother-in-law and the public feels the

BJP is all right, it is only the Shiv Sena which is incapable of governing. Apna Pramod Mahajan remote controls the remote control!'

And if the BJP does not win in Maharashtra?

'If Sharad Pawar wins, Chhagya ban sakta hain, achcha chance hai uska, for the first time we will have a chief minister from the city itself. Chhagan Bhujbal is a Bombay person and also from a backward class. In Congress also there is a backward class man, a good man for chief minister, Sushil Kumar Shinde. But then the Marathas might taang adaao, backward class ka aadmi aayega to unka hawa tight ho jaayega na?' The Marathas might object to a backward class chief minister.

Who will he vote for?

He laughs, a clear, untramelled, almost innocent laugh. 'I can vote for all of them from different booths. I have done it in the past and I have got other people to do it too. But I think this year I will take a holiday, I will go away with my girlfriend to Bangkok if she is not shooting.'

Why Bangkok?

'Aisayich, muh pe naam aaya, bol diyaa.'

Does he not want to make money in these elections?

'There are too many people today and they will do it for lot less money, marna sasta ho gaya hai Bambai mein. I don't want to do it because ghafley ka time gaya. There will not be simply shady things in these state elections, there is going to be blood and guts. The Congress has to win so it will do everything in its power, the Shiv Sena has its own people and the BJP has its Bajrang Dal. Sab mil julkey ek doosrey ko kaatengaa, they will all work towards finishing off each other. But you know what the joke will be? They will all, once again, make chutya out of the public and the public will not mind becoming a chutya again because they will think they are participating in some dharam yudh between patriotism and gangsterism.'

Meaning BJP-SS versus Congress corresponds to the rivalry of two big gangs, Chota Rajan versus Chota Shakeel? Patriotic gangster versus non-nationalist gangster? Supposedly Hindu versus ostensibly Muslim?

'That is all political parties and police ka chutya-panti, you should not listen to their propaganda. The two Chotas are just like all the other big-big businessmen; religion goes into the sandaas, the lavatory, when their long-term interests are at stake. See how the industrialists have been putting one-one kilo maska to both parties, Congress and BJP? Same way you watch, the two Chotas have worked together in the past, they will once again do a mandwali. Now I am thinking that the saala politicians have made chutya out of the gangsters also, they make the two Chotas fight and kill off their rivals and they sit happily in their homes while the public dies and the police dies with it. Pehley bhi gangsters tha, gangsters were always there but the public did not care, the police did not mind and the politician behaved himself because the fear of the gangster kept him in check, hai kay nahi? Then how come all this tamasha is happening only in the last ten-fifteen years? Public is getting affected, gangsters are getting affected, police is becoming barbaad and getting a bad name but politicians are not. Aisa dekhne ko jaayengaa toh public ka interest mein Chota Rajan and Chota Shakeel should do a mandoli.'

Mandoli, corrupted from mandwali, comes from the time coolie-turned-gold king Haji Mastan met fellow-smuggler Sukkur Narayan Bakhiya of Daman—on the Mandwa beach across Bombay's harbour. Their smuggled goods were landing in dhows at Mandwa at the same time and this led to friction on which side could claim the cargo. Mastan and Bakhiya met at Mandwa and worked out a compromise; all gangs since follow the principle of the mandwa-wali agreement.

'No I want to go away to Bangkok because both sides will engineer riots and I don't want to die in indiscriminate police firing. One side will call it a civil war, the other side will say foreign hand, ISI, Rome hand, Dawood, Shakeel, Rajan, woh saala yeda Abu Salem, kuch bhi chalengaa, check karne ku kon jaayengaa? They will say any damn thing, how will the voter check? Remember the time the police said they had arrested an ISI man for trying to kill Bal Thackeray? What did they produce, one thin, crazy-type man who did not look like he had the strength to lift his own prick never mind an AK. Toh abhi kuch bhi ho saktaa hai. Tu bhi jaa Bangkok, everybody go to Bangkok, come back after the elections are over.'

He pauses and peers, almost anxiously, from behind his Ray-Bans which he has, assiduously, not taken off, even when answering phone calls. He has taken instructions quietly with the minimal murmurs and re-punched buttons to pass them on stacatto. 'Am I frightening you with all this kind of talk? I thought you wanted to understand the situation.'

The people will not let this happen, the riots and

bomb blasts have affected everyone badly.

'Konsa log, which people?' He appears to have lost interest in the answer as he looks towards the cash counter.

The middle class. They are a people who are now rising all over the country; they are acquiring a distinctive strength even if it appears limited just now, a great resolution even if it seems dull today.

'Udhar dekh,' he gestures towards the counter. A man has walked in from the street with a snivelling child, he is trying to get a glass of water for the child, he is being refused and told that he must buy a bottle of mineral water instead. The man is protesting, but very weakly.

'Bhenchot sey paani nahi maanga jaata hai, he cannot ask for a glass of water properly, this middle class is going to demand its rights?'

The man's wife pushes him aside in her anger and presses herself against the cash counter. She is trendily dressed, tights and a long t-shirt hiding the bulk of her expansive hips. She flicks back her shoulder-length, hennaed hair with her left hand, she has rings on every finger including her thumb, she begins speaking in fluent English, 'Look here, you have no right in my country to not give me . . .'

Pakya takes off his dark glasses, there is contempt in his eyes, 'She will give her lecture but style mein mar jaayengi.' Style will kill her substance.

She gets told in equally fluent English, with a ma'am thrown in, that this is their rule, no water for outsiders unless they buy something.

Pakya looks, oddly, very angry; his hand goes to his

pant pocket, it is clear that he is about to pull out his gun. He is restrained so he contents himself with watching the woman stomp out with husband and child in tow. He puts back his glasses on his nose and opens the half-eaten bun of his burger to look at the limp chicken cutlet. 'Bekaar hai, taste-uch nahi hai, saala pav bhi meetha hai. No taste and even the bread is sweet. Bas ho gaya yeh bhosra udhaasi. Chal idhar se jaayengaa apun. Let's go.'

He buys two hot vada pavs from near the Khada Parsi and sprinkles his liberally with garlic and red chilli chutney. He is still hungry and orders a zhunka bhaakar only to be told that it is sold out. He laughs, slapping his thigh with his hand-holding mobile. 'Saala, achcha paisa bana liya. Tere ko maalum hai na yeh kya scam hai?' Zhunkha bhaakar is a delicious, nutritious dish of ground gram flour cooked in onion, green chillis and rai-jeera spices to be served with a jowari roti. The state government floated a scheme of zhunkha bhaakar at one rupee, space was allocated all over Maharashtra for the stalls; the politicians quickly moved in floating voluntary service organizations for operation stall-grab. The cheap food centres were also slated to receive Rs 25,000 each per annum as subsidy, its non-receipt being the reason given by the stall-managers for selling everything else except zhunkha bhaakar including multinational potato chips, soft drinks and, in some stalls, non-vegetarian cooked food. The government has, subsequently, announced its decision to abandon the zhunkha bhaakar scheme but the stalls show no sign of going away from the prime locations they occupy. Meanwhile another scheme is being floated by one of the political parties in power, for self-employment, like stalls for nimbu-paani and other hawking possibilites since 'our boys don't want to work as private drivers, they prefer the security of government jobs which we cannot give at this present moment, and they do not want to work far away from their residences'.

Pakya orders another vada pav, topping it with a little hill of red chutney powder. A cavalcade of big cars pass, red lights, police out-riders, several Ambassadors in tow, a police jeep clearing the way through clogged going-home traffic, sirens blare as the low-nosed, long white vehicle bearing yet another very important politician tears through the murky pollution.

'Dekha,' says Pakya, 'gaand ke neechey angaar hain, sidi bamba bankey duniya mein paani phenkne ku nikley.' Their own house is on fire and its occupants pretending to be firemen are drowning the city with water from their hoses. He throws back his head and laughs under the city's night lights, 'Chaggya agar aaya toh ek-ek ko pakad key gaand maarengaa.' Should Chhagan Bhujbal be chief minister he is not likely to let any of these get away scot free. It will be the salt which will impart savour to Chhagan Bhubal's success.

And what will happen to their leader, that man who built up tribal support on bitter bile, the mob leader who achieved huge success by focussed application of limited but deadly means: what will his failure be like?

'My name is Bhujbal, Chhagan Bhujbal. Ex-mayor of Bombay, ex-Shiv Sena leader, an active Congress member until I followed my leader Sharad Pawar. I am confident that the people of Maharashtra will back Sharad Pawar in the upcoming elections, this is not based on wishful thinking, I say this with certainty because I have been a grassroots person all my life and know my state of Maharashtra well. Yes, I was the person who toured the state district-by-district to establish the Shiv Sena, so that it could transform itself from local rabble-rousing to a respected regional party which could be reflected at the national level. That is now a story of missed opportunities, a time for ever gone into the dustbin of history.

'Perhaps it is because I continue to keep my finger on the pulse of my city and its state that I am now being told I could well become the next chief minister. I still have not been able to come up with that perfect facial expression when people and party-workers tell me this. How am I supposed to react? With a tightly-controlled smile, with glee, with false humility? Of course it is an honour, even if it is being unfortunately rubbished by some chief ministers; however I think some people would like to have this greatness thrust upon me only because I have earned myself the reputation for being a successful fire-fighter. This is a scary premise to start a new job on; but I think this is, sadly, going to be the fate of whomsoever is elected as the next chief minister of Maharashtra.

'It is no secret that the state, starting with its capital of Bombay, is in a shambles. I might add here that when Bombay suffers, much more than Maharashtra suffers. There is no money in any kitty, misappropriation runs into multiples of thousands of crores, mismanagement has resulted in anarchy and a completely despondent electorate;

this includes the police and the bureaucrats who were otherwise as law-abiding as the next citizen. Everything has simply fallen down; to pick it up, restart and carry it along will be the next chief minister's job, it will be a thankless one and it is very likely that he will first receive the ire of citizens before he can be there long enough to win back their respect for his post. As the poet said, "Yeh duniya agar mil bhi jaaye to kya hain."

'I sound cautious, I know. It is not that I also don't know that chief ministers get chosen on their ability to survive within an elaborate web of political shackles and booby traps, a system of checks and balances to finally please powerful sections of party leaders. It is just that I have seen enough in these fifty-one years of my life to know that wisdom lies in being a practical realist, not a frustrated idealist. You get more genuine work done this way, the latter turns you into a bitter brooder which I will never allow myself to be. Put it down to my middle class background which does not permit anyone the wholly unnecessary luxury of looking back in anger. And the complete process of my understanding this has been a trial by fire, for which I am also grateful. It has proved to be my rebirth.

'I was orphaned at the age of five, my parents had come from Nashik as a young couple, settled down in Mazagon and set up a successful wholesale vegetable business at the nearby Byculla market. We lived comfortably. We are what is called the mali community, gardeners would be the English word but inappropriate to encompass the ethos.

'My mother went to her parents' home at Nashik to deliver me but we returned almost immediately as my father needed her assistance at the market, I think my first smells were that of fresh vegetables, my first colours were the rich reds of tomatoes, the vibrant greens of peas, that golden shaft of sun lighting up a basket of lemons. My father and mother died soon after each other, my grandmother's sister took me in. I grew up in Mazagon studying at the municipal school abutting Padamsee Wadi while continuing to take care of the family's vegetable business. Education was important to me, it still is, I have set up and run an educational trust at Bandra.

'When I was completing my technical studies at the VJTI in Matunga I became aware of Maharashtrian youth wanting equal employment opportunities, the feeling was that there were too many outsiders bringing in many more. There was also this anger about deteriorating living conditions. Let me take you back a little. There was a drastic increase in Bombay's population in 1872 with the wave of poverty-striken Maharashtrian peasants from the drought-ridden districts of Satara, Kolaba and Ratnagiri who took up jobs in the mills at Mazagon, Byculla, Tardeo, Reay Road, Lalbaug, Parel, Naigaum, Sewree, Worli and Prabhadevi. By 1891 it had risen to 0.82 million from 0.64 million because of the influx. There was no looking back after that, people in Maharashtra left their desolate villages to be with their families, work in mills, set up the markets for mill workers and hawk other goods for these migrants. The population was 1.16 million in 1931, it rose to 1.49 million in ten years; by 1931 there were already 50,000 homeless people in Bombay. In 1947 and early 1948 there was a fresh wave of migration from Pakistan of the refugees straight into the city, over two lakh people within that short space of time; by 1951 the numbers stood at 2.3 million.

'I look back now and realize that this had to happen; it was a disaster waiting to strike, and it did because the sons of the mill workers wanted jobs better than that of their fathers but they did not have commensurate education, the areas they lived in had turned into fetid inner cities. The resentment was enormous, the class divide was very apparent. Thus was born this leader, a cartoonist who smoked a pipe and patterned himself on Hitler, who understood the situation as an opportunity to legitimize his own insecurities.

'I started as one of the soldiers, swallowing all the history that was distorted and fed to me. I discovered only much, much later that the great Maratha warrior Shivaji and Mughal emperor of that time Aurangzeb fought a battle on geographical principles, it had nothing to do with religion. In fact Shivaji in a famous epistle to Aurangzeb wrote, "Islam and Hinduism appear as contrasted terms; but they are diverse pigments used by the Divine Painter to fill in His picture of the whole human race. If it be a mosque, the call is chanted in remembrance of Him; if it be a temple, the bell is rung remembering Him alone. To show bigotry towards any man's creed and practices is tantamount to altering the words of the Holy Book. To draw new lines on a picture is to find fault with the Painter."

126

'I was misled yes, but I also genuinely believed I could make a difference to my life and that of the people around me. I make no apologies now, I cannot be held responsible for leaders who let down their own followers. I was young then, and an idealist. I would like to think I have made some positive contribution, beginning with libraries and ambulances; later the ambulances turned into cars for individual use with red lights on top to cleave through busy roads, get ahead at any cost, rough-ride and scramble over those patiently waiting in queue. A symbol perhaps of what was to follow. Accountability is a word unknown to them, beginning from the top. I remember that instance when a young worker came from interior Maharashtra and he was asked, "How did you come?" By bus, he replied: "Chay-chay, get a car." But how, the young man asked; "Manage somehow, as a worker of my party why should it be difficult," he was told.

'I suppose I was naïve in those days, gullible. But I still say this—I worked hard, I rose to Mazagon shakha pramukh, branch head, and then I entered the city corporation to be eventually appointed mayor. It was I who instituted the privatizing of traffic islands so that corporates turn them into gardens and help in taking care of the city, the Tatas took over the Horniman Circle garden and what a splendid job they did. They even sent the old-style lamps to be specially re-cast at their Jamshedpur factory. It was a proud moment for me when the garden was inaugurated, no less a person than J.R.D. Tata was at the gate to receive me. His active participation helped people understand that city concerns are not merely gutter concerns; you have to be involved in the interests of your city because if you cannot control your city council—and your city councillors do not respond—you have no locus standi as a citizen of that city.

'I also got companies interested in putting up railings on road dividers and pavement fencing. But all these ideas seem to have been destroyed in execution eventually. The city looks disparate today, there is no control at all on design, anything is being stuck on anywhere including hoardings against heritage buildings and rubbish bins suspended on two metal sticks. They fill up with water during the monsoon and tip over if anything heavy is put into them. Take the main road leading from Siddhivinayak temple to the mayor's bungalow, Rs 40 lakh of the people's money was spent on setting up concrete planters which quickly decayed, concrete pavement guards which are an eyesore and lamps whose height is so low that they hardly light up the road. There are many roads like this in the city which have been superficially prettified, costs inflated and money pocketed. There is not a single signboard left in English so that tourists can know where they are going, the earlier intention was to have both languages, English and Marathi. What can I say of a corporation that uses more than 70 per cent of its income on itself as establishment costs and then spends around Rs 4 crore on a mayor and his hurriedly conceived special council's cabin when there is a deficit in excess of Rs 600 crore in the corporation's budget? After which, of coure, they scrap the mayor-in-council system within a year. The corporation worked in my time, it reflected the work ethic of the people of the city. Of course I made mistakes too but these were not acts of commission nor were they sins of omission. And, of course, I am paying for my mistakes; each man has his own private hell, mine came early.

'The first time I realized, albeit faintly, that my leader had feet of clay was when I was arrested during the Maharashtra–Karnataka border row, Belgaum was the bone of contention and the Kannadiga leaders said they would not allow a single Maharashtrian to enter it. I flew to Goa and from there took a car to Belgaum dressed as an Arab. The border had been sealed, the police stopped us, asked who I was, I could not speak a word of either Kannada or Arabic so I just puffed on this pipe behind the false moustache I had put on and the Arab headgear. The driver told the policemen, "This is Sheikh Al-Bhujbal, he wants to inspect some land to set up a big factory in your state." We were allowed to pass through and I drove straight into the city to address this huge rally. Seven people died in the firing which followed and I was thrown into Dharwad jail for one month. My party leader did not even send word to me or ask about me.

'The iron entered my soul when I was denied the position of leader of the opposition. To mollify me I was made mayor again, but by then I had understood that I had a place as long as I stuck to what was handed out to me; I should not think of wanting a post which would be above my standing. It is funny how God teaches you a lesson, I had entered the fray to fight against a class barrier, I was being excluded on grounds of caste. I protested, there was a sharp reaction. I remember that day well, 23 March 1991, I was in a garden I had set up in the suburbs, inspecting the tree stumps I had designed to be converted into seating for elderly citizens, and a copy of their mouthpiece paper was shown to me. It had a cartoon of a donkey and Christ sitting on it, the caption said donkeys should not think they are worth anything because a respected figure uses them. Later it publicly proclaimed, "He is good at cleaning up gardens, let the Congress take him to clean their kachra."

'I thought then that I must simply leave everything and go away, perhaps to Nashik, grow grapes to live without this kind of sadness. My wife Meena dissuaded me, she said it was now my dharma to try and set things right; my children were already settled by then, my daughter Durga is happily married, my sons Pankaj and Sameer run a rubber factory in Mazagon's Anjirwadi and a farm in Nashik. Several political parties contacted me after they heard about what had happened, I understand that they did it because I am a backward caste man and there are 52 per cent Other Backward Castes in Maharashtra, besides a very large percentage of them in Bombay. But I have to be honest here, I decided upon the Congress because I was concerned about my safety and that of my family; you need proper back-up from your people if you are going to stick your neck out for them. I knew I would need this back-up very soon because I could see what the megalomania was doing to what I was leaving behind.

'My instincts were proved right. In October 1991, eight days before the Pakistani cricket team was scheduled to arrive in the city, they dug up the Wankhede pitch and poured oil on it. In that month itself they ransacked the offices of the bold Marathi eveninger *Mahanagar* and beat up two staffers; after the *Mahanagar* attack there was a public protest against their goondaism and they targeted three more journalists, Milind Khandekar, Sheela Rawal and Manimala whose jaw they broke. In August 1993 their union wing attacked the office of another Marathi paper, *Aaj Dinank*, a reporter was beaten up and office furniture destroyed. They even targeted a pregnant woman Kalyani Thombre who was quickly shielded by the office accountant, he was badly hit by the chair thrown at her. On the same day they physically assaulted editor Nikhil Wagle who was addressing a seminar at Churchgate. In July 1996 they assaulted the vice-president of Nippon Denro Ispat at the company's factory in Raigad by blackening his face and garlanding him with slippers, they were demanding recruitment of locals in the company. In the same month Haffkine Institute director Vishwanath Yemul was bundled into a car and taken to their head office where he was detained for one and a half hours. Then there was this hate campaign against him in their mouthpiece paper with a picture of his face being tarred on their front page.

'In December 1996 the women of their party attacked the home of corporation officer G.R. Khairnar because he spoke out against autocracy, they pulled his daughter by her hair and broke his window panes. The women involved included one who later became mayor and another who is the wife of a gangster, she was later given charge of an education committee. The police sat and chatted with the attackers on the lawn, a chargesheet was filed in July 1997 and the matter, as in earlier cases, has yet to come up in court.

'In July 1997 their 600-strong mob ransacked my official bungalow and came after me with iron rods, I locked myself into the bedroom and managed to phone the police commissioner for help. They broke everything in sight including the television. The case is with the Crime Branch and there have yet to be chargesheets. In the same month Ramesh Savarkar, director of Lilavati Hospital at Bandra, was assaulted for the "anti-labour" policies of the hospital, they thrashed him severely, tore his shirt and blackened his face with shoe polish. In April 1998 they barged into the Ghulam Ali concert and indulged in large-scale violence including stopping the show and smashing tables and a harmonium, the organizer got so scared that he did not even file a complaint, he says he has to live in the city. Nothing has been done about the semi-naked men sent to protest outside Dilip Kumar's house either. Tell me, when one set of people resort to sending men in underwear out on the roads, what counter-protest can any decent set of people think of? And what does it tell you about the level of the minds of the protestors? Their families, how must their mothers, wives and daughters have felt when they saw the photographs in the papers?

'Subsequently they have damaged one more pitch, this time in Delhi; we know what they did at the time of the release of *Fire*. Recently they got into fisticuffs with the film people on the sets of a Shah Rukh Khan and Juhi Chawla production because they wanted their people to be hired, they damaged the set. And we all saw for ourselves what they did at the Cricket Control Board of India's office to our hard-won trophies. I reached there as soon as

I heard and I was thunderstruck; the national press and television networks wanted a quote from me, all I wanted to do was sit down on the sidewalk and cry.

'The courts are overworked, the police is completely under their thumb, the people are paralysed with fear. All this is legitimizing the role of these misfits and their deviant behaviour. And—in a peculiarly twisted manner— it is adding credibility to a despot's reputation. He manages to get publicity for himself each time, milking mileage out of every single incident. Can you imagine a legend like Don Bradman reading about the cricket pitches and the man behind it? Or the prime minister of Great Britain? Every one has his day, I suppose, and his had to be when he jumped on the Hindutva bandwagon unrolled by L.K. Advani; I don't think the people of Maharashtra would have voted for him and his party had it not been his quick tie-up with the saffron section.

'But like I said, every man has his day. Soon, the policeman will have his for being so paralysed by his own political master, the much-abused bureaucrat is keeping things on file, the voters are waiting too. And let us not forget that day of reckoning for each one of us in front of our supreme master. When God casts his ballot against you it is the tightest slap on your face and it echoes down the years on the faces of your family and descendents. It is a day to be very frightened of.'

Pakya has not called in a while, quite a while. He has promised, 'aai shapath', mother's promise, to meet again.

He phones late one night, 11.40 p.m. 'Zhoplee hoti? Sleeping? Okay-okay, I will phone later.' Before disconnecting he agrees to meet at a South Bombay five-star coffee shop.

He arrives punctually, looking around warily but only briefly, seats himself by the seaside view window and proceeds to order an iced tea in careful English. 'Suna hai bada log thanda chaay peeta hai'; he gravely thanks the waiter when the tall, faintly frosted glass arrives and stares at the sliver of lemon wedged into its rim. 'Is ka kya karneka?'

What to do with the slice of lime? Leave it there.

'Naakh mein jaayengaa.' He does not like the idea of the slice poking his nose as he drinks from the glass, he plucks it out and plops it into the glass. He takes a few quick sips and grimaces, 'Pisaab hai.' The high-priced drink like urine with its massive luxury tax slapped on, is abandoned and a cappuccino ordered.

Pakya has just returned from his gaon, he had gone to see his ailing father. He looks relaxed, and happy to have gone away for some time. He came from his village in interior Maharashtra when he was a child, the son of a schoolmaster sent to his uncle in a city for the better life: 'padh likh ke kuch ban ne ka'; to have an education, then become someone. Uncle, aunt, their children and more born as Pakya grew up with them, lived in a slum on uncle's salary as a peon in the Bombay Municipal Corporation. Pakya ducked and dodged and held on hard, he helped transport hooch, he sold drugs, he learned how to use a knife, then the talwaar, somewhere along the way a gun; he earned his money through booth-capturing for the Congress then, the Shiv Sena later. This election he takes a break and will return, he says, to do 'big work' for the Bharatiya Janata Party when Pramod Mahajan becomes prime minister. This according to him, is not too far away, 'bas, ek chaar-paanch saal'.

Meanwhile Pakya will move from the world of minor offences—'I have never killed anybody intentionally'—to the legitimate one of political wheeling-dealing, the visible middle-man, Mr Fix-It. 'As it is I am starting late in life, people who started with me are already there.' He gestures towards the coffee shop's ceiling, suggesting a higher level. He already knows how to broker small deals; with simple bribing he—as part of a small informal cartel of unofficial agents—has procured 10 per cent quota flats for several people.

Has he got one for his girlfriend?

He shakes his head, 'Not applicable, she is not Marathi.'

With subtle pimping he has cleared deals at the city corporation; to Mantralaya, the state's main administrative offices he has sent middle-women from small towns who have liaised with ministers to clear files for their area. Pakya's job was to identify ministers and their minions who were 'naadey se dheela'—this is impossible in translation, Clintonesque should provide the gist—and to send in the middle-women to Mantralaya. Fair and fleshy, preferably light-eyed, always long-haired; they would be sent in from areas the files of which needed speedy clearance. Pakya would pocket the cut, he still does as do some more like him.

Is that all it takes, a few fucks to clear a file?

Pakya chortles. 'Kaay shivya kaadte! How she abuses! Tera mister tere ko kuch bolta nahi kya?'

He laughs a lot when he is informed that the mister is continuously agitated about the cuss words.

'One day,' he prophesies without malice, 'he will hit you. Don't blame him then, you will have asked for it.'

Who hits him when he abuses?

'Arrey, apun ko solid maarti hai woh saali.'

The girlfriend smacks him for his language?

'Haath mein jo bhi aata hai uthaa key fekti hai saali.'

She flings whatever is handy when he abuses. Where did he meet her?

'On the sets, she had come to meet a director, the assistant director is my friend and I was there to talk about a story we are writing together. Manjhe, means, we are discussing the story but he feels we will have to make it as an art phillum, it has too much sex for commercial cinema.' He switches to English, 'Might be we can make into television serial, not for Doordarshan but.'

Pakya has also been production controller-cum-casting-director for porn films. 'If you think about them now,' he reflects, 'they were almost comical. In fact the first time my girlfriend accidentally saw a small part of one video I had kept, she hurriedly shut it off but I could see that she was dying to laugh. I cannot find that video now, I think she has broken it and thrown it in the kachrey ka dabba.'

Those were the days when the video cassette player was the new toy. Foreign blue films were to be found with very great difficulty but demand was high; supply was started by setting up a video camera in a darkened, dingy room with the minimum of unit men. Pakya was hired by a politician's son to assist in organizing the shoots with additional charge of getting the actors. The actress was difficult to find so they lined up prostitutes. 'But they were no good, very mechanical, and they charged so much, aaiyeelaa! It was just not economical enough so we looked for fresh girls who wanted to become actresses. We were quite lucky there, we managed to make some money and the girls' facial expressions were also good.'

As the camera began rolling the actor, a beefy-hairy-paunchy type, would begin kissing the girl and in a fairly complicated manner begin taking off her blouse and his pants, she would look ecstatic and they would get underway with the business-of-the-day. The cast of two would be pretty much left to discover their own devices of finding each other's pleasure principles while the cameraman would try and not frantically run around the room to get the best angle for the intended audience. Sometimes the camera would jerk, lose focus, come back too abruptly with an unintended shot of a crack in the wall and then hastily pan to a part of a body. It was as live as you could get, recording all sounds including scrapes of a chair, simulated moans and groans and, occasionally, the couple even enjoying themselves, delaying their own pleasure. In which case the director would check the time left on the tape and yell, 'Chalaa, chalaa, lavkar, jaldi karo!'—hurry up, get on with it; muffled but duly also recorded on the tape—and the couple would hastily strain towards climax.

The production house wound up when too many

newcomers entered the fray and foreign videos became freely available. Pakya also got bored with the proceedings, 'Saala same thing over and over again, no scope to do anything creative because of the budget.' But that was when the bug bit him and he started building contacts with the film industry, he personally funded part of some films, got the funding for others; in the future he is, himself, going to produce a spectacularly creative picture and get the financing from his friends. Pakya talks about the politician's son who hired him, 'Woh bhi mere se bhot aagey nikal gayaa, saala mera koi godfather nahi hai na, problem yeh-ich hai pailey se.' No godfather to prop up Pakya while the hirer later turned legit producer, delivering a huge commercial success before he died young; do the sins of the fathers visit their sons?

'In his own way God has given me time-off, time away from hectic day-to-day government administration and—dare I say this?—politicking, to understand where I was going and where I am headed now. I have been thinking quite a bit, meditating and looking within, reading a lot of good newspapers and books which I never had the time for before, or perhaps I did not make the time. A lot of questions have been coming up as a result of all this thinking, I don't have all the answers as yet but I am seeking them: from within, from my seniors, from the books of philosophers and thinkers. As a consequence I have wound up reading a lot about Bombay and getting to learn new things about it. My staff is, I think, mildly amused at me turning into a bookworm of sorts and has been plying me with all kinds of reading material. The other day they brought me a whole stack of people and time management books from Strand at Fort; that old man who runs it, Shanbag, he is quite a gem giving discounts to everybody who comes to his shop. I think it is Bombay's oldest store for English books, but I could be mistaken.

'Someone else on my staff brought me books on Bombay from a shop which is under a bridge. This intrigued me so much that I thought I should go and see how a bookshop can be under a bridge. I have seen shoe shops under bridges, and barbers, also godowns and this being Bombay, the homes of beggars with their rags, but a thriving bookshop? I had a small problem finding the place, the access under the bridge was lined with hutments and their tiny religious structure—this is what they do, they quickly put up something holy so that demolition in that area becomes close to impossible.

'My driver is very good though, he knows Bombay like the back of his hand, and after that beautiful blue Essar building with its helipad on top, he took the western approach under Mahalaxmi bridge and found the place. Paramount Books is actually an agency which distributes books all over the city though they encourage single-buyers too. The spaces under the bridge, loftily called arches, were given out as godowns and it is to Paramount's credit that they have turned it into a book-holding house designed in such a friendly manner. They have lined up what was otherwise a cavern into neatly categorized shelving, tube-lit the place and let the books sell themselves. You don't feel intimidated when you wander around and browse, it is very easy to feel self-conscious, and even insecure, in new surroundings where people speak posh.

'From the entrance of Paramount you can see the wide, rolling green and open spaces of the Mahalaxmi Race Course. Above is the Mahalaxmi bridge, on one side of which is the railway line and many manufacturing concerns including those of pharmaceuticals. The bridge itself is a very busy one, continuously taking the load of heavy vehicles like lorries and double-decker buses; but Paramount below is completely vibration-free. I must find out who built that bridge and when, he has done a fine job. To me this entire scenario has come to symbolize Bombay as it was, and indeed as it should be. Entertainment on one side, trade and commerce on the other, the bookshop underneath providing knowledge, people liberally using the entire infrastructure to make happy lives—Lakshmi underpinned by Saraswati.

'Mahalaxmi was actually a breach area, waters flowed here and effectively cut-off old Bombay from the rest of the world. Then the governor of that time, from 1771 to 1784, William Hornby, had it all filled up into a permanent vellard, thus forever giving an extension to Bombay. Mahalaxmi bridge turns into a very powerful symbol from that point of view, I really must find out when it was built.

'I have also been trying to find out if I can pin a date on Bombay's beginnings. But this is proving to be difficult, Bombay was never ordained as a city, it has turned out to be a wholly existential experience. It does not have an ancient Indian past, perhaps this is why it came along so unfettered, until, of course, some people thrust their past upon it to change it so perversely. Our history books tell us that the East India Company was the worst, then history has yet to catch up with B Company, C Company, D Company, R Company, S Company; please note that I am going in strict alphabetical order! When they first came the East India Company men were called The Company of Merchant Adventurers to the East Indies—this also gives you an idea of what kind of men they were: no integrity, no moral fervour but very determined in their self-seeking. Just like the current bunch except for two notable differences, the East India men were not cowards and they did not deprive others—while bent on making personal fortunes—using a combination of religion and fear as the key.

'Bombay began as a city of traders, I would like to think of those years as its birth. Depending upon which book you are reading, they tell you Bombay came into its own with the first steamers in 1840, or when the Suez Canal opened in 1869. I think Bombay did not wait till then, it simply used sail ships as soon as the Mazagon Docks opened in 1770 and started trading in cotton with China. To cotton were added piece goods, paper, more cotton when there was a famine in China and they were forced to kill their cotton fields to replant them with grain. Then, of course, came opium; several staggering fortunes have been built in Bombay—big families with fancy names— on the strength of trading in opium; but you have to give them credit, a lot of that money was put back into the growth of the city. I would have liked to be born then— maybe I was, as one of those tough Muslim men who came from the Deccan to lift the heavy loads or may be I was a mathadi, those very strong head-load carriers who came from interior Maharashtra. I would really have liked to be a part of that period—the overwhelming mood of that time appears to have been philanthropic, visionary and practical with good men leading the way. Today it is merely charitable, confused and muddled for all of us, with men of straw posturing as politicians.

'The other distinct impression I get from that time is that the middle class used to make every effort into ensuring that their city was a decent place to live. And because they were so united and clear in their requests—they did not even have to demand in those days—governance listened, and jolly well obeyed! I would really like to see the re-emergence of this in the new millennium; a strong middle class makes for a strong city which makes for a solid country; take the example of any foreign country which thrives and the reason will become clear.

'When I became mayor for the first time I looked up corporation records and came across detailed plans submitted by an architect called Foster King to the city fathers of how a new city could be built on the mainland across the harbour for the upper middle class and rich, his logic was that they would be happy to leave the congestion and live in surroundings more suited to their dispositions. He worked out a harbour transport system too, like what you see in Hong Kong. This was in 1945; after our independence the entire plan was dismissed as "too elitist". By the time they built New Bombay in the seventies they had completely destroyed the original idea and ruined its execution. Just think, what a difference it would have made to the city, to property prices, to housing and to the middle class if the idea had been executed in its intended spirit in the early fifties.

'There was an almost identical response when in 1947 a planning consultant from New York called Albert Mayer and architect N.V. Modak submitted their master plan to ease congestion and regulate traffic flow. They took into consideration all kinds of future growth, from industries to peripheries; they suggested a new township at Vasai, bridge connections at Uran and Trombay, that is traffic flowing in a west-east direction also, apart from the corridor-like south-north direction it is doomed into. They connected the west-east to south-north directions in a pattern of fly-overs and clover-leaf expressways. It was a plan beautiful in its practicality then, I don't know how it would work now with all the encroachments; it was jettisoned because it "largely focussed on improving amenities for the middle and upper classes".

'All reclamation ideas were also worked out in those days between the British and Indian engineers, they had phased in what is now Nariman Point but with more open-spaces, and they wanted to leave Cuffe Parade open, no skyscrapers on the city sea-front. In fact they had thought of Nariman Point as a centre for cultural and recreational activities. The proposed plan had open spaces, a ceremonial avenue all the way till an open Cuffe Parade, public buildings and a waterfront development. Somewhere, sometime, these land use colours changed overnight and all that intended open space simply vanished. Tall clustered buildings huddling together came up and ironically got named after the man who spearheaded public opposition to this kind of reclamation.

'Chalo, what is done is done, but this does not mean the idea is not a good one; perhaps all these ideas can be put together and out of them selected those which can still work and make Bombay look—and feel—beautiful again for the people who really deserve it. This has also been among Bombay's, and consequently Maharashtra's, biggest tragedies—that the people who have always, always, paid for and cared for the city have been ignored the most.'

Before leaving the coffee shop Pakya had turned serious, he had taken off his Ray-Bans to ask, 'Achcha, now tell me the truth. You have been meeting me for what reason? Kisi ko tapkaane hai kya?'

No, no one needs to be killed, thanks for the offer for having anyone of choice knocked off.

'Sachi bol, what do you want from me, this buk-bik on me is all lies, I know it. You want to meet someone from the underworld?'

Uh, no, thanks.

'Why not? Every journalist wants to meet people from the underworld today. Jisko bhi dekho koi bhai se milney ko poonchta hai. I tell them ghar jaao boss, we have no bhais left in the underworld, only big bhenchots and they are all pretending to be politicians.'

He looked mildly annoyed at the laughter. 'Hasti hai? Ajeeb aurat hai yaar. Okay what do you want, tell me once and for all.'

He watched intently as he listened, asked questions about the request, ascertained what it was for, how it would appear, whether sources would be protected.

Aai shapath.

'I will phone you,' he said when he appeared satisfied with all the answers. 'But you will have to come to my side of town, saala I do not want to come here any more to meet you, making me drink cold tea which tastes just like piss.'

He phones on Holi day. 'Can you come today? Okay forget it, women are not safe on the roads today. My chikni is also at home. It is not safe in the trains either, some lady got hit in the eye yesterday with a stone and her contact lens got broken inside it. Today the tracks are being watched by the policemen to protect commuters from being hit with coloured balloons. Garmi mein bichara Pandurang sadtaa hai.' The poor policeman braves high heat—guarding sinking metal railway tracks—to protect God alone knows whom and from what.

He fixes another day with a completely unexpected invitation. 'You come home.' Then he pauses, 'You come to the west side of the station and wait at the main gate. My boy will come to pick you up, he will recognize you and take my name. The car is a blue Maruti with heavily-tinted glass, please sit behind with all the windows rolled up. Be at the gate at eight in the evening.'

He senses the hesitation. 'Kya madam atom bomb, itne mein dar gayi? Don't worry, I will get you back safely home to your mister. If it gets too late one of my boys will drop you on his bike. Bike pey jaayengi na?'

Oh definitely jaayengi; a powerful bike ride through Bombay's open highways by night? Yes, please.

He chuckles softly, gently, 'You women are all the same.' Before hanging up he says, 'Bhiku Mhatre ko phone kar.'

What?

'Arrey, woh Satyawale ko phone kar. Ask Bhiku Mhatre who he has patterned his character on.'

Why is this important? And why can't he do it himself?

'Tu journalist hai na, dhishang-dhishang Englees bolti hai, he will answer you because you are an English journalist. Main phone kiya to uska answer machine pey sab English mein dhada-dhad tha.' His answerphone has an English message.

It is the first question he asks upon entrance to his home. 'Bhiku Mhatre ko phone kiya?'

Yes.

'Kya bola usne?'

He was not at home, a message was left on his answerphone, an assistant called back within a few hours politely saying that he was out of town and that he would return the call as soon as he got back which he did, he is a nice man and his name is not Bhiku Mhatre, it is Manoj Bajpai.

'So what did he say? Achcha thaire, ek minute just wait.' Pakya goes out of his flat and yells to someone down the corridor's long balcony, two flights down. His flat is sparsely clean, with just a gentle suggestion that a woman too lives here, a coloured throw-rug on the floor, a tulsi on the window sill, a used large red bindi stuck on the mirror above the washbasin, a small black one in curlicue pattern under the red one. There is nothing adorning the walls, save a framed degree. Pakya is a Bachelor of Arts with honours from Bombay University. There is nothing at all to show where its occupant gets his manic energy from, his—can this be said?—never-say-die attitude. He comes back into the flat.

There is no picture of any gods in his home.

'Kya farak padta hai?' he asks. 'What difference does it make? In mera-Bharat-mahaan-jaldi-poncho-kabrastan every one is a god. Even a naked man sitting on a tree who puts his foot on a prime minister's head. Nobody objected, not even the prime minister who went to the tree.'

Tea arrives, two steaming glasses of masala chaay. Pakya looks sheepish, more so since his Ray-Bans have been sitting on the television all along. 'I don't know how to make tea. Hey chaalel na?'

Chaalel. Chalengaa. No sweat, it will do.

'Tell me what Bhiku Mhatre said, from the beginning.'

His name is Manoj Bajpai and he comes from Bihar. He returned the call and sounds like a professional, dedicated young man who has suffered a great deal before becoming famous. He is likely to suffer further, as hardly any roles are being written for that kind of talent in their world awash with mediocrity. He is sick of being just Bhiku Mhatre to the people. He has patterned his character on at least three different relatives of his including an impetuous uncle and an impatient friend. He said he was sorry that the police

147

thought youth were taking to crime and copying his screen mannerisms but they seemed to forget that gangsters existed in Bombay even before the biggies like Haji Mastan, Karim Lala and Varadabhai, and they all had their goons with their own styles; so art—as far as he was concerned—followed life and not vice versa.

'Baraabar bola boss ney. Well said. What else, aur kya bola?'

He said he had been invited for breakfast to Bal Thackeray's house and he had tea, biscuits and some mithai while meeting the children of his family. Bal Thackeray and he discussed films and he felt that Bal Thackeray could be a very powerful film-maker. He was also told that Dilip Kumar was his very good friend and it occurred to him for a minute that he should ask why, then, Bal Thackeray had sent a morcha of chaddi-clad men to Dilip Kumar's house but then he, prudently, decided against it.

'Bhejeywala aadmi hai. Tu ne tera kuch Hindu-Muslim bhai-bhen ka dialogue nahi maaara?' Did you not ask one of your usual communal amity questions?

Oh shut up.

'What? Kya boli tu?'

Nothing-nothing, sorry. No, there was no further conversation with him.

'Saali, jhoot bolti hai, Pakya ku jhoot bolti hai tu?' Lying to Pakya?

All right, he was asked whether he had read about the Srikrishna Commission report in the newspapers which severely indicts Bal Thackeray. He said he had not even heard about it. It did not sound like he was lying, so a bit of it was explained to him in connection with his breakfast companion. He was silent for a while and then he made two separate statements. 'Film people are very vulnerable.' 'The nature of urban and rural crime in Bombay has become very similar, just like in Bihar.'

Pakya has been taking notes while listening, scribbling in a thick writing pad filled with similar scribbles using a combination of Marathi, Hindi, English and what appears like shorthand notations. He grins, 'I studied shorthand and typing long time back thinking I could become a secretary, but no one gives secretary jobs to us, they all want good-looking, style maarneywali women.'

What are the notes for.

'Mere picture ka character hai. This boy comes from Bihar to become a hero and he is given only gangsters ka roles, and then he begins believing in the roles being him— like how these heroes think they are big heroes in real life?—and becomes a big gangster himself, a ruthless killer. Apun ka hero thoda psychic hai, Shah Rukh Khan key jaisaa thoda sankhee. Should I ask Bhiku Mhatre to play this role?'

Manoj Bajpai. Sure, why not, leave a message in Hindi on his machine.

Pakya looks immensely pleased then looks at his watch. He calls up the contact and wants to know what is delaying him, he bursts into laughter, 'Maadarchot aadha Bombay ki top-class randi ko control karta hai aur ek puncture fix nahi kar sakta kya?'

He disconnects and says the contact is running a little

late, a puncture has stalled his car. 'You want to read the story for our television serial till he comes?'

He pulls out a plastic-coated marble-patterned pink file in which the pages have been neatly punched in. There are working scribbles, there are typed notes, the first line of the first page of which opens with: 'He puts it in her bum.' It is about a politician doing it to his daughter-in-law.

The file is handed back to him.

'Kya ho gaya?'

This is pornography.

'Akhaa life gandaa picture hai, samjhi kya?' Pakya is angry, he clenches his teeth. He is about to explode when quite literally, a bell saves the situation. He answers the door breathing heavily, a young man walks in, around twenty-five years old, the similarity to Pakya is obvious, his brother. Except that the brother does not have Pakya's sparkle, he looks old and jaded in comparison. Pakya does not introduce him and takes him into the bedroom where they speak in rapid-fire Marathi. Pakya is furious with his brother, 'You will not use my house for your dhandaa, is that clear? This is the first and the last time your business enters my flat.' The sound of something opening and closing and they come out with the young man holding a huge-ish packet of white powder. He leaves without saying goodbye to his brother and bangs the door behind him.

Pakya paces up and down thrice, then stops mid-pace, 'Gandaa? Filthy? You want to know what I think is bhenchot gandaa? In your high society all those women roaming around half-naked is gandaa, their husbands not minding it is even more gandaa. All of you have become like the villains and vamps in the old pictures, Jeevan and Faryal, the men smoke cigars, the women wear small blouses and coloured contact lenses. As for your models and TV-wali girls and women who attend parties every night with men who drive them around like drivers, we all know what you do by night, how much cocaine you all take, which hotels your women check into with their toy-boys and where their husbands take their wives' friends. Okay you do what you want to do; we don't care how many flats or how many cars you buy, how many times you want to get married, or for how many generations you want to make money. But don't call us names then, saying underworld this-and-that when you all are worse than us. You all may have a position in society but at least we are not like you, a hijdon ki fauj.' An army of eunuchs.

Pakya is not done as yet, his eyes have turned red. 'You call my story pornography? Six months back one of your high society memsaabs got raped by her high-society party friend while his high-society wife watched. Still they are going for the same parties, still high-society people are inviting this high-society rapist and up until today that high-society man whose wife was raped has done nothing, nothing! Kya class log hai, wah, your cocaine crowd of Colaba, Cuffe Parade, Churchgate! If this had to happen with our women, we would have taken a long knife and rapist ki gaand mein ghusa deta, phaad ke rakh deta usko. We would have cut up the rapist by now. You eunuchs want to make us like you? Saaley hijdey ho hijdey, tum log to hijdey ho hi, humare ko bhi saath mein hijda banayegaa?'

Apologies, truly. But he is confusing that 15 per cent

of Bombay with its diamonds and drugs with the other larger percentage of working middle class, this is patently unfair on his part. Also, he happens to be part of the latter if his several occupations are not closely looked into.

Pakya runs both his hands through his carefully dyed, thick hair and closes his eyes. When he opens them a split second later he is a different man, almost tired, like his brother. 'Aur chaay?'

Why hasn't he educated his brother?

'He dropped out of B Com. The system of education is like this, you spend fifteen years of your life studying something completely worthless and then you cannot even get a clerk's job in a big office. And worse still it makes you nikamma, unable to understand anything else, once you take arts you have to study only those subjects they tell you to study with very few other choices. Suppose you also want to do, say, accountancy if you are doing BA, you cannot do that in the college, you have to take private classes. More money, more time, for what?' His mobile burrs, the contact is on his way up. Pakya walks to the front door while continuing to talk, 'The youth are even preferring to be enrolled by that mad man Abu Ṣalem, saala yeda whom even Dawood does not like, because they get a bike, a gun in their hand, the gun is even cocked for them and all they have to do is shoot. They spray bullets everywhere, kill all kinds of public also, come back and get Rs 5,000 per shooting. My brother does it when he is called by his friends, along with his other dhandaa. Can this education of fifteen years get our youth Rs 20,000 every month?'

The contact comes in while listening. 'Pakya you should stop saying such gloomy things, specially in front of journalists. They write in the papers and everyone believes them and then everyone becomes pessimistic. Madam, you please do not listen to this man, he has been working for too long in this line and needs to retire or go away. Pakya, ask your boss to export you to Madras to start up fresh operations. They need professionals there, that city is really growing.'

'Chutya hai kya, un log ka andu-gundu kisko samjhengaa?' A language barrier would hamper business transactions.

'Kaayku? Varadabhai came from there, he knew Hindi or what? Theek hai tu Hyderabad jaa, even the film industry is thinking of going there.'

'Tu jaa na saaley, then you go first, lots of girls for you to do dhandaa with. You can even start an export-import chakkar, udhar ka mal idhar, and girls from here flying to Hyderabad for special customers.'

'Madam, please don't listen to this man's nonsense. Things are improving in Bombay, I am telling you. See the other day a whole group of rowdies went to Film City and smashed the sets of Aziz Mirza's picture because they wanted to control things through their shady trade union activities. The film people united and beat the daylights out of these political mawaalis, they also burnt the van in which they came. Then the top shots of the film industry like Pahlaj Nihalani, Surinder Kapoor, Shakti Samanta and Pappu Verma got together and informed the state government very sternly that they would not tolerate any political manipulation because they knew how to safeguard their own interests.'

Pakya intervenes, 'Arrey woh fighter hai, Pappu Verma, he is a Rajasthani. Uskey gaand mein dam hai, he told the Federation of Western India Cine Employees that they should not simply sit there any more and tolerate nonsense, he said people from the film industry should now stand for elections. Maalum hai, South mein film people are so powerful because they take interest in politics, they even become chief minister. But film industry ka baat hi alag hai, khaas jagaa hai; the public is not connected to it.'

The contact patiently shakes his head, 'Madam, I am telling you again, please do not listen to Pakya. Instead see that officer in Thane, Chandrasekhar, every day he is doing so many good things.'

'Saala, tu Thane kaisa ponch gaya? What were you doing there?'

'Apun ki ma udhar rehti hai yaar. Every now and then my mother picks up the phone in Thane to give me a lecture. Now she is telling me I should become an officer like Chandrasekhar, is umar mein she wants me to give up my dhandaa and become a babu.'

The commissioner of Thane, T. Chandrasekhar, spearheaded a movement to demolish illegal constructions to widen a road in this far-flung suburban town of Bombay. He trod on several political toes and they—cutting across all party lines—united to have him transferred out when the people of Thane stepped in to support him *en bloc*. To the extent that authorities running various religious spots—temples, mosques and a gurudwara—agreed for demolitions of structures to make way for his road-widening. The politicians on the standing committee of the Thane Municipal Corporation retaliated by revoking his proposed hike in water and property taxes and slashed his road-widening budget by five crore rupees. The hike proposed by Chandrasekhar would have added Rs 12 crore to the Rs 311 crore civic budget; the standing committee increased this budget by Rs 13 crore by raising the octroi collection target. They also raised the corporators' ward development fund from Rs 5 crore to Rs 15 crore, Thane has 100 corporators.

Pakya is leery. 'These babu log cannot survive without politicians, that is why they want to become politicians themselves. Dekha na, woh Seshan ne kitna dhamaal kiya, kya daring dikhaaya, phir kya kiya? Bal Thackeray key pass ticket ka bheek maanga.' Ex-election commissioner T.N. Seshan who, for all his fire and brimstone, wound up asking the Shiv Sena for a ticket. Pakya then refers to the senior policeman, who frustrated with the workings, shifted to the Bombay Municipal Corporation to be stymied once again by politicians. 'Woh doosra Chandrasekhar, deputy municipal commissioner Rokde, he started the demolitions and was ordered transferred by the Shiv Sena whose encroachments he was breaking.'

The people stood up then too, especially those from Bandra, Santa Cruz and Andheri. The women took their belans and thalis—their chapati-making equipment—and banged them outside their area's corporation office. The Jan Jagruti Manch of Vile Parle held a blood donation drive and gifted the bottles to the mayor. The politicians hit back by not transferring Rokde and allowing him to retain his demolition portfolio but reducing him to a paper tiger—by divesting him of the licence department which verifies the legality of the shanties. In other words, like allowing an advocate to argue a case in court but taking away his right to prepare for the case. Reducing an honest and efficient officer to a rubber stamp despite public outcry.

Pakya dismisses it all with a shrug, 'Yeh sab bhosra udhaasi hai. Kuch nahi sudhrengaa Bambai mein, samjhaa kya? Idhar public nahi, murdey log rehte hai, zombies inhabit Bombay. What happened to that Jayabala ladki? Who came to her rescue? Everybody wants to feel nice, they throw some money for it, but they don't want to do anything themselves for it. Now everybody is saying wah, kya himmatwali hai. Haan, definitely hai. But there is only one Jayabala in Bombay, the rest are like those who did not want to help her at that time. Hijdey, saaley hijdon ki fauj.' Pakya is referring to Jayabala Ashar, a student who was assaulted in a local train for her purse, she refused to let go and the three other women in the compartment refused to come to her aid. Her attacker threw her off the running train whereby both her legs were cut off, she lay on the tracks for several hours with people walking past her as trains trundled up and down; the people living in the buildings running alongside the railway boundary wall threw buckets of water on her.

Pakya has moved to his next point in his chain of no change, 'Congress was the one who brought Shiv Sena into the limelight with its open support to break Datta Samant's union. Now Shiv Sena jaayenga, Congress aayenga; Congress jaayenga, phir jam key BJP aayenga. Sub political party sheher ka sabse upar ka point pey khada reh kay city pey hi muth maarta hai, public kuch bolta hai kya, kaisa bolegaa, murda log baat nahi kar sakta na? Haan, voting ka time pey khud public jaakey booth mein muth maar ke aata hain, bas utna-ich.' All politicians, no matter which party, shag all over every city they claim to govern and the public is powerless to do anything except come out and vote once in a while to vent their frustrations.

His mobile buzzes, his girlfriend is on her way to the station to pick up her father who is visiting from Delhi, the train is very late. He will be coming home with her to stay two nights; she has told him this thrice already and she hopes he has remembered to stock up the fridge. Pakya has not, it is so late now that the markets and shops are closed; he dashes down the corridor and comes back with a neighbour's crisper compartment from his refrigerator and empties it pell-mell into his tiny fridge. He rings another bell and brings back a packet of sliced bread which he flings on top of the television. He throws his visitors out of his house.

'The people's mood is changing, they want a better quality of life and they are becoming increasingly impatient with politicians too; they are seeing through us and the postures we adopt for temporary reprieves. This is being reflected in the newspapers very clearly and I am proud—make that very proud—to see that the quality Marathi papers are proving to be the catalysts in this change. I am not undermining the role which the other language and English papers are playing, they translate our concerns to our children, to the rest of the country and internationally.

'I realized this when the Srikrishna Commission's report came out examining the riots which took place in Bombay during December 1992 and January 1993 after the demolition in Ayodhya. There was an attempt by the state government to bury the report because their leaders were severely indicted in the report, along with their ministers and the party workers and the policemen on their pay-roll. But the committed newspapers really took up the issue, some journalists like Teesta Setalvad and Jyoti Punwani even had the report printed and sold on the pavements for Rs 60 a copy. It is a telling, tearing account of what can be perpetrated in the name of God.

'For Bombay to understand what should never happen to it again, there should be open debate and continuous discussion on Justice B.N. Srikrishna's report. People should come out and talk to each other, argue if need be and verbally thrash out their prejudices instead of allowing politicians and their goons to manipulate them into such frenzy. I am continuously asked if I will want to re-open the Srikrishna report issue when we are in power in the new millennium. I think I get asked this more often than any other leader because of my political past, people think I will want the report to be used as a weapon to settle old scores. My leader Sharad Pawar has committed himself to abiding by the Srikrishna Commission's recommendations: those indicted will be brought to book by us.

'I purchased another copy from the traffic lights, those boys who hawk magazines and books from car to car were also selling the Srikrishna report. It is quite tragic that the state government chose to reject the report's major findings and in the process dismissed the entire thing by giving it a communal colour. Because the report is also a searing document of all that has been wrong with Bombay—and the country—since a while. People from all communities who think such terrible things can be done only by the poor and the backward class living in chawls and slums specially need to read Justice Srikrishna's report. It is the true story of a time when we all collaborated in the raping of a city.

'These riots did not happen suddenly and spontaneously, workers wearing saffron had gone around surveying areas and putting indelible marks on doors, this was during the build-up to the demolition, the culmination of that terrible rath yatra. Homes were marked out, along with shops and they were brutally dealt with during the riots. Similarly sections of the police did not turn communal overnight; their workers were systematically inducted into the police force and, of course, some of the top brass among Maharashtra's police was being wooed, and responding, quite openly. Who does not remember the senior police officer who bent down to touch his leader's feet at a rally in Chowpatty and who has been subsequently severely indicted in the report?

'Whomsoever forms the government of Maharashtra in the new millennium must definitely take heed of what has been said in the report about giving the police an intensive overhaul. They are, of course, points that have been raised time and again by the police themselves and presented to the central government as their own, very valid, concerns and demands. I think what keeps happening is that the police meets with a knee-jerk response: law and order is a part of the home ministry and that is how it must stay one hundred per cent. Perhaps the answer lies somewhere in between, elected representatives of the people keep the control but also ensure a more professional way of working.

'And for this we will have to begin at the beginning; starting with ensuring that a policeman is hired into the force because he shows the aptitude, not that he is just an SSC pass who cannot get a job elsewhere. They will have to be given the right kind of physical training—apart from de-communalization and re-sensitization—like in the armed forces and airline industry with continuous enforcement of physical fitness. There will have to be an improvement in their weaponry, the standard riot equipment for police personnel is a heavy metal helmet and a hand-held shield to deflect stones; these will have to be made of lighter material. When race riots flare up in America, England and Japan, the police use rubber bullets and water cannons, this could be looked into. At a day-to-day level everything will have to be carefully examined: the police's response, or lack of it, to the public is also because of the sub-standard quality of their own working conditions in badly-maintained police stations where they work for over twelve hours every day because of under-staffing. There is also the problem of housing in big cities such as Bombay, police personnel travel long distances to get to work and constables live in slums where they are dependent on slum lords and anti-social elements to obtain cheap housing. Available police quarters are insufficient and there are long waiting lists which lead to further corruption in their allotment. A policeman needs to bribe or use political interference to get himself a place to stay if he does not want to stay in what is increasingly becoming a city of kachcha structures.

'Slumbay is what a reader nicknamed the city in a letter she wrote to *Mid-day*. That hurt, but she is not wrong, around 67 per cent of the city is slum today. Since the last so many years people have been brought in from villages by trucks and encouraged to encroach upon land. Hutment colonies have been coming up with the active collusion of dadas and some municipal corporators who have charged Rs 5,000 per kachcha structure. When there is a demolition, the dadas move in and give loans at high interest rates for rebuilding, the dadas share the income with their political friends. When this lot of encroachers is moved out to an ostensible housing scheme, money is made by a cartel of dadas, agents, contractors, builders and political types; a fresh truck is brought in to move on to the land which was just freed of encroachment. Unemployed youth are also brought in to occupy government land, then government gives sanction to the slums cleared by such squatters, builders buy them out and pack them off elsewhere to grab yet more land. And this goes on, a vicious cycle within a vicious cycle.

'You see slums everywhere today as a consequence: on railway tracks, footpaths, in by-lanes, and traffic islands, on beaches and even several bus stops. Bombay has really been up for grabs in this last decade. When I was mayor I had started demolishing slums but had to stop because a rich woman went to court on behalf of the slum dwellers. I asked her if she understood the full implication of what she was doing, if the court struck down the demolition, it would create a problem in the future for every single city in the country, she said this was Bombay and everyone had a right to live; I asked her if she had slums around her fancy building, she said no; I asked her if she would have gone to court if she did have few hutments around her building, she did not answer. Subsequently several public personalities have been going to the court, as have the slum dwellers themselves.

'Too much kindness can also kill a city.'

Pakya is on the line, laughing so hard that his head will fall off any minute.

'Listen,' he says, 'this is a nice story which my boys have just told me. You will like it because you are so proud of your precious middle class.' He tells it cruelly, enjoying every minute of making his point.

A teenaged boy and his teenaged girlfriend are sitting at a suburban club. They have just come out from a swim and are having a soft drink near the pool. There is another teenaged boy splashing around in the pool who obviously wants the attention of the girl, he is passing comments loudly. The young couple are trying to ignore him but are clearly not succeeding. The boy gets up from the table, jumps into the pool and pushes the other. There are underwater fisticuffs by which time the club's manager intervenes. The boy goes back to the table to rejoin his girlfriend, the other leaves the club and comes back with a group of four elder teens who proceed to beat the daylights out of the boy. No one intervenes anymore, not those watching, not the manager.

The boy tries to run out of the club, jump into a waiting auto rickshaw. The other and his goons attack the rickshaw driver. The boy manages to get into another and reaches home, bruised, beaten and still in his swimming trunks. The boy's father is enraged and finds out from the club about the other's name and address. He reaches the police station with the boy, there is already a complaint lodged there against this boy for 'trying to molest' his girlfriend and being stopped from doing so by the other and his friends. The complainant is the other's father. The boy's father whips out his mobile and calls his friends who in turn phone some local dadas and they all go to the other's house.

There is, however, a rickety satisfactory ending to Pakya's story.

By the time the two fathers are about to clash with their separate sets of goons, the boy's frantic mother has informed the police of this rent-a-riot that can happen at any minute; constables reach there in the nick of time. The boy's mother has also spoken to the other's mother about keeping her son in check; the other's mother has professed utter helplessness.

Pakya's laboured point is that across class lines, today's city-man and his son are not worth it and that the other far outweighs the decent.

'There is a very radical book that has been brought to my attention, *The Rise and Decline of Nations* by Mancur Olson. Olson says all nations need crises to get back on their feet because long-term poverty leads to a hardening of vested interests. These greedy people take all the wealth available and chop it into convenient chunks for themselves and their chamchas. Naturally they are all anti-change and therefore keep resisting anything new, including the emergence of dynamic leadership or entrepreneurial abilities.

'What these anti-change people do not realize is that those who want to keep sharing the spoils only among themselves ultimately eat into a nation's competitiveness and prosperity. The moment the people realize, and react unitedly, a crisis gets triggered off. This crisis unlodges all the old power structures along with their cronies. This bewilders those very people who are fighting for a change but it helps clear the kachra for a new system, and change which brings about genuine growth.

'I like the idea of agreeing with this, specially since the upcoming elections for both India and Maharashtra, will be interesting to watch. If this Olson is right, we should see some very big changes in political alignments and policy promises. We have been burned so badly lately that we might well change in the direction of large-scale political liberalism and economic freedom. This will be excellent for Maharashtra in which we can start building a first-rate educational system which is bilingual by choice, we can have privately funded universities which encourage intellectual capital to rise, and we can allow property values to fall further. It will encourage our people, especially the entrepreneurs and existing industrialists, to concentrate on creating value, thus building a strong economy on manufactured goods and services.

'Bombay will benefit immensely with all this, it will stop this rapid slide into an economic and intellectual wasteland like Patna in Bihar. The city will no longer be too expensive for start-up entrepreneurs if property prices fall; it will also attract all the multinationals who have gone away to other states. With intellectual honesty and a credible strategy Bombay can as yet reinvent itself.

'But I have to ask this: do the people really want a change to strong, all-encompassing leadership which does not break them down into castes, sub-castes? The editor of *Indian Express*, Shekhar Gupta, recently said in a thought-provoking column that we Indians have a fear of genuine leadership and that because we are so comfortable with faceless and spineless leaders we are so winless. The unfortunate truth of our unwillingness to take a stand results in extremist cult leaders like Bhindranwale and Bal Thackeray. We have conditioned ourselves to accept fate as it unfolds. Karma, where we believe that men should not live by fighting evils, that should be left to our gods. Strong leaders can shake all that up, but are people ready to accept change in the form of fresh, dynamic leadership which will not indulge in sops for one lot and reservations for another? Come to think of it, are people willing to be their own leaders, do their own dharma without waiting for another avataar, or expecting everything from a maay-baap sarkar? Are the people of India willing to make necessary changes that may cause all of us some heartburn knowing that you can never have a casualty-free war? I hope the upcoming shake-down provides this answer.'

Pakya's brother died last night. He and his friends had watched games of Russian roulette simulated on television serials.

The man in one serial would dare compulsive gamblers to stick the half-loaded revolver to their temple and to pull the trigger for a high price, payable to the man on the spot, doubled if the man survived the next round as well. The other serial had a mid-thirties successful man given to throwing lavish parties at the drunken end of which he would extract a price from anyone present who would dare him to play Russian roulette with his life.

Pakya's brother tried imitating the second man down to the drunken party. The man in the serial dies but this is only because his friend slyly loads bullets into all the chambers. In the serial the man collapsed neatly, cleanly, on the carpet with his blood flowing elegantly.

Art does not completely imitate life: Pakya's brother's brains whooshed out all over a wall, then some spattered down the shiny, oil-painted wall to the floor like runny scrambled egg dunked in inconsistent ketchup.

I'm depressed. I just can't seem to hack it, nobody's willing to give me a job in Bombay, nobody's willing to give me a column either where I can have my picture every week in the papers and write staggeringly sweet things about the oil slicks I've met and the affluent effluents in the social cesspool. The chuterrati. I've tried, I promise you I have tried. Everyone tells me I have been away too long, there are younger, far more dynamic people who have taken over the spaces I vacated. Besides, the head honcho and chief enchilada of the *Times of India,* king-maker Pradeep Guha, tells me, 'I think you've got attitude.'

This further depresses me, I stand in front of a mirror and stare at my attitude for a long time. Husband comes and stands beside me to complete the rearranging of the fuzz on his face, I stare at him, and then at us. Shankar and his poor, paavam Parvati. Hagar who sets off every morning to conquer the world, leaving Helga to peel her potatoes.

And e-mail. I've got e-mail from my friend in Bangalore, Rina Mahindra. She lives on this stud farm with her husband Martand Mahindra and their teen deviyaan, Amrita, Jahnavi and Ahalya. I hope I've got their spellings right because, being a numerologist, she's particular. She thinks I should change my name and my surname, or at least spell them differently for things to look up for me. She also says 'Mumbai' is all wrong for the city; they should stick with Bombay because that's eight which is a number of financial security, caution, self-discipline and self-control. It represents an intense desire to reach the top and deep inner strength. 'Mumbai' adds up to nine which is a number of conflict with a tendency to make snap decisions which are later regretted and materialism which can only destroy the spiritual side of the entity it represents. Rina Mahindra further splits that up into an eighteen which is associated with quarrels, wars, social upheaval and revolution; the number eighteen, she says, warns of treachery and deception and dangers from floods and fires and earthquakes. She adds that if an 'I' is added to 'Mumbai'—a good idea anyway, people thinking of their city as themselves, instead of mere I, me, myselves—it would total to nineteen which is the Prince of Heaven, one among the best numbers, fortunate and favourable, indicating victory over temporal failure and disappointments. 'Mumbaii', that does improve the vibrations considerably. Now, which politician should I send this idea to? They all understand number-scrunching in political alignments, but would they appreciate numerology?

Now I'm too depressed. I realize I have no close friends left in Bombay—they are in Bangalore and Delhi and Chicago and Ryhaan Sha is in Georgetown running Guyana Television. May be I should phone Shobha Dé, do you think I can call her my friend since she stunned me by calling me her friend in her column? She came to my bungalow in Bangalore and that had touched me; after that I would phone her in Bombay from Bangalore and burden her with all my innermost immaturities. But that was Bangalore, the past, another country, and I should try and put it behind me.

Actually we don't have too much in common, Shobha and I, except that both of us hate our own names and we are Nari Hira's women; in the sense that I think that we creatively came into our own when hired by publisher Nari Hira. That was a hundred years back and Shobha went on to turn herself into a staggering success story and call me her friend in print. I was promptly flooded with invitations to parties because Shobha Dé had acknowledged me. I went for two of them too, a pani-puri do where the pani was strictly vodka, and a mafia party where the men pasted black bindis on their faces as moles, a woman came with this huge black grape cellotaped to her chin but it did not look quite in the right place.

I passed on the cigar party; when a woman smokes cigars they say she is using this phallic symbol to give herself oral gratification. So what should one say when a man smokes cigars, that he has this latent and dormant desire to set fire to his dick? And I gave that Moroccan sangeet thing a complete miss. They had everyone dressed up in diaphanous do-daahs and washed their feet before having them carried around in huge platters. An almost inspired tastelessness.

Not that I take a moral stand against tastelessness. For instance I would have been delirious to be invited to the colours of love party. It sounds Kohinoor condom-like but was not, a Valentine's Day thing with red all over, pillars of red apples, hundreds of heart-shaped balloons bobbing in the breeze, and red roses and red wine and hearts in red satin on the hand towels. What a time the colours of love couples must have had dancing and stomping about on what used to be my playground, red-faced in their exertions and whispering red-hot endearments to each other. But how can I get invited when I don't have a high-profile job? I shake myself, I have to stop thinking like this. 'Dhichkyaon! Khopdi abhi, chopadi mein? Jhatka dey! Phatka dey! Jokeron ki naukri karegaa kallu, bhejey ki sunegaa toh maregaa kallu, goli maar bhejey mein.'

Yes, maybe I should phone Shobha; women aren't supposed to compliment other women but I like her nerve. Another woman, and hers are nerves of steel, is the singer-actress Sharon Prabhakar, who never ceases to amaze me. Spunky women both, even though Shobha's latest avataar is diametrically different from what she has stood for all along. The film industry—which she loves to hate and who refer to her as Shobha Stardustwali—now says of her, 'Sau chuhe maarkey billi haj karne ko chali'. I think they are just piqued that she has done one better than them, made a cult of herself. These filmwalas, and lately some pathetic TV-walas, are just like the other celebrities who raise altars to themselves, then they stand around at parties waiting for people to come and bow and make offerings at their altar; happily, neither Sharon nor Shobha are like that.

Shobha took time off to try and make me feel welcome in Bombay. She invited me for a dinner where she introduced me to her friends the Sisters Garewal, Simi and Amrita who is an astonishingly organized speaker, somebody should give her a column. I told Simi Garewal that the day after she interviewed the widow, so voluptuous in her sorrow, for her popular *Rendezvous with Simi Garewal* on Star, she—that is, the merry widow—was seen hanging all over a slightly embarrassed man and a few weeks after that, draped over yet another, this time very young man. Simi Garewal rolled her eyes delicately, Shobha never invited me again. Quite often I've tried rolling my eyes the way Simi did so elegantly, my eyeballs hurt.

I've also tried doing a ladies-who-lunch, playing languid lady suitably weightless and desultorily disconnected; we meet at this partially illegal Chinese restaurant where at the next table sit Hindi film rejects. They must be because they tear the Bollywoodwalas to shreds, each one by first-name, and then they speak at great length about how, as TV-walas, they really cannot address social issues because it is not the medium for such things and it is such a pity that

171

the film world does not do it because it is the burning need of the day, Bombay is really going to the toilet. 'But,' interjects one brightly, 'the people will rise.' Everyone else at their table says, yes, yes, the people will rise, they have to now, and then they help themselves to some more crab.

About four minutes into our lunch one of the ladies says she is so exhausted because she has given this party for her husband last night where she had ordered a naughty cake. She has to stop herself from going nudge-nudge wink-wink when she says this, adding that she has got the address from a socialite list-lady who makes it a point to include 'naughty cakes' among her foodie tips and supplied numbers. 'My dears,' she says, 'they looked so real, with, you know, the pink-brown tips and everything?' I wonder what kind of woman would bake this kind of cake, I wonder what kind of woman would publicize it, I wonder about this woman who has ordered it so that her drunk husband, while his friends cheer, can sink the knife through the cleavage of his birthday boob cake.

Another lady tells me about this book she is writing. I ask who the publisher is and she says, 'But darling, why do I need a publisher when I never intend finishing this book?' Another agrees and says, 'Quite right, one simply does one's work; if a book comes out of it well, that keeps the publishers in business. India is, after all, all about merit.' I don't see the connection but I ask Ms Prissy, since she coordinates with so many non-governmental organizations and speaks with such authority about meritocracy, if she has ever heard of the Mandalization of India. You don't want to know about the desultory and weightless fight which follows.

After that I decide that I do not want to have fun where I have no real friends, I am sick of trying to have fun, I have begun to find this kind of fun traumatizing, difficult even. But Shankar insists because it is an important party. I am feeling particularly fat this evening, I have nothing to wear because my hips are now wall-to-wall and each time I speak my words come out in bubbles, like in the comics. But the party is nice, high up in a penthouse overlooking the sweep of Haji Ali, valet parking, no smoking on the premises, the food is vegetarian Mexican, nobody present who is known only because of their well-knownness, no model behaving as though she is the constant object of scandal or desire, no society columnists, no photographers, no loud music, no dancing and everyone actually talking to the other and mingling, waiters attending to everyone since the crowd is small, and guards positioned on the terrace just in case anyone has too much and decides to fling himself a few hundred feet down.

I feel slightly stupid because I'm wearing this designer pyjama from Sangita Kathiwada's Melange since the dress code said casual, all the women are wearing elegantly-tailored salwar-kameezs. But I don't feel too out of it because below my designer t-shirt I am wearing my special, underwired, Victoria's Secret push-up, just for that additional confidence. The increase in weight around my back is making the push-up tear a bit into my side and I think one of the underwires is threatening to escape its lace and harpoon me directly into my chest. But I ignore it and help myself to a chilled martini with extra olives, I am happily absorbed in sticking my fingers into the glass to fish out the olives and pop them into my mouth when I feel an incredibly disapproving stare from a few feet away.

I look up to have cricketer Mohammed Azharuddin shaking his head in disapproval while all the time staring at my Victoria's Secret-ed area. I raise my eyebrows, what? Again he goes, no, no, no. Oh crud, may be the underwire has finally pried itself loose and is popping out from the top of my low-necked, big-scooped t-shirt. I set my glass down on a table and move away to, you know, casually inspect the damages. Mohammed Azharuddin smiles and nods his head in immense approval, yes, yes, yes.

I can't handle this but I don't know what to do, so I decide to brazen it out and walk right up to him and again raise my eyebrows.

He smiles, a very shy smile. Then he puts his tongue slightly between his teeth and again shakes his head, no, no, no.

What? What? Tell me!

'Muslims should not drink,' says he softly.

How does he . . . oh lord, my locket hanging around my neck, nestling on my designer t-shirt.

I wonder, does Sachin Tendulkar 'drink'? I hope he enjoys his well-deserved flutes of champagne.

Begum Ayesha Azharuddin—Bijli to Bollywood—is also standing without a glass at the party. She says they slugged the photographer trying to take a picture of them strolling down Bangalore's Sankey Road because he 'did not respect our privacy'.

This kind of thing always makes me see red. When

celebrities want to be noticed, they go all-out for photo-ops, courting photographers with coy smiles, but when a newspaper lensman is merely trying to do his job the same celebrities suddenly turn into vestal virgins.

What privacy should celebrities expect in public? She nods, we chat briefly; I wonder why as women we tend to heap it all solely on the second woman. Our well-defined areas of self-interest which wobble when faced with such incidents, I suppose. Somebody should ask Sangeeta Bijlani to start maintaining a diary, which could be later published as a book; it should make for interesting reading if she tells it like it actually is, all that grime behind the cricketing gloss.

I also meet architect Hafeez Contractor who insists that the environmentalists are killing Bombay with their 'eco-terrorism'. 'You want to build a bridge over the harbour and they go "Oh my prawns!" It's amazing how everyone manages to kill everyone else's genuine interests. If sensible growth patterns had been followed, the rich of Bombay's Breach Candy, Peddar Road and Malabar Hill would have moved out by now to fancier places leaving those flats for the middle class at an affordable rate. The kind of money a Ratan Tata or Dhirubhai Ambani have had to spend in South Bombay on their housing would get them palaces in London or New York.'

I ask him about the incredible amount of vegetation growing out of Bombay's plumbing, every building has its own set of trees growing out of its sewage pipes. Outsiders keep saying Bombay is full of shit anyway, but such verdant offal?

'That's sacred stuff,' he replies. 'It is the peepul and banyan berry which the birds eat from all the trees planted all over the city and then they sit on the leaky spots in the plumbing and before you know it, Bombay's weather has helped trees grow right into the building's brick-work, roots and all. It really should be removed because it's very bad for the building, but I don't see too many people doing it.'

I come back and tell my building's secretary who looks totally unimpressed, he also looks at me askance since as a renter I have no business caring about a building in which I don't own a flat. Now, every day, I monitor these trees getting bigger and bigger from the plumbing and even shifting the sanitation pipes in the process.

On an impulse I phone Shobha Dé, I am going to have this light, frothy telecon with her. I am horrified to hear myself sound hysterical.

'Poor you,' she says, 'you never have re-connected with the city.'

My brain wants to know, is that pity in Shobha Dé's voice?

Bheja shor karta hain, goli maar bhejey mein.

A MODERN MORALITY TALE

Ek. Here is a man; barely a man because he is on the brink of tears. He is being driven co a house ablaze with lights, and surrounded by dogs and men-dogs with guns cradled into their chests. The head office of Hades, with the reigning god of it awaiting within. It is his aadesh that has brought the one who is about to weep to this house built upon what was once swamp.

He bites his lip as his car slides to a halt at the gates, suddenly he taps his driver on the shoulder and gestures that he be driven on, the car jerks back slightly and purrs forward. Anger is beginning to flare in the pit of his stomach, how dare they.

What's an aadesh, he had off-handedly wanted to know when the phone call came with the summons.

An aadesh is what you don't fuck with.

He is chewing on his lip now, ferociously trying to draw blood to convince himself with its metallica that this is not just a badly-shot scene from some C-grade flick. Anger is now trying to convert itself into rage, how dare they. They? He? Who? Who was it that had taken word to the head office of Hades that someone had sworn out at their master? Then came the aadesh. Come, come and personally apologize.

One more round of the once-swamp, and one more. Come. Or else. Now he bites back his tears and blinks as he steps out of the darkened interiors of his car into a harsh pool of light. He tries not to feel naked. They are expecting him, still there is a frisson of excitement at the sight of such a well-known hero. The guards and the servants and the hangers-on will go home to tell their families of who had obeyed the aadesh today. And the halo around Hades will brighten even more into a fierce light, to which will be hypnotized many more vulnerable moths; and we know what bright lights do in big cities, don't we?

He is ushered into a sitting-room festooned with light fittings, crammed with flowers; no orchids, he notices as he tries breath control, no carnations. Above a cane basket indiscriminately stuffed with hideously wilting tubers is a photograph of a woman, garlanded with scrunched sandalwood shavings. Near the basket sits a woman on a sofa, exuding sad glamour.

She addresses him by his first name, familiarly, enjoying the idea of being able to do so.

'Come.'

The anger in his veins turns into lead with the shock of recognition. After a concert, not too long ago, this woman in the throng of fans backstage, trying to reach out to him, that let-me-touch-him-look on her face. He pulled her forward, smiled as she had a picture taken. He had been seeing her photograph since, in a tabloid which fawned all over her; but he had never bothered to connect the face to the name in the caption below the picture.

'Sit.'

She would sound imperious if she did not pronounce it as seet.

He closes his eyes for a fraction to mask his rising hysteria. He sits opposite her, he holds his knees tight against each other, he places his sweaty palms on them. She uncrosses her legs, and then recrosses them the other way.

'You have drink?'

Dreenk.

He shakes his head. 'No thank you.' He pauses. 'Ma'am.'

She preens, she approves of his manners. 'What you say about saheb?'

'Who, me? Who is saheb?'

'Do not try to act funny. You abuse him, do you not, at the Aleef-Kabir party?'

'No, no, of course not. I swear.'

'You say, what is that bastard and what he thinks he is?'

He slumps, his upper body held up by his face in his palms, his elbows resting on his knees.

'No,' he whispers hoarsely, 'that was not how it was meant to be. You misunderstand, it is only an English phrase.'

He had attended that party reluctantly, film people flung far too many artificially boisterous parties to reassure themselves of some social standing. He had been carrying his licenced revolver; there had been several extortion threats, anyone with an uncouth voice, a phone and his number was calling with a demand; the police had suggested he arm himself. The master of Hades was to attend the party, he really liked playing this role in the Hindi film industry. And so had been erected a metal detector for everyone else invited; security insisted that he hand over his revolver when it had been detected.

'But you guys asked me to carry it,' he had protested loudly.

No weapons allowed when saheb attends a function.

'But this is a private party, goddammit, not a public place!'

Orders are orders. Hand over your weapon or it will be forcibly taken away from you.

'What about my safety, I am at risk too! Who does that bastard think he is?'

He raises his face from his palms, looks directly at her for the first time in what has become a very long night. 'It was only an English phrase.'

Her mouth parts slightly, her lips glisten. 'You are teaching us English now?'

The tears are beginning to flow, freely. And he is crying because there is no shame left in his surrender.

Doh. Here is a story about a happy ending. It is the kind you see at the end of every Hindi film. Why is it being inflicted on you here, in a book about Bombay? And why should the Hindi filmwalas—so insular, so contemptuous of the rest of us—be included in a book on a city? Patience, we must find time to be patient with idealism. Remember, that is all we have got left to hang on to for our future. All this nimble moving from black and white to all those shades in between, no wonder everything appears so gray.

Flashback then, in time and space, to Veerender Devgan at the Golden Temple in Amritsar. He raises his forehead from the cool, stone flooring and implores kay hey bhagwaan, you have got to make me a hero. The year is 1957, he is all of fifteen and he is running away from home with four of his friends; between them they have forty-five rupees in their pockets.

It is thirty-six hours on the Frontier Mail and never has a ticketless ride held more promise. They are already heroes in their own reckoning. Bombay. Fame. Fortune. Hard cash which can be regularly money-ordered to the family back home. The Frontier Mail reaches Virar station and one of the five detrains to drink water. He is caught by the platform guard, the other four get down too in support. They are fined ten rupees or seven days per head in jail. Rope is loosely looped around their waists, with twenty-five others who also do not mind breaking journey at a Bombay jail.

Veerender quite likes his stay at Thane jail, it is giving him a chance to get used to the language—what kind of Hindi is this? Dev Anand does not speak like this on the screen! But alas on the fifth day, all five are let off despite Veerender's protests that their sentence is a seven-day one; the policemen suggest he goes to Sion Koliwada where there are many from his part of the country. Three of the five return to Punjab immediately, they do not like the way Bombay smells.

Veerender enters a photo shop in Koliwada. He used to hang out at a studio in Amritsar and knows a bit about developing and printing and box cameras.

'What zamaanat can you give?' asks the shop's owner.

'Zamaanat? I want to work here, why would you want me to pay you bond money?'

'Because this is Bombay, it might make you run away with my expensive equipment back to Punjab.'

On the sliver of pavement outside the photography shop Veerender feels his forearms. They have been toughened enough for mehnat mazdoori and any kind of strenuous work; at four every morning back home he had set off for the akhaada, his langot around his neck, a bottle of oil dangling from his wrist. He had worked out hard in the gymnasium. It pays dividends when the sardarji at Sion asks him, 'Randhaa khichengaa?'

How many days, from morning to night, at two rupees per day, does he unflaggingly plane wood with the randhaa, shaves flying furiously to turn them into school desks. Now he is upgrading, polishing the desks on which a new arrival from Punjab is plying the randhaa. And now he is subcontracting the work. He is beginning to feel good about himself when he looks up and all at once he's a child again, in Amritsar hiding from his nana behind his mother's chunni to escape those well-aimed whacks of the walking stick.

His nana, Pandit Kedarnath, what is he doing here—in this Koliwada slum, so far away from Punjab, and how has he found him? Veerender ducks behind a desk, Pandit Kedarnath raises his stick and points it at his errant grandchild from ten feet away, freezing him in frame.

'You will not move from there shameless boy, until I tell you to do so. Your mother is crying every day at home. I have yet to see a more besharam son.'

Pandit Kedarnath. Who gave his dead brother's daughter in marriage to the head postmaster at Attari, near the Wagah border, and she was sent back with her nine-month-old son Veerender as a young widow. So the granduncle became both grandfather and father to the boy whom, he sometimes suspects, has not one single scruple in his wiry body.

Pandit Kedarnath now draws himself to his full height of six feet three inches, all the shanties of Sion Koliwada appear stunted and sullied by his majestic presence, his fair skin, his luxuriously upturned moustache, his bullet-studded belt slung around his shoulders. It is time to tame Veerender.

No, it is not. Back in Amritsar, Veerender pays no attention to his private tutors—his nana does not want to take the risk of sending him to school and have him escape again. He manages to stage a convincing failure in the eleventh standard. A family meeting is called in the courtyard—his mamas, his nana, they sit in the aangan on charpais, and they discuss whether they can at least salvage something of the situation by making him a policeman.

'You have to let me go,' Veerender tells his mother Shantidevi Devgan in the kitchen which skirts the aangan as she gets the rotis ready for dinner. 'Look at them talking, your brothers specially. Would they ever become a policewala that they want to make me one!'

Shantidevi continues to make the rotis; he can see the kitchen fire reflected in the wetness of her eyes and he is filled with remorse.

'Please, let me go, forget about me. Don't even remember that you gave birth to me. And if, by chance, I do something right in Bombay I will prove that what is dross now is not forever worthless. You can have the satisfaction of knowing that your khota sikka has turned khara.'

Shantidevi Devgan gives her son fifty rupees which she takes from his nana. This time there is no arrest for ticketless travel. Washing taxis for five annas inclusive of sleeping in them in the nights, crisp kaanda bhajiyas with steaming glasses of tea, four rotis with one dal free at one anna per roti. This is the life, make no mistake, Veerender Devgan is about to become a Hindi film hero.

He trams it up and down Bombay on the two anna ticket, the tram tracks embedded into the city charting his journey from studio to studio. Outside Shree Sound Studio at Dadar, a long line of good-looking hopefuls wanting to become heroes. Outside Mohan Studio at Andheri, even better looking men anxious to make it big, no one paying any attention to them. Outside so many studios, the same story. Veerender takes a long, hard look at himself in the rear-view mirror of a taxi he has just finishing washing; he is not hero material. It is back to polishing fifty benches, subcontracting, peticontracting for Hanspal Industries in Kurla which makes school desks and chairs.

Then wrestling comes to Bombay, brought by a combination of enthusiastic albeit slightly eccentric Parsi-Muslim promoters and the cut-outs go up in an arch facing the sea at Haji Ali. Dara Singh, Randhawa, Gama, Majid Accra, Bholu; all and more wrestlers in freestyle kusti on the NSCI grounds in Worli. Veerender does not miss a single evening, there are season passes. The oofs, the grunts, the flying kicks, the thumps as corded flesh falls in the raised and padded ring with its red corner and blue corner, the look of horror on Mallika's face as she leans forward in the VIP stand to try and not watch her husband Randhawa being pasted into pulp by some Pakistani in a green chaddi; and then Dara Singh for the last bout—Rustom-e-Hind, victorious, legs and arms akimbo as the crowds roar their pleasure in the crisp wintry night, the triumph of lassi and assi-tussi.

Veerender makes enquiries, takes a decision because he cannot spend the rest of his life making furniture and there have already been too many days of hunger between making tables and chairs. He locates the address of Abdul Sattar who had worked at the Mazagon Docks before switching tracks as fightmaster in the Hindi film industry. Veerender Devgan goes up to Abdul Sattar and touches his feet, be my guru. He learns from Abdul Sattar and watches how other fightmasters work. Azeembhai who specializes in equestrian stunts and Douglas whose fencing is legendary even while he is alive. Douglas Master starts the Movie Stunt Artistes Association, five rupees per membership, Veerender Devgan is among the first three cardholders.

It is time to get into the thick of things. Veerender turns fighter, the guy who falls down when the hero delivers what appears as the knock-out punch on the screen. He falls down quite a bit subsequently as a fighter, and then upgrades to falling down as the double of his hero Dev Anand. He doubles over for several directors, Chetan Anand, Guru Dutt, and his enthusiasm is noticed by fightmaster Ravi Khanna who makes him a contractual offer and even suggests a place to live—a stringed cot set up near Sunil Dutt's horse Dara, inside Mohan Studio. Veerender Devgan shifts in as Dara's immediate neighbour. Beats sleeping on Bombay's pavements with rats, cats, dogs and the occasional cow as bedmates.

Both Dara and Devgan appear in *Mera Gaon Mera Desh*; Devgan as fight composer and double to Sunil Dutt. By which time he has doubled for every hero in the film industry bar Raj Kapoor, from Dilip Kumar to something called Sailesh Kumar. Free time is spent sitting by Dara's side on the cot inside Mohan Studio making up punches which heroes can convincingly throw on screen. Veerender also adds wrestling, punches mixed with acrobatics, where do you think that famous scissor-kick-in-the-air came from, where the hero phatkarke knocks off the gun from the villain's hand? Mind you, the gun flew in a gracefully victorious arch. And who do you think first picked up the camera and jumped with it several floors down just so that the audience could feel the falling, this long before Steadicam? And the conceiver of those repeat shots, the hero whooping into the air and kicking the villain in the face, again kicking the swine in his by now bloody face without coming back to terra firma, again kicking in the face, again . . . it becomes so popular that directors start using repeat shots in their song picturizations.

It has to happen, of course. One day as Dharmendra is saving himself and Asha Parekh on the screen in *Shikaar* and Veerender Devgan is hurtling his body through all kinds of complicated aerial manouevres as the hero's double, there is an audible snapping. The double has dislocated his shoulder apart from breaking his other hand in a few places. The Parsi doctor at Grant Road who treats him for the dislocation mutters, even as he marvels at Veerender's capacity to withstand pain, 'Kevo saand jevo chhe.' Asha Parekh translates the Gujarati for the saand, that the doctor thinks he is one tough bull.

Bulls and china are a lethal combination, Veerender Devgan smashes through glass like Superman avenging evil, which indeed is what he is doing for the hero on screen. Lesser stuntmen have died when simulating jumps through doors and windows and shards of glass have sliced through their veins. Veerender is focussed, the scene replays itself in his head—over and over—with clarity and the precision of a stop-watch before he attempts it. Manoj Kumar observes this and offers him *Upkar*. This is it, the interval is over, it is the beginning of where the men come in to do their thing.

Doubling for Pran in the famous well scene with one leg tied behind him to appear lame, setting punches all day and having them thrown by Manoj Kumar and Prem Chopra on screen, having food given by producers on the sets and conveyance being paid too since the Movie Stunt Artistes Association has been organizing itself creditably for its members; this is the life, and it can only get better. It does, if you do not consider the falling out with mentor Ravi Khanna and the resultant bad blood thereof forever. Manoj Kumar offers Veerender Devgan *Roti Kapda aur Makaan*, and who do you think is responsible for conceiving the film industry's first motorcycle jump over burning barrels on screen? And who scores another first in the history of film-making in India with a special credit? 'Introducing', it shines on-screen, 'Fight Composer Veeru Devgan'. To understand how this must really feel, your name up there in the lights, you could ask a hero, any hero.

He says it became Veeru on the sets of *Mere Apne*, Gulzar rechristened him; it was used as Dharmendra's screen name in *Sholay* later. He has done, he cannot remember, how many films since then. 'Maybe 400, including work with the Southwaley, badey disciplined log hai, they really know how to work in Madras.' Someone has told him that the bridge collapse scene he did for *Henna* has been copied by a Japanese film, this pleases him but does not particularly impress him. 'My high point, my biggest thrill, was not in seeing my name in 70 mm, by this time I had already decided that I wanted to move on and become a director. It was that first motorcycle stunt, after which I did another over a long line of cars for *Agent Vinod*. I even got letters from Hong Kong from their filmwalas saying "too good". And look at me, I simply had a drink and I was happy that my work was being internationally recognized, I did not think of taking advantage and going there to see if I could do any action and stunt pictures for them. Later the Londonwalas sent a message through Shashi Kapoor congratulating me, again I sat on a terrace with my friends and had a few more drinks.'

To use Veeru Devgan's lingo, maybe his brain ka track did not open at that time because bhagwan did not want it to for a specific reason. But there are no complaints from life, he has yet to cry after that one time when the first love of his life let him down. Those were the days when he was polishing benches and she would stand and watch from her house on the third floor of the next building. He made friends with her father and her little brother buying the brat more biskoots than he could ever eat; one day they all went away to Punjab and he went in search of her to this little village near Amritsar. He changed from his pant-shirt to a proper Punjabi shirt and salwar so that no one would doubt his intentions and went to find her address from the patwari of her village. The patwari looked a little doubtful, as a village elder he had to tell Veeru that it was said she had a chakkar going with another youth from the village.

Veeru Devgan nevertheless walked up to her house and stood outside it until she came on the roof to dry some clothes, from there she saw him standing down on this dusty, suni village galli and she turned her face away. He walked down the lane, many lanes like it, until he came to a charpai set out by someone in the deserted dusk. Lowering himself on it, he pulled out his checked rumaal from the pocket of his kurta and cried into it as much as he would have ever wanted to for the rest of his life.

And this is how his personal life would have then stayed, Veeru in Mohan Studio near Dara, planning punches and executing fights, had his pals not pointed to a girl across the road and dared him to line lagaao her. This has to be said here, our hero is a virgin. He believes in love first and that which follows is only a culmination of love. Which is why, when everyone else goes to the women of Golpeetha to get their rocks off, Veeru declines; he has honestly not felt the need, work is his physical release, prayer takes care of the spiritual side. Thus it is through work he discovers that there is something called a Nirodh.

It's like this. On the sets of *Bhai Bhai* an effect is required whereby the bullet hits the hero and he falls with the impact and blood simultaneously gushes out of where the bullet has hit him. A blank is used, a suitably armoured Veeru doubles as the hero, he flies back eight feet when the bullet slams into him. This will not do, it does not look real enough, the bullet is chopped into half; half bullet, half the number of feet for a hero to look less like a wimp who cannot manfully take a bullet's impact. Now for the blood bit. Frances the electrician of Mohan Studio who handles all the blasting scenes has an idea—let us wire an eff ell.

'Yeh eeful kya cheez hai?'

'Veeru, eeful nahi, eff ell; such a tagdaa man like you and you really don't know?'

'Sincerity-sey I am saying I do not know.'

A box of condoms is procured and the latex sacs filled with red liquid whose consistency closely resembles that of human blood, the camera should feel that this is human blood flowing, it should not splash down like water and it should not take forever like honey, therefore consistency is as important as colour. The special effects shop in Dadar has begun stocking this liquid now that the Bombay film industry has begun asking for it quite a bit, a bottle is sent for. The condoms are filled with the liquid with the use of ink droppers, the tops are taped shut and all of it is taped to Veeru's body exactly where the bullet is going to hit, on the top of a lot of protective padding.

Frances the electrician wires the sac in such a way that impact will result in immediate bursting. Lights, camera, action! A marksman fires the gun, on screen it is the villain's face; the sawed-off blank hits Veeru exactly on his eeful, Frances' wiring works immediately, the sac bursts, blood gushes; on screen the hero gives the effect of being temporarily vanquished by evil like a man, gracefully staggering a few steps backward as blood nobly pours from his divine being. Hereinafter this is christened as the Body Effect; to be pronounced—without fail—as bawddee effac. Frances's son Anthony today carries on his father's tradition of electrical and blasting techniques in the Hindi film industry.

Okay, so this is how real love happens. Veeru Devgan is teaching Vinod Khanna action for a Sunil Dutt film and they are taking a chaay break at Railoomal da Hotul near Mohan Studio. Across the road is Tone Func Radio Components owned by a Sindhi who hires Sindhi girls to work in his factory. She comes out from the building every day, at the same time, to the same bus stop, never once raising her eyes towards anything except oncoming buses.

Veeru is nudged, 'Yeh wali.'

'This one? Okay, I will get her to talk to me in fifteen days.'

'Ha, ha, ha! Some of us have already tried and failed.'

Hmmmm. So Veeru starts making it obvious that he wants to talk to her, he continuously gives her what in filmi language is called 'loud expressions'; to no avail. He jumps into her bus and sits next to her, she ignores him. Her lunch, like all the other lunches for the Tone Func girls, goes from Railoomal da Hotul. Veeru takes to making her dal-fry separately, preparing that entire plate himself, putting in one specially roasted-in-ghee plump cashew in the middle of the dal. The plate is handed over to Najundaa the delivery boy; he is actually Nanjundaiah from Karnataka but no North Indian is ever going to get the pronunciation right at Mohan Studio, and he has settled cheerfully for Najundaa. Veeru gives Najundaa a new set of instructions every day with a new plate of dal. This has some effect, she waits for him to sit next to her in the bus and gives him a firing.

'Don't even look at me,' she storms.

Veeru takes to angling the mirror at the barber's kiosk next to Railoomal da Hotul so that it catches her reflection in it, across the road at the bus stop. She crosses the road and addresses him. 'I want you to stop this immediately. Why are you harassing me?'

Veeru is stunned to hear the words coming out of his own mouth. 'But I love you!'

Well, now that he knows he starts turning to his brain for directions on how to proceed. She responds by telling him that she is aware of the differences in their religious beliefs and her family will never allow this, so please to leave her alone, this is her kasam to him, and if he really loves her he will not break this promise.

Hmmmm, kasams can only be broken with your khoon, this Veeru knows from his childhood. But he is also a fight composer and he knows what can happen if you mess around unthinkingly with blood, guts and mindless violence. He scours all the stationery shops in Dadar and finally finds a pure pin, the kind which will not instantaneously give him tetanus. Back on the bus, on the seat next to her, he pulls out the pin and sticks it right into his finger. Luckily for him and the effect he desires, it is not merely a ruby red dot which rises, blood spurts out. She grabs his finger and puts it into her mouth. Heroine wooed. All that is left now to deal with is her family.

His reputation as a fighter helps greatly in this regard. When Veeru barges into her home in the Kurla Sindhi Colony and announces his name and intention, her father and brother recognize him and freeze for a bit before they can react vehemently; yielding enough time for him to take her hand and lead her away. They get into a taxi and from Bandra she phones her father who says come back, then we will agree to this match.

'No chance,' Veeru says. 'Marry me first, then go to say hello to them.'

They marry in the Arya Samaj mandir at Goregaon, he buys a satin kapdey ka suit for her for the simple ceremony on 22 February 1968. He takes her to a friend's room in a chawl at Oshiwara, these are frightening days because the kaanpatti killer has been stalking poor people in Bombay, he has been taking some sort of blunt object and pulping them in the area just above their ears. The chawl dwellers have been collecting in the nights to stave off each other's terror before going to bed; eventually a constable does catch the kaanpatti khooni wandering around with his killer hammer at Masjid Bunder.

Their first child is conceived here, in his mind Veeru names him Raju; he also decides that if it is a son, he will make him a Hindi picture ka hero. But there are more frightening days, the Hindi film industry embarks on a strike which threatens to pull on. How is Veeru to feed his wife, clothe her, nourish her womb? He has eight annas in his pocket, he joins several other jobless in the film industry in playing matka, he gambles all day and by the evening he has won forty-one rupees, chalo, one month's ration for the house. She refuses to spend the money; I cannot feed my child with khotee kamayee she says. Veeru takes her to Delhi to where his mother now lives, with his brother who is an officer in the government. Their son is born in Delhi, on 2 April 1969.

But Veeru does not bring them back to Bombay until much, much later. He returns to being Dara's neighbour, he works even more than Dara does, he manages to buy a flat three years later, 450 square feet in Prabhat Colony at Santa Cruz East for Rs 21,000, for which his nana lends him Rs 4,000. He goes from being fighter to fight composer to stunt director to director, apart from star-launcher.

Now they live in a duplex-penthouse near the sea with the sun setting behind their plush condominium in Juhu, the director and his Veena, their hero son and his heroine wife Kajol, nanaji was with them until recently when he gently died at ninety, his mother followed in February, his daughters Neelam and Kavita visit with their husbands, it is nice. It is how families who work hard towards happiness should be.

He has had to work a little hard at changing too, it has even been painful in parts. Raju wanted to marry a heroine; this made him uncomfortable, with what he could not understand; but there were arguments and angry words and, yes, even bitterness. Then he acquiesed, his brain ka track told him that he had to look at things differently. Why, because the zamaana is changing and most things are changing for the worse? His brain gave him the direction, because jab aadmi main pe aa jaata hain, nature ne usko tamaacha maarna hi maarna hain. Veeru thinks about that, yes, when a man reduces life to just himself, events do tend to twist around and slap him hard. Then he thinks about it some more, why should his son not marry a heroine? What is wrong with heroines anyway, are they not somebody's daughters and hard-working women? And when a self-made man like that industrialist Dhiru Ambani can see his son Anil's point of view eventually in wanting to marry the heroine Tina Munim, inspite of all that she has been publicly put through in her personal life as a heroine, how can he, Veeru, hold on to his ego? And what a mard ka bachcha that Anil Ambani is, wah, he really protects his wife. On and on and on, the thought process of a man who understands that to evolve is to be alive. That's it, settled.

And now he sits on his terrace and has a drink, when he feels he will burst with the contentment God has given him he drives to his farm in Panvel and fires a few quick shots in the air with the revolver nana left for him. An astrologer had told his mother in Amritsar that he would find his life samundar ke kinare, near the ocean, and that his work would be something to do with colour; the man also said his best creative period would begin in the year 2002.

He has but one question which only his wife can answer and she refuses to—will she ever give him permission to gamble? Instead Veena looks towards his expanded middle and says, 'Badal garjenge, sardiyaan aayegi, after all that beating you have given your body your bones start paining the moment the monsoon clouds hover or at the first chill of winter. You have had open-heart surgery, now you are directing movies, this is enough gambling for any woman.'

Hmmm.

Teen. Here is the hero Ajay Devgan, Veeru and Veena Devgan's son Raju.

Are you clucking your tongue in irritation, what is this cutesie stuff à la the saccharine sweet, virtually diabetic movies of Rajshri Films? Are you thinking: happy-happy crappe—get real, this is about life?

Patience, patience. Ajay Devgan also knows this is about life and he too is playing patient. Every now and then he erupts in a controlled sort of way, his quotes to non-film publications define the grey area and give focus to his paradigms; you may recognize him as a long-term thinker in the film industry, notorious otherwise for converting everything they associate with into a Golpeetha.

So, big deal?

Look again, and Ajay Devgan could well be about the Men of the Tens, boys who might well make the difference in the first ten years of the new millennium. Him, and Aamir Khan. Heroes in their own right, men on their own terms. Something that all of us yearn for but think that we can never achieve because we are so trapped between the past of our parents and the uncertain politics of the future with the present revealing that we do not even fit into this never-ending nightmare.

Wait, look at Ajay. And Aamir. They could never be considered hero material for all the obvious reasons, valid only until they changed the rules—skin colour of the former, height of the latter, attitude of both; neither believe in the artificial dignity tradition insists must be accorded to mindless events and brainless people. And both are working towards understanding what cannot be seen so that they can eventually make some sense of it all.

Sure, for them money is important, like Shah Rukh Khan they take all payments in cheque and pay hefty income tax; but unlike them Ajay Devgan does not dance for it, not at weddings, not at concerts.

Oh yeah, well who is asking him anyway?

Ah, but you will be amazed at the star-struck out there—understandable, because in this country where are the real heroes otherwise; pitiable, that they should think stardust is worth being bought. Then why do the non-resident Indians do it—pay packets in dollars and pounds to have stars visit their homes and eat off their crockery? Who knows. And why do these film folk charge for being guests and fed? Who cares.

Ajay Devgan does, he who was launched by his father in a spectacularly conceived motorcycle scene in *Phool aur Kaante*; and so what if the rest of the movie is a rip-off of a B-grade British teleflick. He is on the outdoor sets of a movie the climax of which is being shot, he is wearing all-white clothes and in a minute he is going to be called for the shot where he is to get into a crane and swing the fork of it around to hook the villain into it and throw him with a flourish into the wild blue yonder. All around the crane are the signposts of communal amity, a gurudwara, a masjid, a half-crazed wandering-singing mendicant; all kinds of political correctness to appeal to different sections of the masses out there. He grins. 'It's like the things you do for love.'

Ajay Devgan is a chain-smoker and his father has tried very hard to get him to stop. Veeru has even bought a whole pile of cigarettes and smoked them in front of his Raju, bang on the opposite chair on different sets. Ajay's laser looks have assessed the situation so—Veeru is smoking cheap cigarettes, why should he at this age and stage in his life, expensive packets have promptly been purchased for Veeru and handed over to him.

'We have grown up together in these last few years, dad and I. Things were difficult until some time ago, then he understood some and I understood the rest with mom playing middle-man. Actually it was nana who understood me well, I think I have learnt the art of stillness from him. Nanaji could sit in an absolutely empty room with bare walls for hours on end in complete meditation and then emerge in an instant, completely refreshed.'

He does not say so but if he could he would, too, go into meditation and come out of it only when the circus has left town.

'Some of us just want to work, and want to be known for our work as professionals. I want to be in front of the camera, I want to be behind the camera as director, and then when I am confident enough I want to act in plays. So why am I feeling so marginalized? Because I don't want to lick arse and call some politician's daughter-in-law bhabhi in public? Because I am not working on building some charisma so that I can sell myself to the highest bidder? Because I do not even want to see myself dancing on the stage when I am fucking fifty-five years old?'

He looks a bit apologetic about his outburst, as if these are things he should only be thinking about and not voicing. Ajay thinks, Ajay acts accordingly—in reel and real life; Aamir Khan also thinks, perhaps a shade too much, and they both get called by their tradewalas, 'Lambi race kay ghodey'. Ajay does not agree with them, he is not a horse in any race, he is not even a role model for anybody because he thinks actors make for unreal heroes. And how does he feel about being touted as the next Amitabh Bachchan? His lasers have already seen through that hype, 'I'm not going to fall for that and get trapped in it.'

Every now and then Ajay indulges himself, he opens a map in his mind and charts the places he will go away to forever—America pops up instantly because he has friends there, his friends from childhood like Gufraan Rizvi and Mahesh Punjabi. His other close friends, executive Vijay Nakhra and leather exporter Navin Chopra, are also not from the film industry, bar ace cameraman Sameer Arya. But his serious girlfriends—Karisma Kapoor, Twinkle Khanna, have been only from film families as is his wife Kajol. Point out that all the girls also come from incomplete homes and Ajay looks astonished; testimony, nevertheless, to the happy family atmosphere Veeru and Veena have set up and which attracts. And to their shared sense of destiny.

Ajay nods while exhaling smoke, 'I am really grateful for that because I do not see this shared sense of destiny in too many homes any more. I do not see it in Bombay either, I used to earlier when I was a kid. Of course I have never seen it in the Hindi film industry though it is still somewhat evident in the South, their film guys and their people. In a sense the people of the South are still heroes in their own lives, Bombaywalas used to be like that once upon a time. And now we have all become like the worst of the Hindi film actors—we play roles all day and in the night we are still playing roles at the dinner table and everything has meshed and we have turned into pathological liars who come alive only at the sound of money.'

Money, he exhales some more on the word. 'Money, even religion is about money because religion controls and keeps everyone stupid so that some people can make more money. Why have we turned into such morons, or were we always incapable, genetically, with one small flash of light in 1947? When people talk about brain-drain and how Indians are leaving for other countries where they can get a favourable chance at exercising their intellectual muscle, I wonder about our country's gene pool. Isn't this also a gene-drain? I don't like declarations, they make me sound like, "I am saying this so listen to me because I am Mr Know-It-All and you don't know jack-shit." But something has to deconstruct to make way for fresh infusion; and it isn't just the film industry which we are talking about.'

Maybe, now he inhales on the words, 'Maybe things will change, may be the old guard will let the younger guys who are already in place do some good work.'

Maybe. In the meanwhile he, and Aamir, and a few million more working Indians, are trying to find that balance between their father's idealism and tomorrow's hardbitten new liberalism—for want of clever coinage let us call it practical professionalism.

And for now exit Ajay Devgan. He has to go out there and vanquish a bad guy. It takes a crane to do that these days.

Char. Where is the heroine of our story? Glad you asked, she exists but does not feature. She plays a role, but it is not a new one because no one is going to let her experiment with anything between feminist and ultra-feminine. The greys are for the guys, the chicks have to stick with the black and the white until the very end. And even the women are not going to let them do it, witness their burning posters and breaking windows to protest against an over-the-top lesbian film called *Fire*. Look at their expressions, just like those of the madmen around them, the only way of differentiating them being the sarees they wear. Oh look at the one in a salwar-kameez smashing the glass at Delhi's Regal theatre and the mangalsutrad-wali in Bombay, this is sad, they look bestialized in a brainwashed way. What a combination has been stuffed into their minds, the explosion of sex and religion. They are the workers of a party whose rudraksha-wearing boss had Michael Jackson perform in his city. Jackson is a child sexual abuser, but that's all right.

Now, now, let us be fair and not get carried away. One *Fire* does not make a movie industry. True and of course there have been powerful heroines in powerful roles. Remember *Mother India* and how we became the permanent pall-bearers of Indian womanhood after that—provider in the kitchen, comfort-giver on the bed with a nipple on the ready to be proffered to the perennially anguished Indian male, worker-drone in the fields, cracker-of-the-whip for wayward sons, controller of daughters so that they never let go of their puja ki thalis.

In those days, and perhaps even today, *Mother India* goes under the category of idealism of the fifties. Then came the Green Revolution and romance of the sixties—woman in the fields holding her man's hand as he holds the sickle, looking towards the fleckless sky and smiling. The seventies, aha, the woman is coming into her own; she is smoking, she is wearing tight saris and extra-small blouses. Makes sense, it is the first phase of disillusionment in the country, the need for real heroes is beginning to be felt because Indira Gandhi is making the men jump through rings of fire. The eighties; confusion, hope and then despair—weeping, widowed mothers in a parody of *Mother India*, raped sisters, supportively bright-eyed and bushy-tailed girlfriends—it has been the age of Amitabh Bachchan. The nineties, anarchy; and in the late-nineties escapism, women back where they belong, wearing chiffon saris and smiling and smiling and smiling till it hurts—*Hum Aapke Hain Koun . . .!, Raja Hindustani, Kuch Kuch Hota Hai*.

But it is women who like this sort of thing, insist the film trade pundits, they have been weeping while watching *Kuch Kuch Hota Hai*. Women do not like change, they add, Indian women actually just want to be at home waiting for husbands to show up to marry them or come home after office. Why, the biggest hit of all time in ladies-ka-pictures has been *Jai Santoshi Maa*, and lately the karva chauth crowd has simply loved *Hum Aapke Dil Mein Rehte Hain*. So there.

And so here is the heroine who has never emerged from the shadows; she will not emerge now. Of her you shall only know this: she hates playing Mother India. But after they have messed up everything that they possibly can—be it cities or values—they will insist on putting her back on the pedestal. That role, play it again mom.

Till then she may experiment with some hutt kay

roles, this is film lingo for token difference. How much hutt kay? That depends upon the craft of the woman, the heroines of yesteryear did not have roles really written for them either, but they shone did they not? And that was because of the strength of their performance; then came Rajesh Khanna and Amitabh Bachchan and admittedly the women's parts got mechanized a bit, but really you can be as hutt kay as you like! This is after all a democracy and women have to be left free to either hug or rattle their binding chains.

P aanch. Here is a gangster; barely a gangster because he is a politician. He is watching a card game in progress in an ante-room of the head office of Hades loosely called club only because you are expected to join it when you are invited. The invitation may have started as an aadesh, now it is the inner circle, albeit with members in a continuous state of flux.

Let us see now, today's guests are among the legendary from the film industry; all male, goes without saying. They are drinking, scotch, warm beer, wine, vodka; nothing so crude as harsh whisky. Saheb is in his element, cracking the kind of colourful jokes he has become really good at, every one guffaws. Men never titter, that is left to the women and the wimps.

'So I told him, chhodo yaar, do not worry so much, just go ahead and stake your claim to the land. Nothing will happen, that Mohammedan will never get into a pangaa with you. Your holy men roam around naked, aur nango se toh Allah bhi dartaa hoga.'

Guffaws. Ditto when saheb tells this story of an ancient politician who looks like his poodle and keeps pet boys. And this middle-aged politician who prefers virgins. Girls, he adds. And the reason why this politician keeps a girlfriend is because her boyfriend used to drown in her, that's why the Madrasis called him nakki, licker. More drinks, more rounds of cards, the gangster-politician watches from a respectful distance. More guffaws.

'Pura wax karvaati hain. Full and completely. To maine kaha, bhai, women use hot wax to take out their hair, then this does not burn her there?'

'Garam garam sambhar main doobi idli.'

Guffaws.

'That one who was here yesterday, she claims to be a virgin still.'

'Haan bhai, uska thoku must be content with coming between her breasts. Or Monica style.'

'Doodh doodh piyo glassful doodh.'

Guffaws.

'That producer whose payment problem you sorted out with his financier? These days he gets them to tie him up. Then they have to do all the work, kehta hain it's like body massages in Bangkok, only better because Indian girls have bigger mammey.'

'Likho script apna apna.'

By now the guffaws are a given. The gangster-politician shifts a little in his seat, there is a faint stirring in his groin. Drinks, laughter, derision, conversation.

'Your wife is no less a teekhi mirch. Chakne ko dil chahata hain. Whenever I watch her old movies on television

I feel like tasting the tang of your wife.'

Small, infinitesimally small, pause of silence; then laughter, the loudest from him whose wife is the chilli. The gangster-politician looks at him laughing and feels his cock uncurl. He excuses himself from the room with a small, self-effacing gesture.

Out, in the garden of the head office of Hades, he breathes in the murky night air and pulls out a mobile phone from the pocket of his trousers. He goes into the cell phone's memory and presses dial to be connected to another. Ring, connect, crackle.

'Where are you, this line is not clear.'

'I am on my way to the office.'

'Office, at this time?'

'Haan, tonight has suddenly been a very busy night, lots of calls and the diary is in the office.'

'Theek hain, you reach there, I will phone you on the land line, keep it free.'

'Haan saab. Aaj raat ke liye kuch hukum tha?'

'Kuch teekha chahiye.'

The man laughs. 'Chatpata ka mood hain saab ka. Kaula maal bhi hain, aaj hi aaya hain, maske ki tarah hain.' He adds that she looks just like a popular actress, and he has more heroine look-alikes as saab knows.

'Bola na, mirchi chahiye.'

'Arre saab, the asli chilli has already been chosen by your boss's family. Suna hain, the brothers play passing the parcel with her?'

He disconnects, dials another number, a woman's voice at the other end. 'Baiyee, aaj kaay programme aahe?'

Come, coos the woman, we will tailor the programme to suit your needs.

He dials another number, a four-star hotel which keeps a tart chart, is connected to the man in guest relations who keeps track of the chart's availability. The names of starlets and starlings feature in their conversation. He looks at his watch, 11.30 p.m. He redials the woman and issues rapid-fire instructions, she says that one requires advance notice, he agrees on the actress who is immediately available.

It does not take him long to reach a building by the Dadar-Chowpatty sea, the roads are not all that empty but the detachable red top light and siren help, any politician worth any standing in the city keeps one in the car today. His driver screeches to a halt at the entrance, the building's watchman does not question, he has seen several such important cars in the last few months. The man takes the lift although the guest house is hardly high up in the sky and enters a completely air-conditioned, sealed-to-the-outside-world, flat. Chandeliers with dimmers, thick carpets with plump, satin-covered bolsters, a television and video set at one end of the room.

A girl appears silently at his feet as he makes to take off his Reeboks, unshods him, he looks down at her and sees the deeply scooped neckline, her bountiful cleavage. He feels his cock take shape. She leads him to the bolsters, runs a pearly pink long nail across his lips teasingly; it scrapes, he has chapped lips. She smiles with her heavily kohl-ed eyes and leaves for an inner room. The baaiyee whom he spoke to on the phone chit-chats, offers political gossip, suggests who he can speak to for a role for this actress since he knows the producer well, gives him a drink with lots of ice in a glass of heavy crystal, flicks on the video cassette player with its remote control, and vanishes for the night.

Crowds fill the small screen, disco lights, cheering, the high voice of a woman asking the audience playful questions. 'Kyaaaaaaa' the crowd roars; she re-enters the room.

Ding rang ding, ding rang ding rang ding rang . . . the heroine on screen is wearing pink sequinned shorts, she is wearing them in green, the heroine is wearing a one-shoulder pink sequinned blouse, she is not . . . ding rang ding, ding rang ding rang. The drink enters his bloodstream like a shot of heroin.

Her breasts are fresh, succulent, they bounce as she does backward dance steps on the carpet. Ek, doh, teen, char, paanch, chhey, saath, aath . . . he lurches to his knees and makes to grab her, she side-steps . . . nau, dus, gyaarah, baarah, terah . . . he downs his drink, gets to his feet and joins her on the carpet; him, her, the heroine on the screen, the crowds roar their approval for all of them . . . aaja piya aayi bahaar.

He has opened his shirt buttons, she is dancing across his chest, grazing it with her lusciousness, his cock is rock hard. He pushes her onto the carpet, mashes her breasts, mouths them, pinches her nipples, tweaks them between his teeth, she protests at the sudden pain. 'Kaad,' he mumbles, she obeys, reaches for his belt, unzips, holds his hotly oozing penis, he reaches her other hand down to cup his hairy testicles, he rips off her velcro-fastened shorts and sticks his beringed index finger into her in one savage movement, she gasps. He tears into her flesh, he gnaws at her bones, eventually he will spit her out.

Chhey. Here is an art gallery, located at what is being promoted as Bombay's art crescent, the area is called Kala Ghoda. There is no black horse here anymore, it used to be where the parking lot now is. That expensive statue gathers bird shit and rots elsewhere, along with a number of other statues pulled down from their pedestals in a we-hate-the-British-wave; it seemed at that time that no other autocracy would be allowed to flourish.

Kala Ghoda is crammed with security personnel, policemen whose job appears to have become solely that of protecting from the people those whom they voted into power and fame. There is a very important inauguration on this evening and people who think they are very important are spilling out of their cars this very minute. The art gallery is the venue for an exhibition of a potential political successor. Several invitations have gone out, the phones have been busy, to attend, to not attend? You cannot not attend if you have received an invitation with your name on it, they will notice you were not there, and then, who knows what they will do. Why bekaar mein take pangaa, if the successor feels happy that your presence as a famous personality adds weight to his exhibition, just go and smile for a while. Sure their party has tried to lay down the rules on what culture is supposed to be and are now trying to appropriate art; but what the hell, apne baap ka what goes, right?

Later there is to be an exhibition by his brother, the

other political successor; hoardings have been illegally propped up in the middle of busy traffic intersections like the Bandra–Mahim highway announcing it. You will have to go for that too. These are the heir-apparents, you cannot displease either, and anyway you are doing it because who knows when you will need them? You privately agree that this shenanigan is being handled very unaesthetically, but you are modern, progressive, looking-ahead and looking after your backside. You smile and sweetly say that you do not think that art should be confused with politics, which is why you do not see these two boys as rioteers currently on reprieve. You are here for their art, and c'mon guys, admit it, these boys are artistes-in-the-making! And they are so pleased you spoke to them in their language, you must remember to write about them in your column and sincerely advise them that they must give up politics and stick with art for which they show, as aforementioned, soooo much promise.

Columnist and retired income-tax officer Iqbal Masud sighs at how quickly the ostensibly influential people of Bombay accepted such trivialization of the city's culture be it work or individual merit. Dr Aroon Tikekar, editor of the popular Marathi morninger *Loksatta*, feels that its intellectuals have let down Bombay. Intellectuals. The meaning of this word encompasses another word—thinker. Then what do you make of the intellectuals who supported Hitler in his country; and others of this ilk elsewhere?

Thinkers. Those who will live with less of everything—fame, money, power—than take from the state. Oh dear, this really discounts a number of intellectuals, along with sportspersons and singers, poets and painters, directors and dramatists; this list is getting a little longer than necessary, of those who have taken fancy government appointments and chaired state committees and fought for 10 per cent quota flats and other favours in exchange for intellectualizing fascism. No wonder then, that there is hardly anyone left to speak up in protest when hoodlums storm into the Board of Cricket Control of India and smash everything in sight, including the few big trophies India wins with such difficulty in any sport.

And it is these supposed intellectuals who scoff at the Bombay film industry—which has never had any pretensions, this has to be acknowledged by all—for glorifying sex and violence.

Cry, beloved city.

A brooding view of which is available for 360 degrees from Sunil Veerappa Shetty's high-in-the-sky residence at a plush building on a plush road. Veerappa Shetty came to Bombay when he was nine years old from Mangalore to wipe tables in an Udipi. Soon he began to manage that Udipi, then he bought it, then he purchased another, and then there were four restaurants. Plus one clothing store strategically placed at the corner of Breach Candy and Nepean Sea Road called Mischief which his son Sunil handled. Soon enough there was More Mischief and a Mischief Dining Bar; then Sunil Shetty also became India's answer to Arnold Schwarzenegger on the silver screen.

When Veerappa Shetty was running his Udipis in the days which memory reduces to misty-eyed better times, this murderous political movement was born whose first target was the South Indians and their hotels; there are enough records in the Bombay police books which register the arson, the rioting, the killings, with started with the slogan, 'Bajaao pungi, hataao lungi'. The lungi—the veshti actually—being the best way to identify those who were 'coming from outside, crowding Mumbai and denying the sons-of-soil their jobs'.

Today the hardworking inheritor has been invited to the exhibition of another kind of inheritor who needs patronage, so desperately it would appear, that he and his family would much rather forget those records of those riots in the Bombay police files. If there is any irony in this it is so gentle that it is lost on the intellectuals.

Sunil Shetty has just returned from the art gallery to his apartment artistically decorated with Ganesh figurines and the view of a city which has turned so spectacularly seedy so quickly. His pretty wife Mana, clad in a salwar-kameez softly fused in mauve and rich green, moves in and out of his line of vision, gently keeping their denim-clad daughter and son in check as they run in and out of their flat to Veerappa Shetty's flat next door. Sunil is on the phone, talking business softly in Tulu, a language comfortable enough with itself without needing a written script or people killed for it. He hooks up the cordless phone, absently taps his cowboy boot as he looks at the headlines in *Mid-day*. Then he asks of no one in particular, complete dismay written all over his face, 'What is going on here?'

The *Mid-day* story talks about a bag of bones, several bags of bones actually, dumped in an open area of suburban

Andheri. Most of the bones are proper skeletons and most of the skellies still have their clothes on them—suits and women's formal dresses. The police have given a statement that there is no need to panic, the skellies have been dug-up by some builder on his site just before he commenced construction and because he did not want anyone to know that he was building on a Christian graveyard, he has had the bones stuffed into gunny sacks and tossed out into the night.

There is a picture of a paunchy policeman, surrounded by the skelly bags, upending a sock. Out pouring from the sock are little pieces of something, ah this must have been the big toe, and this dust must have been the smallest one. There is a question hanging over the picture, and over the minorities in the city, which is yet to be convincingly answered. A lunatic lot has been at work on the outskirts of the city and are advancing steadily into the city wherever the Christians reside, pray in their churches and die. They have stopped a Christmas dance, a concert of a Goan singer has been cancelled because of this, there is a hushed story about a waltzing party stopped in Bandra and the youngsters made to perform Bharatanatyam in its stead. So many more instances which are not coming into print because no one wants to confirm them, not even those who know it has happened. Could this fringe have dug up graves? They did it to the Muslims and that building in Ayodhya. No, let us not even voice our grief and turn into sitting ducks the way those Muslims are. Let us not spread fear, let us just try and send our children away to Australia and New Zealand because this is the beginning of the end over here.

Several of Sunil Shetty's very close friends are also thinking of leaving the city, consequently they will wind up leaving the country. Not all of them are minorities, least of all financially. But they have children and they do not want their offspring to fight-fight-fight-fight for a sane way of life the way they have. Enough, already. 'I do not blame them,' Sunil says, 'these days you can get killed by a bullet aimed at someone else on the streets. The amount of sophisticated arms now available in the city with all kinds of people inside their homes and offices is unbelievable.'

Would he leave?

'I thought about it when my friend, and an excellent producer, Rajiv Rai left. He got these calls and then men landed up at his office with guns, they wanted money, they threatened to kill him and his wife Sonam. It shook him badly, but just when he was beginning to calm down, some drunken idiot with his private phone number, called up Rajiv and threatened him. Maybe Rajiv could have handled that too, but then the Super Cassettes owner Gulshan Kumar got shot by the same guy who had first threatened him. Rajiv and Sonam and their family have shifted to America. This time when Mana and I were in the States with our kids, having a completely hassle-free and happy time, I felt so tempted. But I cannot leave, I have too many workers in my business dependent upon me. I look at it this way, if I let down one guy whom I employ I am abandoning his entire family because these are such tough times that the guy is not going to get a job anywhere else right now.'

And so Sunil Shetty makes these samjhautas, he compromises and attends exhibitions.

'I am a businessman, I cannot get apologetic about what I am doing when I know I am not hurting anybody consciously or otherwise. I am not asking for property to be vacated, I am not taking somebody else's life or money through their help. One set of people are in power right now, what makes anyone think the set coming after this is going to be any better? As a businessman I have to keep my businesses running and if I do not use some connections, there is just no way I can cut through the crappe which I have to face every single day because I want to make an honest living and provide employment.'

Veerappa Shetty's very first Udipi is what Sunil Shetty has been trying to convert into multi-tiered, multi-cuisine restaurants. 'Every single goddamn restaurant is turning into a beer bar with dancing women, but when I want to do something that is not offensive and actually gourmet, the rule book is thrown at me. A licencing inspector shows up, a corporation official follows by an elected representative, another wants to know why my wiring is going the way it is. I am standing there and answering every single question patiently because I know I am in the right, I know I am following every single law correctly, archaic though the laws may be. But I am harassed, and am I harangued, and my people are tormented with continuous visits of slime balls who want money, money and more money. So what choice do I have?'

The devil and the deep sea. Always, always.

And yet it was never so bad earlier. 'I have been in the restaurant trade for what appears like a hundred years now. I have watched the underworld grow, but it has never been out there on the streets the way it is today. It is an over-world now, unemployed youth with guns in their pockets, firing for five thousand rupees. I have never felt more under pressure, for the safety of my wife and parents and children and my workers who are my backbone. But I find comfort in the fact that I am a somebody—a celebrity in a star-struck environment—and so I can be the passport to safety of all my people.'

The self-appointed celebrities who work so hard at being only, and just, that will hate Sunil Shetty for such a statement—that he can use his celebritydom for mundane matters. But they hate him anyway, because he has not conformed. Here they were patronizing his sweet little shop, getting him to make foreign rip-offs and allowing him to feel that yes, he was one among them, the South Bombay snobs. And then, good grief, he develops muscle and, the embarrassment of it all, joins the yucky film industry. Of course he has no voice and no charisma and he can only flop. Which will also put paid to those high-flying dreams of marrying his long-standing girlfriend who comes from such a good family. Oh well, what can you ever expect from new money.

Sunil Shetty, student of the fancy Palm Beach High School, resident of the old money area, clothes exporter and retailer, hotelier, becomes a hit in Bollywood. His fight scenes are all the rage. Nothing changes from within him though, except that the roles he plays on screen make him a fighter for life personally. Of course he continues doing whatever he was doing before the Arnie Schwarzenegger avataar began, and so keeps one foot in South Bombay and the other in the suburbs where Hindi films are invariably conceived and shot.

He marries his girlfriend of long-standing, Mana Kadri, daughter of the eminent architect I.M. Kadri, in the face of enormous opposition, much of it from his own family since Mana is a Muslim. He starts doing charity work and he expands his business and he happily cuts down on his maar, dhaadh and dhishum films to concentrate on better offers because the businessman in him knows that Arnie, too, has to age. The money manager in him also sees the general recession in the country as the best thing to happen to the film industry. 'There are far too many beautiful women, an excess of glamour and the highest returns in Bollywood, no wonder it has always attracted the wrong kind of money. Now this lull should give us some time to cut out the flab and turn lean, we can look inwards and do some long overdue spring-cleaning. If we learn our lesson from this I am sure the new millennium will begin with a bang for the film industry. I can already see the signs of this, good production houses like the Chopras and the Barjatyas are playing a bigger role, the golden days of the studio may well return by the year 2000.'

Sunil Shetty's business plans for the new millennium include the starting of 'enducation' centres for children, where the kids can get some entertainment coupled with education, maybe even go into a national franchising with it; and in the meanwhile he has already opened a mom-pop-bachcha video arcade called Astro Mischief, on the top of which he is going to open a bistro with stand-up comedians performing for the diners.

Here is more for the brittle celebrities who believe that to be is enough, to do is to wear oneself out; Sunil Shetty is using his self-confessed passport to sort out the confusion in his own building. 'There were some older guys who just would not give way and would also refuse to do anything good for the building. So I bamboozled everyone into demanding an election, and the fresh lot not only has managed to get twice as much money from the building's society members but has provided five times more amenities.' The experience has also made him think in terms of standing for elections from the city. 'Maybe I should; Bombay has given me, my family and my workers so much, I should try and give some back.'

Just one question because both politicians and gangsters are known to call in their favours. What happens if the exhibition-ists lean upon Sunil Shetty to stand for elections on their party ticket? 'Cause if he can win some now, he can lose much more later especially since the run-up to the next elections is expected to be the final countdown.

He taps his other cowboy boot, he looks at where he has tapped, inspecting it minutely, Mana is in the background, listening.

'That will really be my defining moment, won't it?'

Below him, hundreds of feet below Sunil Shetty, and as far as a pair of eyes can swivel, the city swelters in the heat, appearing as though shimmering with rage, the kind which on explosion will make Arnold Schwarzenegger's escapades look like a baby's day out.

S aath. Here is another outdoor set, except that it is indoors, in the basement of a hotel near Bombay's airport. The set in the basement is for a film that looks like it is never going to get completed. Not for now at any rate, shooting has been stalled for want of a special camera. The special camera is required for a special kind of fight sequence that is to be shot between Shah Rukh Khan and hordes of policemen who are a very special kind of policemen because they do not wear uniforms. Their special mode of clothing is white-and-tight T-shirts with faded blue denims and guns in holsters strapped right across their chests. This is also unusual for policemen, the bodies of the guys in the ganjis are tough, well-built, with chests which can be wept on or hidden behind for protection, depending on who is complaining to the cop. The top cop on the set has the best chest, he is adman Bharat Dabholkar and he is doing a hutt kay role in this picture which is going to have a very hutt kay police station, one with no bulging files and no messy papers, only sleek computers. The director of this picture is Shashilal Nair who makes movies which take their time to be released, not that he ever sets out to let this happen. So whenever he is asked when his next picture is going to hit the silver screen, Shashilal Nair replies, 'Friday, one of these very many Fridays in these ditto number of years.'

Now everyone is waiting for the special camera which is on another set somewhere else in the suburbs. It is a camera so much in demand that its owner feels compelled to rush it, eight-hour shift by eight-hour shift, from location to location. Shashilal Nair is a bit antsy and is shooting looks which could kill towards the production controller whose job it was to ensure that the camera got to this set on time. The production controller is getting upset that Shashilal Nair is giving him the bad eye, considering he has been phoning the camera owner and is being told, since the last two hours, that the camera is on its way. It is just a normal day in film world in other words, so everyone else is fine, sitting around, chatting, cracking in-house jokes and drinking chaay from those special kind of tea glasses with the thick bottoms sold in wholesale from Babliseth's shop.

But the daggers being thrown between Shashilal Nair and the production controller are turning a bit pointy, blood is being drawn. A fight simply has to happen. In good filmi tradition the fight must also have several swear words, the first swear word should have something to do with a mother or sister and the reply swear should ring with indignation that a swear word was used to start with.

Lights, camera, action. Fight on cue.

Someone tries to break it up, several people join, someone goes running to Shah Rukh Khan's air-conditioned camper parked above the basement to tell him.

'Hand to hand?' Shah Rukh Khan asks, miming if it has already turned into fisticuffs.

It's getting there.

Shah Rukh swings out of the camper which he has smoked up with his chain of cigarettes while waiting for the shot to be called. He starts walking towards the basement, the crowd collected around the hotel just to see him goes berserk and sets up a chant, 'Shah Rukh, Shah Rukh, Shah Rukh!' The private security on duty move their hands slowly to their batons.

'Shah Rukh, aye saalaa Khan, idhar dekh!'

Shah Rukh hears the saalaa bit, his nostrils flare, he looks in that direction, pauses, smiles and waves; the public goes berserk afresh. He disappears into the basement.

Cut back to camper, more cigarettes, more rounds of chaay. Shah Rukh Khan sips from two glasses, alternating and meticulously maintaining an equal level in both.

When he came from Delhi he was the arriviste who wanted to make a difference. He wanted to act in meaningful movies and he wanted to be known as a good actor. He did not even bother to get his words right, yet his idioms on idealism only amused an industry smug in its own mediocrity. The first senior film journalist to give him quality time and generous space was Nishi Prem, she saw him as being an innocent from abroad but talented, brusque but bloody right in his thinking, brash but preferable any day to most of the stars struck by duplicity; he was that crazily happy gust of fresh air desperately needed in a fetid film industry.

In an early interview with her, Shah Rukh Khan was blunt but not malicious, overtly judgemental but not resentful. 'I've just joined and there are guys wanting to hold my cup of tea, tie my shoe laces, hold an umbrella over my head. What for, am I a fuckin' retard? What's this fashion here, seven people walking behind one actor? And I could be the world's biggest fuck-up but I have got ten directors wanting to sign me because six guys already have. Nobody is even considering my capabilities. This whole thing is making me laugh.'

He was still Bollywood-bashing after hits like *Dewaana*, *Raju Ban Gaya Gentleman* and *Chamatkar* . . . 'I am not going to fit into the scheme of things as they are, this is trash. Commercial gains are just an excuse for making mediocre films. If someone comes and tells me that I am supposed to do something only because someone else did it and it worked, then I am not going to take it. They say I do not respect seniors. If respect means touching everybody's feet, then maybe I do not. And I am not going to any producer's office to give haazari, this system is too warped.'

Shah Rukh Khan refused to include the film industry in his success. Producers who wanted to be a part of his new limelight felt slighted. Female co-stars seeking favours were snubbed by Shah Rukh's open statement that he loved his wife Gauri. Then came more success, *Baazigar* and *Darr*; Shah Rukh Khan refused to fall flat on his face inspite of his open contempt for the film industry, he refused to give his detractors the opportunity to belittle him. And he still refused to share the limelight, 'I think stardom is my birthright, I fully deserve it, this is the conviction I came here with otherwise I would never have come. The problem is not me, it is this place which is filled with people who have got success they do not deserve. Or if they deserve it they do not want to believe they do, that is why they are so insecure. Here humility is only about fear and lack of conviction. I am not being arrogant when I say I am good, I believe in me.' To prove this, even a *Kabhi Haan Kabhi Naa*, dismissed as a commercially unviable film, turned out to be a hit.

And then they began hating him, openly. He said, 'I am tired of meeting eighty people in a day, listening to stories, shooting, dubbing. It is somehow overtaking me and I don't like not being in control of what I am doing. A lot of people want to cash in on my success but I am feeling crowded and I have become more edgy and a little less understanding. I do not like it. I have everything to feel happy about with this kind of success and I am trying to enjoy it. But should not joy come spontaneously, why am I still trying?' So saying he imposed a self rule—only five films at any given point in time. They promptly called him brash, arrogant, disrespectful to his seniors, condescending towards his co-stars, cold towards his heroines, uncooperative with the film press. Some producers insisted that Shah Rukh Khan's stardom was overrated, that he was never really a hero in the interiors of the country, he was just a city slicker. Every statement he made subsequently was blown out of proportion, every step he took flogged to death.

That was in 1995, several people have changed their tune since. *Joh hit hai woh fit hai.* Shah Rukh Khan remains the same, only much more battle weary. But he has understood, and accepted, that those who lead from the front tend to get shot first, and for all his bullet wounds he has paved the way for the rest towards no touching of feet and no haanji, haanjis—all part of the fake dignity only the mediocre need, that which the truly talented and secure should find gratuitously offensive if they are professionals in any field.

Shah Rukh Khan is smoking up another storm in his

camper and talking about books. 'I read this book on how to write screenplays and I thought I had learned it all but at the end of the book the writer says, "And then there is Pulp Fiction." Cool, huh?'

So life is too cool?

'Where, in the basement?'

There too now?

'I am busting my butt for this movie and I am giving dates in bulk because I really want this picture to be made, I have sat nights with A.R. Rahman on the score, I have told Ju (Juhi Chawla-Mehta) that come what may we must finish this picture. And what do these guys do? They fight. I have told them in the basement that they are going to drink in the evening and they are going to fight anyway, so why not just hang loose for now and wait for the Steadicam instead? They wanted to pack up for the day, I said take the money from me but now that we are here, let us shoot.'

Ergo, life is too cool?

'There is only one time when you are too cool, and that is when you are dead. I never want to be too cool, I want to work eighteen hours for a film and I want to get demented about it. I want to have loads of fun about getting a story right.'

You never stop to think?

'I go through these sessions of sensitivity of who I am and what I am doing here. Then I go back to being demented about getting my film right.'

What is right?

'Did I cry? Did I feel uplifted? Was the comedy cute

and not crass? Did I get entertained when listening to the story? This may not be the only way, but it is certainly one of the right ways.'

Is it right for you to have danced at Lakshmi Mittal's son's wedding in Calcutta?

'We were paid, Karisma Kapoor and I.'

Precisely.

'You mean I should have danced for free for him because he is supposed to be the world's richest Indian?'

No, it means how can you make a nautanki of your art.

'You going to hit me for this, or you are just going to hate me forever because I am being an honest performer? Hey, I have no qualms about who I am, I am just a bhaand.'

What is a bhaand?

'I don't exactly know. When I did that booze ad and a few others because I needed the money for my dream home some people—with a terrific amount of contempt in their voice—told me I was just a bhaand. I liked the word because I thought it applied to me, so I use it to describe myself.'

A loose definition would be performing bull in the villages. How long will you go on playing bhaand for your dream home?

'Naw, that's covered. Now I have to do it for my dream project, a studio-in-the-head, which Aziz Mirza, Ju, her husband Jai Mehta and I are initiating. Some day we will have physical space for it too. When we do I will stop being a bhaand. I want to make this clear, you pay, I perform.'

You performed for an AIDS concert without money recently.

'Yeah, great cause.'

Do you know how much money is being made by people in the name of AIDS? You, and other people from the film industry, performed for free and the audience gave a lot of money to see you. Television rights were sold for astronomical sums. How are you so sure that the money went for the tom-tommed cause?

'I don't. I know what you are saying, I'm not stupid. When was I asked to perform I tried to say "no", the permanently bathroom mey hai technique, the old trick filmwalas use when they never want to talk to you. But then I realized there was no way out, I got scared because of the political clout of the organizers. So I just fooled myself into thinking it was okay for that one time.'

In effect you were held to ransom.

'Who is not holding me to ransom? Who am I not scared of when it comes to the safety of my family, my wife and child?'

Therefore, you cannot be your own hero.

'I am not even a role model, anyone who thinks he is can only be deluding himself. Anyone who thinks he is anybody is, in the final analysis, only another arse hole. Me, I am a coward, I would rather be scared than have my family dead. My father was a freedom fighter; me, I am going to leave behind just forty video prints of my films for my son, I can only hope he will not be ashamed to rewind some of them for his friends.'

Achcha, now we are in maatam mode, self-flagellation.

'I am just trying to do my own thing. Some days I feel like a jester, most days I am just a joke. And since I do not have three sixes on my scalp like the devil's chosen one, I know I can keep trying to get it perfect. Or as near to perfection as humanly possible; passion should not be diluted.'

But you do sell your soul for money.

'And now I have decided that I am going to be proud of it, should I tell you when I decided this? Who is the ultimate hero for any Indian? Mohandas Karamchand Gandhi? Ram? No. Any politician? No way. It is Dhirubhai Ambani. I wanted to have that stature, and then they sent the CBI to his house. To his house! These guys in safari suits messed around the man's home looking for stuff they never found. I was shaken.'

Let's change track. All these women who fling themselves at your feet, you never notice them?

'I love my wife.'

The question is, you never notice them? In other words, you never feel tempted?

'I notice them, yes. Feel tempted, no, not as yet. I am not going to say I shall never, ever, feel tempted because in life, I have learnt, you should never say never. What I will say is that I will not make an effort to destroy what Gauri and I have together.'

You believe in goodness and God?

'I believe in Allah, in jannat and dozakh; heaven and hell which starts with right here, right now.'

You pray?

'I say a small dua, "Nasr u min illahi wa fateh um kareeb".'

That's beautiful, what does it mean?

'I don't know but I hold on to it, something to do with asking Allah for granting victory in the war.'

That is it, no five times namaaz?

'I speak to him in English, every now and then I pop in these requests.'

What do you ask for?

'I have never prayed to Him that my film should be a hit, that would be uncool. But whatever else I ask for, I believe Allah listens to me. My mom sits up there with him and slaps him on his wrist if he does not.'

What was that show of yours abroad which took on communal overtones? Do you feel less upset about it now so that you can talk about it?

'It makes me sick to even think about it. That was insanity even if it was at a time when everyone loved to hate me. It was an item that I performed regularly on stage especially in Delhi. It is written by Johnny Lever and he too has performed it often. It is really a very funny piece, not at all derogatory to God or any religion. You know that scene at the end of *Deewar* in which Amitabh Bachchan crashes his car into the temple and tells God, "Aaj tu bada khush hogaa"? Well, I do this whacked-out version of confrontation scenes between God and Amitabh Bachchan, Rajesh Khanna, Mithun Chakraborty and myself and God replies and makes fun of all of us. I had done this item a million times before and it drew the maximum number of taalis from the audience in India. So when I had to do these shows abroad, in London, Birmingham, New York and Vancouver I included the item. It was mainly an Akshay

Kumar and Saif Ali Khan show but I was a part of it because of my relations with the organizers. When I reached London I fell sick like a dog, 103 degrees fever, but there was no backing out because my name had been announced and the public would feel cheated, so for Birmingham I took this personal doctor and a nurse along and they kept giving me medicine. I did not even do the item at Birmingham, I made an entry with Juhi for the song "Jadoo teri nazar", finished it, collapsed and almost had to be carried off stage. The next thing I know is that there is this item in this odd publication saying that I insulted Hindu gods in Birmingham.'

And it was picked up in India and turned into wildfire. Your effigies were burnt in certain parts of North India and then the nightmare started.

'Anwar, my secretary, received the first threatening call. They told him I should ask for forgiveness or else, achcha nahi hoga. Anwar did not bother me about it until he started getting many calls saying the same thing. Then the telegrams started, "You have humiliated our gods. Apologize in public or else." Then there were similar letters, I tried not to tell Gauri about them but then there was this avalanche of phone calls and letters and telegrams and hissed threats and the whole atmosphere in my house was rent with complete fear. And I did not even know what the hell I was supposed to apologize for. I had bystanders passing remarks like, "Kya bola tha, kya bola tha re tu?" To be pushed into a position where you have to explain these things, that you believe only in Indianism and hate communalism, is to belittle what you truly believe in. The funny thing is, people are still very thoughtless about their reactions to communalism. When will we ever learn?'

Do you feel you have to subsume your identity as a Muslim, sort of be whiter-than-white to be accepted?

'I think the film industry is the only place left in the country where there is no communalism. Kudos to us for showing India how it can be kept out of the work place, out of our streets, out of everything except our little prayer spaces. But to answer your question, I have never taken a stand in any of my films not even as a hero, I have just realized that my characters in my succesful films don't ever veer to the moral right or indulge in chhaati-patkaaoing, the way all heroes have to breast beat a little before the climax. Come to think of it, I have only run after other people's women in my films so far, all the way till *Kuch Kuch Hota Hai* where Kajol is engaged to Salman. So I have not consciously not played a Muslim in any of my films. My son, I named him Aryan only so that it could get pronounced both ways, and be an easy name to deal with abroad because he might well be an international bachcha.'

Are you completely over that ugly incident?

'I can go into joke mode over it I suppose. I could put out this ad asking the world if I should circumcise my son or not. My mother-in-law thinks I should not. I have to find books which explain the entire thing scientifically so that I can make up my mind.'

You do a helluva lot of charity very quietly.

'I don't want to talk about it. I am doing it just for me.'

You are doing a lot of ads, may be far too many which could dilute your star value.

'That is okay, that day has to come when I am no longer a star. I am human so it will hurt but it cannot be the end of the world, right?'

Right, but why push it?

'It gives me a chance to vent my hatred in playing different kinds of roles. With the money I will put up a studio, make some good films which will bring us international recognition. I don't want to work for some upstarts of C-grade cinema abroad who are going to suggest that I act in a movie which shows everyone wanking off and into kinky sex in Delhi's Lajpat Nagar.'

You are referring to *Fire*?

'It was a great black comedy about the way we see sex and religion in India.'

Politics?

'They all keep phoning, telling me I should join politics because my father was a freedom fighter. I ask them, "Where the fuck were you when he was sick and we—my mother, sister and I—were starving?" They say oh well terribly sorry about that but we will give you whatever you want now, whatever, if you join us and stand for elections, just ask and we will do it for you. I say sure, why don't you try making my next film a hit.'

Any last words?

'I am not here to get my kicks from five sidies holding out chairs for me. I know I have to keep my bathroom clean, I am working on it. Whoever else does it will also have a clean bathroom and a better smell in his own house.

Think about it, soon enough a stink-free country. Now that would be way cool.'

A ath. Here is a number. Such a nice, plump number. Say it: six thousand. Say it aloud, Rs 6,000 crore. Let them scoff at the Indian film industry; let them cringe at Bollywood's crassness; let them ask, snidely, whether the movie moghuls know their totals; but this is good enough for the film industry to clutch all the way to the coffin: Rs 6,000 crore.

Six thousand crore rupees, is what it is worth, insists the Indian film industry by the dint of sheer endurance. More numbers roll out easily, perhaps far too easily like the six thousand, because an industry so disorganized cannot possibly be in command of such water-tight statistics. It employs eleven lakh people directly and approximately fifty lakhs indirectly. In many ways the film industry is like government, over-staffed, evident on the sets of even a medium-budget quickie with a hundred hangers-on doing precisely that, hanging around.

So much for the lies, damn lies and statistics. Here are the facts. The Indian film industry makes three-fourths of the world's films; do not consider 1998 please, where only 690 films got made. The average number of flops in any given year: 80 per cent. And while the Hindi film industry may, unconsciously or otherwise, appropriate the sexy six thousand as theirs, it is the overall Indian picture, encompassing Assam to Kerala with Punjab in between.

Get the picture?

But the film industry will not learn, oh no, it is now

working conscientiously towards insuring itself. What is wrong with insurance? Of what use the cart before the horse? But Subhash Ghai has done it, you see, and everyone must now rush in. Subhash Ghai is the first feature film director in India to insure his film *Taal* with United India Insurance. He has projected his film's cost as eleven crore rupees and, in exchange, is paying peanuts as premium, only fifteen lakh rupees. Subhash Ghai may well have quickly anointed himself showman after Raj Kapoor died, thus causing some heartburn in an industry famous for rejoicing at others' failures, but the other hard fact also remains: Subhash Ghai sticks to a work schedule and film-discipline.

The neo-showman also puts work above hero-worship. Govinda, the boy from Virar with the overactive pelvis, wants an image makeover. He wants to speak English correctly, as he puts it, 'Main English faad faad ke bolna chahata hoon.' He does not get anywhere with this because he lacks the discipline. He does not get anywhere with getting a role in Subhash Ghai's *Taal* for the same reason. He keeps going to Ghai and talking about the role, he agrees to do it for a price cut, he insists that he will show up on time and no, he is not going to report at 4 p.m. for a 9 a.m. shift as has been his habit with the other producers and directors.

To use a Ghai-ism, uska sirf furniture badalna padegaa, just the furniture needs re-assessing, the house and its foundations are fine. Subhash Ghai knows that Govinda has a lot of untapped talent, he can see how the role can be easily tweaked to cap Govinda, and he likes the challenge

233

of presenting him in as a mature actor, it would even be a coup of sorts for him moving him out of David Dhawanesque mould. But finally he does not take Govinda, because the man refuses to sign a contract.

Bollywood is full of paperless contracts. An international finance company discovered this in 1993 when they flew into Bombay to examine the feasibility of film insurance in India. In 1992 the country had made a record 930 films and the company saw this as an untapped market. Then they realized that almost no working person connected with any film signed a contract because they wanted to evade tax and, therefore, took payment in hard cash. Further shocks included information that stars arrived late on the sets and producers saw it as a blessing that there had not been a no-show. The company was also informed that there was hardly ever such a thing as a bound script; there was only this wafer-thin story revolving around the hero and roles were given their hutt kay elements on the set itself with dialogues being scribbled on the equivalent of slates with chalks; and that inspite of all this there was no method at all to this madness, the whole process of making one picture took twenty months. The end.

Today the Hindi film industry says things have changed and points out to the production of the blockbuster *Kuch Kuch Hota Hai* taking a mere eight months. Bollywood badshahs also insist that more and more stars are signing contracts because lowered income tax slabs by the Indian finance ministry encourages them to do so. Words like 'more and more', when used, suggest some kind of trend. It is not an untruth, but it is not the whole truth either. As for scripts, where one in a million came bound this year, two might in the next year, and the film industry could well tout this, too, as 'more and more', or even a 'one hundred per cent jump'.

Bad film debts stand at around 30 per cent, a figure so high that it has kept all formal financing away; getting insured cannot change this. Getting disciplined can. But the film industry is filled with get-rich-quick sharks who are in it for the high turnover, the handful who are in it for love plus money are those who then have to get singed as a consequence.

Not that it has ever made any bones about the fact— money has always been the mainstay of the Bombay movies. On 14 March 1931, Ardeshir Irani released his *Alam Ara* at Bombay's Majestic Cinema. It was India's first talkie; the world's first talkie, *The Jazz Singer* had been made more than five years before that. And the world's first sound feature, *The Melody of Love*, had been shown in India in 1929. Indian producers had taken for ever to make their talkies for one reason and one reason alone—money; they did not want to lose the Ceylon and Burma markets with the introduction of Hindi as a language. And the reason for them deciding that they should go for Hindi is yet again linked with money—*Alam Ara* started the black market trend, four anna tickets sold for four rupees.

The dye was cast, the enduring tragedy of the Indian film industry was about to start unfolding—the wrong kind of money was going to start coming into the industry; and then the money would not remain in the industry for plough-back purposes. 'A tyre manufacturer called

Sabharwal strolled into the studios one day and opened his briefcase to flash stacks of cold cash, the stars reached out and shook hands with black money,' recalls film historian B.K. Karanjia who edited several film magazines as the film industry grew. 'There came a point when the whole thing went crazy, the stars were willing to pay for awards so that it could flatter their vanity and help them increase their price.'

Clearly not much has changed since, one award and the price hike is prompt, resulting in the balancing of a film's budget going entirely askew. In Hollywood the payment for top stars never goes beyond 35 per cent of the entire film, here it can be as high as 70 per cent. And today's stars include directors and music directors. So the producer—who need not use that star but is doing so because he wants to gamble on the high returns and obviously does not mind taking the very high risk—goes to a financier. The financier can be a gangster called Dawood in Karachi or another called Chota Rajan in Kuala Lumpur. The financier can be a lieutenant of the above-mentioned, or a politician connected with them. Maybe a glamour-struck businessman with spare cash or just a simple Shylock who will charge two-and-a-half per cent per month. The producer will have to pay the financier six months interest in advance and the film will start rolling.

Film ready, around two babies or nineteen months later, and the producer has to pay up the financier before its release. For this he can borrow short-term from elsewhere or sell the film, territory-wise, to distributors and take the money from them. The distributor then has to sell the movie to the exhibitors, the men who will physically release the film, in theatres under their territory. A chain is only as strong as its weakest link, one snap and the end.

The audience's taste has perhaps been the biggest—and most tragic—victim of the several imbalances in the trade. Which comes first, the char anna front-benchers or the sex and violence stuffed into the film supposedly for them? Sax and voy lens—as the film industry tends to call it and it is never clear why they equate the two in the same breath to start with—is what the audience wants, has always been the popular refrain. Indians have this nasty habit of taking what they get, this does not necessarily mean that they get what they want. What the public needs—and this tends to get dictated by film distributors who are middle-class males—is thrills, spills, romance, action, mystery, beauty, religion, occasional significance, cultural respectability and complete release, paisa vasool. Pack it all in then, and start the movie with a bang, continue with more bangs and end the film happily with an even bigger bang.

See why most are not bothered about bothering with a bound script?

As for those who want to feel enriched after seeing a movie—perhaps feel that there has been some participation in a pilgrimage to a shrine of meaning—well, they can just go and see an English picture, or they can buy a book.

'The more things change the more they remain the same,' muses B.K. Karanjia. 'I remember the time I had taken this delegation to the minister of information and broadcasting's secretary so that they could explain why the entertainment tax on the tickets could be done away with.

They shouted, they screamed, they got very excited and then when the door opened and the minister's secretary walked in, they turned into little lambs, saying haanji, haanji, nahinji, tussi great ho ji. The instantaneous transformation would have been amusing if it had not been so frustrating for me.' The entertainment tax—levied on a film through its theatre ticket and passed on to the audience—is not just an encroachment, it is the complete violation of any human being's right to relax. To pay a tax for being entertained is a government declaring that its people have no business doing anything but working, perhaps toiling in fields from dawn to dusk.

When it is a reasonably decent film and the entertainment tax has been waived on it, more people have gone to see the film. Thus at a time when active—and sorely needed—joint lobbying against resolving the entertainment tax issue for all time can help both, the Bombay film industry and its audience, some film-makers have instead been individually approaching its utterly star-struck state government for tax exemption benefits on individual films, most of dubious quality. And the waivers have been granted, indiscriminately and with a flourish—in five years, fifty-five films, around Rs 19.01 crore in taxes—including the state's first family's in-house production which gave itself tax relief inspite of the hero being a sadist; he whips his wife on her legs and then parts the same legs in the very next frame to roughly enter her.

There are less than five instances of the Bombay film industry standing united since 1947, and half of these too are of them doing so for negative reasons. Like when a bunch of oldies band together to ban English films dubbed in Hindi because the question is not that these films could eat a bit into their own mediocre market but that they 'corrupt the minds of our people'. And on the insurance sector, are they very certain that they are not looking at gains on their typically short-term basis? For decent people to try and make good films there has to be access to institutional financing; for institutional financing to come into play there has to be corporatizing; how can corporatizing come into effect through the backing of an insurance company unless the systems are not already in place? What is to stop the shady operator doing precisely that which he has been doing all along to make money, any kind of money as long as the end justifies the mean? Imagine a whole new set of scams hatched by a people who look only for the loopholes—if people can be killed and their insurance collected, a film can always be done in likewise.

The insurance companies undoubtedly have their work cut out for them, as do the banks trying to work out financial schemes. They are probably enjoying the role they are playing, not unlike Dawood and Chhota Rajan and Remote Control who fall prey to similar kiss-kick-kiss emotions when it comes to the Hindi film world. The younger lot in the film industry feel that the lure of institutional financing and insurance might help change some age-old habits, perhaps enforce some self-discipline. Something that went straight of the window when a tyre-maker came in with his little bag and the studio system collapsed. Since then Bollywood has only resembled a lunatic asylum mismanaged by its own inmates. No wonder they always need some kind of remote control to control them.

For as long as anyone can remember, the Bombay film folks have been insisting that they be recognized as an industry, or else matters cannot improve for them. This has been granted in 1998 by the Government of India's information and broadcasting ministry. What has this 'film industry' done for itself since? Nothing. Except ask for some more special favours and sops like discounts on electricity for theatres and studios. How can we corporatize, they now whine, when there are no incentives to set the ball rolling? When we want money to make our pictures, we ask our traditional financiers and receive the amount in twenty-four hours flat without any paper work, no questions asked; why cannot the banks do the same, after all we are now an industry; this is their latest whinge.

Shakti Samanta, veteran producer-director of films like *Kati Patang*, *Amar Prem*, *Aradhana* and *Kashmir Ki Kali* goes on record in his capacity as the chairperson of IMPPA, a key film association, 'All this talk of corporatization may be good for lively debates and media columns but given the nature of the Indian film industry, corporatization will not work.'

That number, say it again please. Six thousand. Now add to it just one more win. One more. That of professionalism. And you have the perfect role for an industry—and this too has to be acknowledged by all—which holds the country together. There is only one more organization in India which plays the identical role of connecting this entire country as successfully—the railways.

Nau. Here is a bank of washing machines, whirring and clanking away, with a fine sea view from the spacious balcony on which the washing machines are ensconced. Different servants approach different washing machines with nary a glance to the sea, so absorbed are they in sorting out the laundry—loads of it from a large family which appears to be forgetting several items in the pockets of their clothing: small coins, crumpled notes, headphones of walkmans, bits of by-now mushy candy.

Salim Khan is enjoying the view though, as he narrates super stories. Salim Khan, father of hero Salman Khan, director Sohail Khan, actor Arbaaz Khan; father-in-law of Seema who stays in the shadows, the 'chaiyya chaiyya' maiden Malaika Arora and among the finest television actors Atul Agnihotri; proud nana to his daughter Alvira's children Alyzeh and Ayaan; husband of Salma Khan and Helen Khan.

Ah, this is about the famous cabaret dancer Helen being the First Lady of Second Marriages in the film industry, isn't it? It is about Muslims allowing four wives, Hindu bigamy and garlands being exchanged in temples and how the film industry always sets a bad example for us normal folk, and they are so always in the wrong, right?

Nope, it cannot be. Because finally it is not about whether Dharmendra became a Muslim to marry Hema Malini and Mahesh Bhatt followed suit to wed Soni Razdan and Mona Kapoor—the first wife of producer Boney Kapoor who garlanded the actress Sridevi in a temple—said that she would never allow their daughter Jahnavi to be legitimized. Now this might upset Mahesh Bhatt since he luxuriates in the tag: all children are born legitimately, with rights they can expect from their natural fathers and mothers if they need to consult the laws of the land. First wives need to approach the court too if they are so utterly incensed about their husband's second marriages, nobody else can help them there, and they have to prove that there has been a marriage. As for anyone converting to marry, that is silly, evolving society does not need it any more, the converter is merely confusing sexuality with religion and trying to use an archaic law to feel less guilty. And in a time when the world over laws are changing to protect people who cohabit a home—whether married or not—the whole issue takes on tedium legally.

This is not even about how Bombay used to be before the riots and the bomb blasts and how a small section of it still is: Salma Khan's sprawling home and her all-encompassing family. Her Pathan husband came to Bombay to become a hero, he became a story writer, he married her, the city girl, they had children. He married again this dancer called Helen who had physically trekked from Burma to be used and abused by the filmi society and Salma watched as he gave her succour and a life and taught her how to do her own accounts and deal with her own driver. Salma suffered, of course she did, but then so open-hearted was she, that when she gave she became First Lady for ever. For her offspring, their offspring, all their loves coming from lands unknown to her and their lives so complicated, and her husband's wrecked writing career when his partner wanted out and he lost his muse thereafter, and for her sons whom through her small actions she showed that her acceptance did not mean they must hurt another woman, not in their father's life, not in their own. Like Salma Khan today, once was Bombay.

The washing machines by the sea have exhausted themselves, their front-loading doors are left open for some airing. Salim the story-teller is on yet another, 'So Rajesh Khanna invites me for breakfast, maybe he feels bad that I have had a raw deal after my partner breaking up with me. I cycle down to his house, I have to very careful about money by then because I know things are going to get terrible for me and my family, I have stopped using the car. We chat over breakfast, he is a superstar and I am this ho gaya, this has been. Then it is time for Rajesh Khanna to be kind to someone else so I get up to leave, he insists on seeing me out. He walks with me to the gate, he starts waving and then he notices that I am not in a car but on a cycle. I am looking at him, okay, because I have never seen anybody wave to anybody on a cycle before, except in the Hindi pictures when the gareeb father leaves on his postman ka job or something and his long-suffering wife stands there at this broken wicket gate and waves slightly but courageously. So I am looking at him and Rajesh Khanna is looking at my cycle and his hand is still waving out of reflex; and then he looks at his hand because he realizes that there are so many people outside his gate looking at him waving to a stupid cycle when as a star he should be waving to at least an Impala; and he quickly goes away inside his house, his hand still somewhere up in the air.'

Then Salim Khan tells an Arabic story about a scorpion

and a fish, to show how the Bombay film industry behaves with itself. There is this scorpion waiting by the sea, on the shore. The scorpion is waiting patiently, for days and days. Shoals of fish swim past and look at the scorpion from under the sea but they know that they must not surface to find out what the scorpion wants, or what he is waiting for, because scorpions cannot be trusted since they sting. The scorpion waits, his is to be patient.

Finally one day, many years later, a fish surfaces because she can no longer stand this sight of the scorpion waiting so patiently; she has been admiring him for his tenacity.

'Why are you waiting like this, oh scorpion? What do you want?'

'I want to cross the sea, I want to see the other side. I need a fish to give me a ride.'

'Oh no,' the fish says, 'I cannot do that. You will sting me.'

'No,' says the scorpion, 'I swear I will not.'

She is now perplexed, she is a good fish and she believes in goodness which her religion tells her is inherent in all beings. But how can she trust a scorpion?

'Please,' says he, 'please give me a ride on your back. Otherwise I will never see what is on the other side.'

'You promise you won't sting me?'

The scorpion explains to the silly fish that he is the one who wants to get to the other side, then where is the logic of him wanting to sting her and kill her when he would much rather she be his vessel?

'Okay,' says the fish, 'my conscience tells me I must

give you a chance. Hop on my back.'

And the scorpion and the fish swim out into the sea with her taking care that he should not get wet. In the middle of the journey the scorpion stings the fish. The fish starts dying and drowning and the scorpion starts drowning with her.

'What did you do!' wails the fish, 'You promised, now you are killing us both. Why did you this?'

The scorpion says only this before he drowns them both forever, 'Main aadat se majboor hoon, I am a victim of my habits.'

The scorpion and the fish. The Congress and the country. The Bharatiya Janata Party and bharatiyata. Lal Kishan Advani and Hinduism. Self-styled leaders in collaboration with manic maulanas and Muslims. Bal Thackeray and Bombay. Us and our cities.

This is what it is actually about.

Dus. Bus, here he is, the film industry's perfect ten. Except that no one will ever come right out and say it because he does not look right, he is getting on in age now, he was never a hero in the agreed sense of the term to start with. But the critics think so; the audience thinks so—for his screen, television and theatre performances and the fact that he moves between these disparate media so effortlessly. And the different generations he walks with and works for with equal ease would nod too.

The pretty young things from Bombay's colleges have also woken up to him being all man. Eavesdrop on a conversation in the cloakroom of Eros Theatre after a screening of *Bombay Boys*.

'Oooh, you saw how he kissed her? Do you really think he really, really kissed her?'

'That was a throat massage he gave her!'

'He is such a good actor, he must be a good kisser also, no?'

'Idiot, good actor means he can fake his kisses cleverly.'

'Must be good in bed also, no?'

The kisser in question is Naseeruddin Shah, playing the mock-manic bhai in the movie. The girl being given the tonsil-job by him is Tara Deshpande, a spunkily welcome addition to the world of acting. When asked how it felt to be smooched so resoundingly and soundly, twinkling Tara replies, 'But it just looked that way, he was so convincing, wasn't he? People on the sets were kidding me that no one would marry me after this, and Naseer said he would put an ad in the papers saying "Wanted groom for good Maharashtrian girl, only slightly kissed".'

Those lips are now hard at work on dubbing, the practice of getting the dialogues at their right pitch, synchronized with what was earlier shot on the sets. This has to be done in a darkened room with the film unreeling in silence, so that the fresh dialogue track can replace all the noise which intruded on the original audio during shooting. It sounds simple, it is not. Moods vary from the day the scene was shot to the time, perhaps a half year later, when it comes up for dubbing; intensity certainly varies along with interest. Dubbing is thus an art, which when under or overdone can ruin even the most author-backed role.

This dubbing studio is situated under an automobile servicing centre in the middle of the Western Express highway, undoubtedly the facility is absolutely sound-proof. Nothing is disturbing Naseeruddin Shah, at any rate, as he is looking back in anger. Most Hindi films, like much of its country, looks back in anger; it does nothing but look back in anger thus forever forfeiting a comparatively blemish-free future and ruining the present in the process. For India it is the Moghuls, the British, the Brahmins, the Muslims, to which now may be added the Christians—look back, and simmer on slow burn. For the Hindi film industry it is those treacherous thakurs, wronged ancestors, murdered fathers, mauled mothers, raped sisters—look back, and ditto. Bingo at the box office! The audience goes back home feeling relieved, and curiously released, but as history seems condemned to keep repeating itself in India, not entirely spent.

Right now Naseeruddin Shah is working on getting his rage right. Something about the forefathers and how they were traumatized and he as the protagonist is not going to take it lying down any more, no way, no sir. His voice rises, the pitch, no the pitch is not matching his lips on the screen, his voice rises again, and yet again and finally he gets it, the rage at the right point without his voice cracking with the exhaustion of it all. He has to catch a flight to Calcutta from here; theatre, his latest play, beckons. But he makes the time to think aloud about the Hindi film world.

'It is a depressing state of affairs. Our films are only pseudo-progressive when not overflowing with pseudo-patriotism. The hero tells the erring heroine, "I would have raped you right now but you know what? I cannot, because I am a Hindustani!" Why does this get the maximum applause, I wonder. In these last thirty years we have only moved backwards and we are deluding ourselves if we think otherwise. We happen to be pathetic technically. Here technically means only stylish photography; fifty horses against one great sunset is good photography, not anything else. All we have done is borrow something from the Busby Berkeley type of musicals and feel happy with it. We have taken only the superficial aspects of Hollywood, even in our lifestyles.

'The self-seeking so-called middle-of-the-road cinema was also finally twisted into a vehicle of self-promotion for the maker. How could we expect it to survive then? We had statements like, "I despise commercial cinema, I will not have songs in my films and I will certainly not have stars." And everyone said, "Oh wow, this must be a great movie even if I do not understand what the hell is going on in it." No wonder the audience ran away fairly quickly. Sure we have *Satya*, *Bombay Boys*, *Hyderabad Blues* and more happening, but I have to strike this note of caution since I am a bit of a war veteran on the subject, it is too early to celebrate.

'The largest section of our audience today, in the cities at any rate, is the college-going crowd. And how are we supposedly tapping this? We are giving them powder-puff dreams and pink sets and individual college lockers with basketball courts. Everyone is wearing Tommy Hilfiger. God! Tommy Hilfiger is a racist whom Oprah Winfrey had thrown out of her show because he said that if he knew that non-whites were going to wear his clothes he would not have taken the trouble of designing them as carefully as he did.

'No attempt is being made to reflect reality the way it should be reflected. People simply see today's films for what they are, I don't think they remember them very much afterward. Makers like Guru Dutt and V. Shantaram and Vijay Anand made more modern commercial cinema and far more progressive too. Pictures which get remembered till today.

'I am told now that I must look at the young guys who are making movies. Who, twenty-four-year-old Karan Johar who has the heart of an eighty-year-old? *Kuch Kuch Hota Hai* has got to be among the most regressive films ever made. It is also big, made on this big canvas, and I suspect things are going to get even bigger. Here too we will follow the folly of Hollywood, they finally unmade themselves with *Cleopatra* and had to come to their senses with an *Easy Rider*, a film about two bums on a motorcycle.

'Let us talk about comedy. Bar Johnny Lever who has raised the level of mimicry to an art, where is the comedy. Why don't we see it? Because comedy takes hard work. And why don't we want to work hard on our movies? Because it is one big party, what happens in between shots is more of consequence. Swapping anecdotes is all that really happens in the Hindi film industry, the shooting is what happens in between.

'In spite of all this I hold out, I hope, and then I hope some more. I would like to make a movie which I would want to see and maybe I will direct one. I am also impressed with the young lot of actors today who are very disciplined and who take their work seriously. They are educated, this is important for the film industry as it needs people with formal education. I am sure they all want to make good movies, and in fact it is high time Aamir Khan directed one. But I am not sure, and I wish I would not sound so pessimistic, how much of a change these young men can bring about. There are a zillion inputs which go into making one movie—and these young men are not the key elements; this is the abiding irony of an actor, they are only heroes.'

Ah, not entirely true anymore. Agreed that inspite of being 140-films old and dying to direct one, Naseeruddin Shah is not being offered a shot behind the camera by an industry unsure of his slotting. But there are heroes trying to effect changes, Ajay Devgan being a case in point. Through the movies he has also now begun producing, Ajay Devgan is laying his foundation for a future of films— nice pictures, some mistakes, then nifty pictures—which Naseeruddin Shah might even enjoy watching.

Gyaarah. Here are two ones, one and one which do not total two and for now do not make eleven either. Two number ones who started their careers at the same time, their cars entered the shooting gates at the same time, on the dot at 9 o'clock, before they went to their respective sets—one grand, bombastic, big, the angry middle-aged man; the other—quite simply the common man. Both had hit pictures and their films ran parallel to each other without in any way cutting into the other's box office appeal. AB and AP. Amitabh Bachchan and Amol Palekar.

Now we all know what happened to AB and his ABCL which has struck a big blow to films being financed by institutional means like banks. We all know that Bombayites feel let down by him doing everything only for himself and never anything for them, not even setting up a garden for a city which prayed for him when he was grievously wounded. His film industry feels cheated by him for not doing anything for them either—not as that member of Parliament, not otherwise. He knows it too, so let us just let the man be, he must feel ancient now and probably equally tired trying to stay afloat over-banking on himself for himself. As thinker Iqbal Masud points out, 'There is no basic reason why Amitabh Bachchan should have been a better man than he has turned out to be.' But then he adds, 'The film industry as a whole likes to take the outwardly stand that they are artistes and therefore cannot be political persons. After which they dine with the very devil who ordains the killings of entire communities including creative ones. Nobody even notices that they have utterly demeaned their artistry. What a surreal time this is turning out to be. Politicians and gangsters pretending to be artistes; artistes drinking with fascists and pretending to be businessmen.'

You need to grow up to grow tall, most celebrities grow tall without growing up, now we know this too; happily Amol Palekar is not among them.

Among the top stars of that time, Amol Palekar is perhaps the only Bombay-born. A bank clerk who took up

the fine arts at the J.J. School and dabbled in experimental
theatre; his interest grew, so did his fame. He came out on
the streets during Indira Gandhi's draconian Emergency,
helped the underground movement then. He never forsook
his mother tongue either, Marathi films in which he has
acted and directed are still the most powerful in the
language. He continues to work in the language, *Kal Ka
Aadmi* is being simultaneously shot in Marathi and Hindi.
It is the story of R.D. Karve, son of Maharishi Karve, who
was a man before his times, promoting population control
until the day he died in 1953. The film has Kishore Kadam
as Karve and Seema Biswas as his wife.

AB's movies sputtered to their finishing line when age
caught up with both their angry young man genre and
him. Time also turned AP's kind of films towards the
video which turned into the middle class's latest acquisition.
That audience simply stopped going to the theatres, that
was the decline of parallel and viable cinema. But Amol
Palekar sees the world coming around once again, 'The
opening of boutique cinema halls in several cities, specially
Bombay, means compact films can once again be made for
specific release. You need not make this big budget dhamaka
and release it with one thousand prints all over the country
to get back your money; the small theatres ensure niche
audiences, ergo niche or concept films. Let us not forget
that once upon a time, as will soon be again, mainstream
cinema meant different kinds of streams. We may go ga-ga
over Bimal Roy today but we forget that films like
Madhumati, *Bandini*, *Parakh* were the black-sheep films of
those times.'

Amol Palekar is equally upbeat about today's distributors, 'In the middle the distributor had turned into a Hitler of sorts, today's distributor is younger and comparitively open-minded, he is looking for middle-of-the-road viable movies. Ronnie Screwvala, Bharat Shah, Balakrishna and Shyam Shroff of Shringar Films are some of the names which immediately come to mind.' Amol Palekar's directorially acclaimed *Daayra* has not been distributed in India not just because of a distribution bias. And herein hangs a tale.

Daayra was conceived as the Hindi film industry's first corporatized picture. There was a project report complete with shooting schedule and cost breakdown. The film was shot in the specified number of days, the film's financing received institutional backing. It won several awards all over the world, it was screened in important theatres in big international cities and it brought in the audience show-after-show, *Time* magazine praised it. So, why did it never get released in the country? It is a question that the insurance companies and future financiers of films should look into if they really want to get to the crux of why the film industry finally malfunctions. It will also be fascinating to see how banks can levy interest on egos and insurance companies charge premia on them.

Amol Palekar, himself, does not want to elaborate. 'I am sorry that this film which I directed and which has got international acclaim is not being shown in my country; I still hope that some day it will. Not because I am to gain any money out of it, I cannot evaluate what a creative kick I get out of my work in terms of rupees and paise, that

253

would be too simplistic. I have been working as a professional driven by a creative urge all my life, that is the only way I want to look at it because otherwise there is the other risk of getting too self-centred. My wife Chitra's and my work—in several languages on screen and the television— may not be a 70 mm experience filled with sound and light and fury but at least it signifies something. That is how I would like to keep it.'

There is this fable about the hare and that tortoise where the hare gets off to a flying start while the tortoise inches ahead—slowly but determinedly—to reach the goal post. Contrarians like to argue that Aesop really wrote this fable for the 'tortoise market'—the middle-class plodders— to comfort themselves with while all the upper-class hares raced ahead; they add that Aesop exhausted the hare before he reached the finishing line for precisely this reason. But, now it appears, doesn't it, that fables have a way of ringing true in real life?

Baarah. Wait a moment. What happened to Veeru Devgan and his Movie Stunt Artistes Association, are they not here too? Sure they are, jeena yahaan marna yahaan and all that jazz. Veeru Devgan retains his card but is not himself actively involved in the Movie Stunt Artistes Association; his phalanx of office staff does so, him having moved from action director to director as also big daddy of Devgan Entertainment, their production and distribution network which releases films all over the country.

The Movie Stunt Artistes Association has also moved, from strength to strength. A nice spacious office in the suburbs with a mezzanine in a decent building and twenty-four hours security. A television set with a video-cassette player for the members to stay in touch with fight scenes and techniques from all over the world, the idea—apart from 'taking inspiration'—also being that by the time they reach stunt director level they should also be able to visualize a scene and edit it themselves complete with sound effects. The association office also has a carrom board, a fridge, for its 500 members. The members are all chosen by a five-man committee which takes tests in fighting including sword fighting and swimming. The age qualification is from eighteen to thirty years because no man lasts for more than twenty years in the profession in fit condition, and life membership is Rs 25,000 with one son being admitted at Rs 15,000 if found eligible. Upon retirement the members' money is given back to them. All of this ably managed by the colourful Verma brothers, general secretary Pappu Verma and president Tinnu Verma, who also supply horses to the industry out of the forty in their stables.

'It is not as if we liked the idea of hurting our own horses during shoots, so we always took care,' Pappu Verma says. 'We would prepare these beds for the horses to fall on but then the animal rights activists objected and we got a guideline from the censors saying that all shots showing horses falling must be deleted. If you cannot use the shot why should we be putting our horses through all that?' There are seven brothers Verma, four in the stunt line, one in another kind of stuntbaazi as he happens to be a Congress worker, and the rest in different aspects of the movies. Together they have seen a lot of changes, for the better, in the stunt world of the movies because their association, for as long as they can remember, has never not fought for a better working situation.

Now they are trying to get life insurance organized for all their members and personal accident insurance on the sets with a minimum of Rs 50,000 and life insurance at Rs 5,00,000. 'We have to do it,' points out Pappu Verma in a practical sort of tone, 'just as we have to keep alert for our association on all other points including non-payment. We had this situation recently where a guy would not pay up and threatened that he would shoot in Madras with their people instead. We said fine, try, and we told our colleagues in the South to watch out and not shoot for him till he paid up, he had to. Similarly, they had a problem with one of their top directors and they phoned us, we co-operated. It has got to be this way, nahin toh producer hume kachcha khaa jaayenge. We don't want to be chewed up and spat out like the gutka the producers eat. In a way they are the leaders and we are the voters who can get forgotten— or made to fight with each other—after each election is over. So we make sure for ourselves that they remember that we do the most risky work and yet are completely absent on screen.'

Precautions are taken but accidents happen. The stuntwoman doubling for Rekha was to keep pace in between two motor cycles on full throttle. She got caught in the wheels of one of them and was dragged along the road on her face for a considerable distance. Suraiya got several stitches on her head, plastic surgery on her face and three months in bed; she is back at work, 'I like this job, it carries much more respect than that of the junior artiste. And I get so much applause on the sets.' There are other stuntwomen too, a total of six members in the association, like Reshma and Anwari who like that special thrill after a stunt successfully accomplished; the men would describe it as a rush of testosterone, adrenaline, what the bungee jumpers must experience; these women say, 'It feels nice.'

But people die too—in spite of the best precautions taken like crash boxes and air pads and rush mats—last year four stuntmen succumbed to stunts. Two young men fell on their heads when jumping from one hundred feet, for some reason they could not turn their bodies in the air at the right moment; another cracked his skull during a car stunt despite wearing a helmet; the third broke his vertebra during a simulated hand fight. Then there are the famous freak accidents like that of the very experienced Haji. He got into the car with a life jacket, padding on his knees and elbows, the works and the car's hinges loosened so that when it hit the lake it was supposed to plunge into, he could easily escape. Haji was doubling for Dharmendra and drove this car right off the cliff's edge and into the lake. The car started sinking, there were bubbles, but there was no sign of Haji. The others dived in and looked for him— he had had a fatal heart attack somewhere in mid-air.

Neither Pappu Verma nor Veeru Devgan feel that computer special effects will in any way eventually edge out their stuntmen. 'Special effects are still far too costly in India,' Pappu says, ever the practical man. 'A stuntman will do a seven-storey fall for his usual shift rate of Rs 580 plus a lump sum of say, Rs 20,000. It is still one-tenth the cost of doing this with computer graphics which can go up to Rs 8,000 per second.' Veeru Devgan likes the idea of enhancing the stunts with computer usage, 'I want to show a man on fire. I put on this very small fire around my stunt man and then use computer effects to make it look like a roaring one. This saves my stuntman and the shot also looks good.'

Blue mat shots are all the rage now in Bollywood, an Aamir Khan climbing up the pipes to the twenty-second floor of his girlfriend's building to meet her is Aamir Khan actually doing the shot at ground level against a blue mat and the computer then taking over. Veeru Devgan is very clear that the virtual world can only assist in their reel-to-look-like-real world. 'Computer ko leke kitney Titanic banayenge?' he wants to know. 'And tell me, is it ever possible for a computer to faithfully replicate the kind of violence we keep seeing on Bombay's streets?'

He pauses, 'Punjab is safer now. Chalo, duniya gol hain, what goes around, comes around too. Like the terrorism finally ended in Punjab, terrorism will also come to an end in Bombay. But see, terrorism stopped in Punjab because the people held their politicians accountable and, most important, the people became answerable themselves for their own actions. Yahaan abh aise ho sakta hai? Can things improve in Bombay? Have not the people themselves become too vulnerable? Log shaayad apni hi nazar se gir gaye hai.'

Terah. Here is death. Now wait a minute, is somebody going to be foolish enough to suggest that a city, or a country or an industry—film or otherwise—which keeps committing hara kiri out of sheer reflex, must necessarily impinge on a someone who is working towards his own individual inquilaab? Do your dharma, say all religions, and the rest will fall into place. Ekla chalo ri, exhort the songs, walk alone. And it matters not that there is no caravan behind you because hum honge kaamyaab ek din, we shall overcome some day.

Try telling this to the star whose mobile has just buzzed, that one day we will be victorious because behind us we have hundreds of years of terrific tradition and ahead of us is a panasonic future and what is the present but a matter of time, just keep the faith and in the year 2002, India will be the next superpower, has not Nostradamus or Veeru Devgan's astrologer or somebody also said so?

The star's mobile buzzes insistently. He glances at the number on display, his chartered accountant. He clicks on his hands-free, 'Ya man tell me, you want more of my money? I got nothing left to give you.'

The chartered accountant's voice is frantic, apologetic, quivering with rage. 'They want to see you.'

'Which they is this, man? They are just too many fucking theys in this city.'

'The tax guys.'

'Aww gimme a break, what for?'

'He says you should come to the office and meet him.'

'Whatthefuckfor?'

'He just wants to see you, I guess, before he signs on the dotted line and clears your file.'

'But what for? My papers are in fucking order, I must have the most streamlined file in the entire fucking film industry of the country, South combined. What is going on here? My papers are all clear. I know that, you know that. He knows it, it is right there, my file is under his fucking nose I'm sure.'

'Yes, look I am as upset as you are, I'm sorry but I have been trying my damndest to get him to see this, he is being obstinate. He says if that Kapoor girl can come to a tax officer's house in the middle of the night, why cannot you come to his office?'

'This is shit, absofuckinglutely shit. No man, no way, I refuse to get harangued like this. Tell him to fuck off.'

'Look, I would advise you to go and stroke his ego. I know your file is in order and he knows it too and so does everybody in his office, but if you don't go after he has made an issue of it, he could create problems for you in the future. Maybe he will be promoted and get you later, maybe one of his chamchas will screw your happiness just when he is about to retire and you are pretty old yourself. Maybe he is just doing this because he wants to go home and tell his son that he summoned you and you came. All of them are not like him, there are honest and decent offiicers too. Our bad luck that we have got jammed with this guy. Go, please go and see him, I will set up an appointment.'

'So how long will this go on?'

'What do you mean?'

'How long will I be punished for being a success and being honest about it?'

'Oh come on!'

'No really, tell me man, explain this to me because I

really want to understand.'

'Until the system changes.'

'System? What system, am I not part of the fucking system and am I not trying to make changes—doesn't what I do count?'

'I don't know, I really don't know.'

'You don't know, I don't know, who the fuck does?'

'Look why don't we just work on the assumption that the system will never change? Half of this city, maybe it's more than half of the country, is in bad shape and hates the other half for getting ahead.'

'So why don't that screwed-up half do something about their lives?'

'They are farmers, they are helpless, India is actually agricultural, remember?'

'I'm talking about these big city bhenchots, shit I hate abusing, why don't they get their lives in order? I mean, God knows, everything seems to be aligned in their favour while I have to work that much harder and, of course, get buggered for it.'

'Maybe they themselves don't want to anymore since they get it all free in the name of poverty, religion, caste and the rest. Maybe the politicians like to keep them that way because it helps them if we remain a nation of beggars.'

'Maybe I should migrate, huh? You make us sound as though we are some fucking prick-led third-rate banana republic. Okay listen, I gottago, my shot is ready. You let me know what to do because now I'm lost.'

The star feels even more lonely as he sits in front of

the officer, he feels so vulnerable that he aches all over. The officer smiles at him, 'Did not take too much of your time, I hope, to come to our office?'

Bastard! 'No, no, of course not. I just have to drive from my home in the suburbs in the peak hour traffic to get to your office. It did not take more than ninety minutes.'

'Ah, but you see if you had sent a message that I could come over to your place, it would have saved your time. My wife would have liked to meet you, my daughter is a great fan of yours. It would have been a pleasure to meet bhabhi.'

Bhabhi? Who is this motherfucker's bhabhi? 'Oh, I did not know that you would have liked to take the trouble.'

'But I mentioned it to your chartered accountant.'

'Did you? Oh yes, right, right, he did say so but then I thought let me come personally and say hello to you.'

'Good you did. Can I order some tea for you? And I will just phone my family to tell them you are here, they will be over soon. Some day perhaps you could come to our humble home.'

'Sure, sure.'

'Meanwhile we can discuss how best to keep your file closed.'

'Closed? I don't understand. Why should it remain open?'

'Ah, the complex laws of this country; we have inherited them you see, these laws from the British, so what can be done with these clauses and sub-clauses, one has to do one's duty and keep examining them.'

'I'm sorry, I do not understand.'

'Don't worry, I will explain.'

'Maybe you could just explain it to my chartered accountant and he can handle it for me. I will tell him to speak to you.'

'Haan, haan, but now that you are here and waiting for your tea to arrive, I can try and make the explanation short.'

'Okay, tell me.'

'You see a file can stay open forever. But I will not be here forever to safeguard your interests. So let us say that I can make sure that the file is not re-opened for the next three years.'

'This is very kind of you.'

'No, no, it is a pleasure since you have come till here and we must try to keep our good relations going.'

'Yes of course.'

'One crore.'

'Sorry? Beg your pardon?'

'You can afford it, don't forget I have studied your file.'

'What are you saying? You are asking me for a bribe?'

'Come, come, surely you are not so naïve as to look so genuinely shocked?'

'You are asking me to pay money to clear my file, and that too for a limited period . . .'

'I am telling you that I will be protecting your interests.'

'. . . when I know, and you know, that my file is perfectly in order?'

'One crore over three years is nothing per year for

you, you make that kind of money even with a flop picture.'

The star's vision is beginning to blur, everything is going black around the edges of his eyes. He leaps up from the chair, it clatters over. 'Listen,' he says, 'listen to me you little arsehole,' and he walks to the door and turns around so that he can deliver the best line a hero ever can and then he can walk out of here, victorious, and it will be the end: 'I pay all my taxes.'

And then just when he is about to close the door behind him there is this soft voice, amusement mingling with contempt, from the desk and he has to look back because he cannot believe that the final, closing shot is not his.

'See this pen in my hand? See this paper I can write on? How much do you think this costs?'

'I don't know and why the fuck should I care?'

'Ah, but you must calculate these things, young people these days forget to calculate hidden costs. Come, sit down, we have to wait for the tea. We can calculate till then. See, you have come in your fancy imported car which costs so much, you have spent so much of your time when you could have earned much more during the period, you have spent petrol and energy. Think about this, doing this again and again and again for three years. Spending all that time and money. And all I will have to do is use this pen and paper, totalling eighteen rupees, to make you do it. I will call your wife, in the future somebody will call your children.'

Our hero comes back to the chair, he picks it up from floor, uprights it, sits. The edges around his eyes have curled to black. 'Why are you doing this to me? What have I done to you that you want to terrorize me and my family!'

'Don't take it so personally. I am doing it for the same reasons any other middle-class man has to make money; better clothes for the wife, better car for us, later more bedrooms for the children. Yes I admit that we middle-class people have become a little adventurous now, we want the best school for our child so we will pay one lakh in donation, we want to immediately take that advertised grand trip of America because we are seeing so much on satellite TV these days. Would you not agree that all those foreign channels have opened a whole new world for Indians?'

'I could complain to your superior.'

'Mujhe upar tak dena padta hai.'

'I could call a press conference.'

'Nobody from your precious film industry will let you. You know for yourself how many of them would much rather give us some money than pay taxes. They will never allow themselves to be exposed.'

'I could always issue a personal press statement.'

'And I could always deny it. Nobody believes filthy rich people in this country, and definitely not film stars who have such a bad name. The system is like that.'

'I could give you the money in marked notes and then have you arrested by the anti-corruption bureau.'

'That only happens in the Hindi pictures. Some of us have front companies into which you will make a friendly business deposit by cheque.'

'I could go to court.'

'You really are very naïve, I did not realize that. You know, very well, how long things take in court and what kind of money and time has to be spent to move files there. It's worse than us, but then that too is a British system you see. Certainly the system needs to be changed.'

Psycho babbling son-of-a-bitch! 'Can you please consider a reduction in the one crore, it does appear a little on the high side.'

'Surely not for you? If you make so much in white, it can be well imagined how much you have in black.'

'But I don't, dammit. That's why I pay all my taxes.'

'This remains to be seen, does it not, in the file?'

'Okay listen, let us re-start this conversation correctly. I have expenses for which I need the money, you may find this hard to believe, but it's the truth. Could you please, I'm saying please, make a 50 per cent reduction?'

'Fifty per cent is unreasonable.'

'Look, I am a hero with a limited life-span, I have to save for my future. You have to understand this. Please.'

'Okay, you can tell your chartered accountant to talk to me tomorrow.'

The best kind of death is the one which comes physically.

O ne to thirteen, ek sey teraah; such a pell-mell tale. But is there any moral to this story?

Can there be?

Every event in life is chained to the next, and how do you ever separate the links?

THE LALA IN WINTER

Grant Road. Perhaps they have changed the name of this busy avenue from which the Parsi doctor was rushed in to coax Veeru Devgan's broken bones back into place. Have they, does any one know? All of the city, and Bombay too, has been rechristened with names which mean nothing no more. Long-winded, double-barrelled, triple-decked re-namings which twist the tongue but impart no flavour. Chowks—merely those spaces between traffic lights where roads converge absent-mindedly—have also been allowed to be named by a city corporation making money on it; feeding the utter mindlessness of anointing ill-defined squares of cement, concrete and tar upon which no postman will ever be expected to deliver a letter, no child will play hop-scotch.

Grant Road, once the hub of any Hindi film's financing with scores of distribution offices dotting the office buildings in and around the area till Lamington Road; does this road also not exist officially anymore in the corporation and on its city's maps? Wonder which came first, the film financewalas or the cinema halls around them. Theatres with names that took pride in their meaning even if a trifle bombastic, and felt special—Dreamland, Super, Novelty ('theatre magnificient'), Naaz and on the other side, Minerva where *Sholay* unspooled for non-stop years and Apsara with its blue-tiled fountain-stream snaking around the foyer and a curving gangway going up to its balcony above it. Outside Apsara, at the entrance, a vaguely phallic column rising into the sky with a bust by its side, of a Khajurao-ish woman and her perfectly round, basketball-like breasts competing for attention with the night's attraction on the garish poster by her side—macho men strutting their stuff in a blaze of guns and glory, wistful women at variance with their bodies, trying to hold up their hugely padded bosoms by will. The entire effect perhaps also providing a glimpse into how Apsara's architect perceived the Hindi film industry and, indeed, how the filmwalas prefer to see themselves.

Time has not been kind to Apsara but the audience continues to flock to the nearby Novelty; always designed to provide, well, that novel experience of feeling plushy while being a part of those wonderful dreams unfolding forty-five degrees overhead. Deep seats, rich red carpeting, chandeliers: not plasticky ones with their fake glitter, but the real stuff. And, outside Novelty, for some obscure reason but extremely popular, a weighing machine; even if the rest has lost its lustre, the weighing machine continues to look comfortably in place on a public pavement. Urchins play around it just now, there are huge plant-holders near the machine, the elders among the urchins are surreptitiously trying to set up a small shanty between these planters. To foil this attempt Novelty's watch-and-ward man desultorily swings his danda in their direction.

Interval is about to happen, the hawkers flex to start selling their snacks and smokes. The dry fruitswala, his 'khaali paanch rupya packet' losing out to the sibilance of 'sendweess, sendweess' from the garam sandwichwala. Or is it sandwichwaley since one man is making them and two men are lying on a chattai chatting desultorily, ignoring the man who is requesting that they start the toasting? The cigarette-gutka vendor, the vada pavwala, far too many hawkers; this also is how a city loses its magnificence. Interval, three men straggle out, two for chaay, one for vada pav which he tears into pieces before popping them into his mouth. Auntie Maisie would have been appalled as he chomps, he burps, he rinses out his mouth with his own phlegm, he spits—pachhack! against Novelty's wall, and goes back into it to see *Hum Aapke Dil Mein Rehte Hain*.

The film stars Anil Kapoor who marries Kajol for one year on prior contractual understanding, she wants money and support for her dead-beat family, he wants his nagging father off his back. Kajol takes enormous offence each time Anil Kapoor tells her that she need not wait up for him, wait with dinner for him, women are equal to men, and so on. She climbs thousands of temple steps, sings many songs, sighs a lot, but at the end of the contract, he tells her to buzz off and she is so offended that she gives him a very difficult time when he wants her back. The realization of this hits him like a bolt from the blue when he gets up one morning and the tea the servant makes is not as good as her brew. Besides, she is pregnant with his son. They reunite in two hospital beds, pulled alongside and close for the camera.

The film is a hit, it has good drama, it is made by D. Rama Naidu—yes, also called Drama Naidu—with his own studio unit in Hyderabad which his sons, producer Suresh and actor Venkatesh, help run. D. Rama Naidu Studios is set upon a higher point on the Deccan Shield—the Deccan Shield is among the world's oldest rock formations, in Hyderabad it is called Banjara Hills and Jubilee Hills. New money in this old area has been reducing the rock to kankar, very small pebbles, and mixing them up in the construction of their set-like homes. Not Drama Naidu, things have been built around the rocks, history and geography has been given its due place in this commercial venture where a producer can enter with his cast and leave with his film in the cans, the posters of it tightly tucked under his arm. Elsewhere in Hyderabad, Ramoji Rao—media baron, producer of quality pictures and manufacturer of delicious Priya Pickles—has his five-star version of such a film nagar, an awesomely defined one thousand acres complete with residential facilities.

Several Bollywoodwalas shoot in these places, Hyderabad is but an hour's flight away from Bombay, they can hold their stars captive and disciplined while they quickly finish shoots. Many in the Bombay film industry will buy land on the hills, reduce it to some more kankar and partly shift there.

Good people should not leave. Some are shifting out of Bombay directly to the West; some have already left for Pune, Hyderabad, Bangalore; the diamond cutting-polishing trade is slowly moving out of the city all the way to China; the art world is concentrating in Calcutta and beginning to flourish in Madras and artists don't really need to live in Bombay anymore; service-oriented sectors are also looking at bases in the South, the computer world is already there in the Silicone Triangle; publishing is being concentrated in Delhi. Bombay did have something that was its very own which no other city could have taken away, its culture—that is all but vanishing, all gratitude to its own state leaders which have compelled the installation of what it insists is the 'people's culture'—mediocrity over meritocracy; pelf over professionalism. Watch crabs in a bucket, the bigger ones never allow the smaller ones to climb out of it out of sheer reflex. Why, then, should a thinking people not attempt to leave?

Abdul Karim Khan Sher Khan, alias Karim Lala, agrees. 'Aaj ka bachcha log apna watan chhod key bahar jaataa, kya karega woh itna pareshaani yahan jhel key?' He says this in his as-yet lilting Pushto accent, empathizing with the sons who have left because there is no point anymore in suffering at the hands of hukumat ka zulm, the tyranny of an elected protector. And they will never come back, Karim Lala thinks; because once they have seen a better life their roots will not matter; they will only pretend to pine for them. As examples, he points to the non-resident Indian and the poor who have been crowding Bombay from their small towns and villages. He unconsciously paraphrases poet John Donne, there is no such thing as going home again.

He should know, this six-foot-something Pathan who came from Kabul and never went back, he who inspired Bollywood characters like Sher Khan, played by Pran, in *Zanjeer* and Badshah Khan, played by Amitabh Bachchan, in *Khuda Gawah*. The character played by Balraj Sahni in *Kabuliwallah*? He looks concerned, wags his index finger in honest humility, raises his dyed eyebrows in remonstration, 'Oye, aisa nahi bol ne ka.' Karim Lala does not remember his age—he is touching ninety—but insists that his eyebrows have turned white not because of it but through all the 'English medicine' he has to take for blood pressure; his eyelashes turned white when he had to take more of the same after his two cataract operations. He dyes his lashes lustrous black with slender glass mini-wands dipped in black surma powder; during his Dongri days pearls were crushed into this powder for Karim Lala's rapier-piercing eyes.

Karim Lala abandoned his studies in the third standard and trekked from Afghanistan, through Hindustan to Dongri, one of Bombay's original islands, to grow up here and understand the city's demand-supply situation; every city with an over-burdened judicial system and corrupt politicians needs an underworld, and maintains it with gratitude as long as it stays there. Karim Lala grasped this and let it be known that there were Pathans available, with their fabled honour, for contractual work. A lot of work came his way, from ordinary people embroiled in family disputes, bar owners wanting debts settled, the police who preferred some kind of work done by the dons, and the dons themselves—Mastan Mirza who post-Mecca added the Haji prefix and Varadarajan Mudaliar, Varadabhai of Matunga. Karim Lala sent his Pathans for Haji Mastan and Varadabhai, making it economically viable for him to buy up a building on Jail Road South in Dongri and start the Karim Hotel underneath.

He also became good friends with Haji Mastan, born in 1926 in Padikul near Pondicherry, who arrived penniless in Bombay to sleep on its pavements, sell chikki and polish shoes. Remember that scene from *Deewar* when a young shoe polishing lad tells someone called Jaichand to pick up his thrown money and give it to him in his hand? Who later becomes a licenced porter at the docks? The life of Mastan Mirza, who at Bombay's docks saw how corrupt customs officers preferred not to levy duties and take it under the table instead. Haji Mastan began cutting the deals for them, he never cared for the nick-name 'godi ka chuha', dock rat. Soon enough he turned gold smuggler, the laws of India in those days frowning upon the use of this yellow metal by the rich.

Haji Mastan interned as a gold carrier with Daman's Sukkur Narayan Bakhiya and Talib of Jamnagar before eclipsing them to turn Gold King himself and use a sword-shaped golden toothpick, always kept in his shirt pocket. He met Varadarajan Mudaliar in jail; Varadabhai had ordered fifteen lakh rupees worth of walkie-talkies meant for the military to be stolen, the need for cell phones and mobiles had clearly been felt by the underworld long before the general citizenry. But this over-extension of his role landed Varadabhai in the CID lock-up where he met Haji Mastan. Upon release, Mastan bailed him out and had him surrender the walkie-talkies to the police.

Haji Mastan died in 1994, Varadabhai also had a film made on him but only after he died, *Nayakan*. Karim Lala is the only surviving don of a time when the underworld kept itself underground. Not that he sees himself as don now in the dusk of his life. 'I did not hurt the common person in any way, no good man suffered because of me, in fact he was helped. I have been careful not to cross my own line, which is why Allah ne hum ko bakshaa hai.' Small memory lapses there, God has had him hauled in—even if not exactly over the coals—when he was told to go back to his country, tadipaar from Bombay. He went storming in to the office of an aazam, the authority, and demanded to know why he was being sent away from his watan.

'This is not your watan, Lala, Afghanistan is your country, you must go back.

'Bombay is my watan, I say so, and so do all the people who have come here like me. Watan is that which gives you your roti, rozi and good sleep. But you tell me on what grounds you are asking me to leave, where are the charges?'

'No charges Karim Khan, no charges. Nothing that we

have found on you can be proved. So we are just telling you
to go tadipaar because you fight too much.'

'With whom?'

'Oh how does it matter with whom?'

'Oye, only this matters, with whom I am fighting.'

'Okay, you are fighting with other bad characters, and
you are leading all the Pathans to fight with them.'

'Pathan hai, junooni hai, taaleem nahi hai, maramaari
toh karega hi.'

The externment idea was abandoned because it would
have been difficult to prove in court that a man has been
sent away from his city only because he is unlettered,
impetuous and fights to keep his own underworld in check.

Other memory lapses include that day in August 1983
when two businessmen approached him for protection
against another gangster with an offer of one lakh rupees,
they took shelter under the body guards he supplied and
when he allegedly asked for four lakh rupees more, they
complained to the police. And that other day in October,
1994, when he was handcuffed and charged with criminal
intimidation when a woman at the upmarket Breach Candy
struck a property deal and later wanted out of it to sell to
another set of builders at a higher rate.

The only intimidation that Karim Lala is into now is for
his cigarettes. His daughter is visiting from Ahmedabad
with her husband, she has locked up his smokes on doctor's
orders. 'She has hidden all my packets before going out to
visit relatives,' says he mournfully, drawing on a bidi which
he is, very clearly, not enjoying. He yells for his man Friday,
'Oye, cigarette laao.' The man hesitates upon receipt of a

surma-laced murderous look, he leaves for the shop near Novelty ('theatre magnificient') to buy a packet of 555.

Karim Lala moved into this lane near Novelty forty years back, the top floor of a building which he has had partially landscaped into a lush terrace garden. 'I bought this place for only Rs 30,000, can you imagine? There is sukoon here, peace, no noise, the Parsi neighbours go to sleep by eight every night, decent people.' The decent ones were horrified when he moved in, his reputation had preceded him. Karim Lala proceeded to clean up the lane to his—and their grudging—liking. 'There was a bootlegger on this side of the building, every night labourer-types would drink and do dangaa in the lane. I had the bootlegger thrown out. There was also this other problem of extortion, a man would come and want money from the shops below for protection, all this time the shopkeepers had been giving because they were scared, when I moved in they told me about their problem. I said do not pay, we will see what happens; the man came one night when I was resting and started a fight with one of my boys, he attacked him and got shot dead.'

Karim Lala got summoned to the police station and asked why he shot a man dead.

'I did not shoot him, I have never touched a ghoda in my life, ask anyone they will tell you that Karim Lala does not use fire arms, he keeps only a rampuri in his pocket.'

'Well, somebody has shot him.'

'Yes, that appears to be the case.'

'Who did?'

'You are the police, it is your duty to find these things

out.'

'Lala, it would be in your interest to present the shooter in this police station.'

'And how can that be?'

'The man who was shot was a history-sheeter, if your man surrenders we can see what best we can do for him and you. If he does not, we will feel compelled to take very strict action against you and the rest of your boys. Justice is done by the courts, but the responsibility of ensuring that justice must also be seen to be done rests upon us, the police. If we do not arrest your boy, it will send out the wrong signals to future criminals, tomorrow they might start shooting ordinary citizens and walking away.'

Karim Lala went back to his lush terrace, smoked several 555s, drank some Chivas Regal, and turned in the shooter. Such were those times; clear lines demarcated for all—including the gangsters and the Bombay police—who was the mazlum, the oppressed, and who was the zalim, the aggressor. Today—under the guise of caste and class—the politicians of a city twist society into playing a double role, to being both the zalim and mazlum; the police are but a part of this society.

Karim Lala thinks more among the minorities should join the police force, it will be good for the watan. 'Not just constables like Ebrahim Kaskar, but afsars, officers who can wear their uniforms with pride, speak with dignity to the hukumat and pull up the juniors to their level of understanding. I am told their salaries are being increased too. And the awaam will benefit, the constables will not feel instigated to turn into killers during riots.'

But there is always this greed for more, greed just for greed's sake too, and sections of the police have turned as corrupt as the rest. People would be better off, minorities included, in educating themselves to take up more professional non-government jobs. Karim Lala's reply should delight the police, 'Why should the police be seen as a part of government? Yeh galat baat hai, police ka apna darjaa hona chahiye, answerable only to the President of India. About greed, why just the police, the hukumat has forgotten that it has to finally answer Allah. I think the people have also forgotten this. Paisa, paisa, paisa, kitna banayega paisa? Kitna leke jaayega upar?'

This was the thought uppermost in his mind when Karim Lala saw drugs coming into the trade. 'Sharaab bura, powder bahut bura. There is a lot of money in drugs, but I stayed away from it, can I even take a paisa up with me when I die? You can never leave drugs, not the buyer nor the seller, powder sey aadmi kabhi nahi nikal sakta, sharaab phir bhi chhuthta.' Karim Lala—enjoyer of Chivas Regal and the mujras at Bachoo Seth Ki Wadi—stopped drinking overnight when he felt that he was enjoying it so much that he would definitely die in a drunken haze, and how then would he face Allah in that alcoholic state?

For all this, Allah rewards him and protects him. 'Allah bahut bachaata hai humko. During the riots people were selling sophisticated arms to anyone who wanted to buy them and could afford AK-47s, I was tempted to buy one for my protection but something told me not to.' Came Bombay's bomb blasts and the sellers were arrested. They listed the names of their buyers. 'I must have done

something right to reach till here and be rewarded with this
level of contentment. Haan, bahut maaramari kiya, rampuri
chalaaya, par uske liye bahut bura din bhi dekha.'

A lean, handsome man with swift indentations as
features turned jowly, folds of grief on his face. It was that
tumultuous time when there were bloodbaths, constable
Ebrahim Kaskar's son, Dawood, was trying to take over
Bombay's underworld. In the late sixties and early seventies
the Pathan syndicate had flexed its muscle, sending
Dawood Ibrahim scurrying for cover. Alamzeb, Alamgir,
Amirzada and Karim Lala's nephew Samad Khan were hot
on his heels. In the early eighties Amirzada had Dawood's
brother, Sabir, shot dead. Amirzada was arrested and
produced at the Esplanade Court, Dawood had him shot
dead on the court premises itself by David Pardesi to whom
he had given a supari; a contract, of Rs 50,000.

Samad Khan, incensed at the killing of his childhood
friend Amirzada, went on a rampage. He also picked up a
carbine and tried to storm Dawood's then bastion at
Musafirkhana, 33 Pakmodia Street in Dongri; he sprayed
the huge door with bullets. Dawood waited until Samad
Khan was returning from seeing his girlfriend, twenty-six
bullets were pumped into him as he was coming out of the
lift. Later Karim Lala's younger brother, Rahim Lala, was
shot dead by the Dilip and Aziz duo at Sankli Street in
Byculla.

Karim Lala swore revenge, he chalked it out
strategically, before he set out on his mission he went for
Ummrah, the main Haj he would do later; and at this minor
pilgrimage he was roped into a truce effort with Dawood

Ibrahim. He met Dawood Ibrahim in Mecca, after that they left each other alone. 'He invited me to his brother's wedding in Dubai a long time ago, I went,' recalls Karim Lala. 'After that no contact, I am told he is in Karachi.' He shakes his head, dismissing Dawood with it, 'Yeh aaj ka maahaul bahut ajeeb hai, gang war nahi naukar war ho gaya. Today's times are strange, there are not even gang wars any more, they are servant wars. Someone is sitting in Dubai, someone else in sitting in Malaysia, someone is sitting in hukumat, and they are not coming out to fight themselves, like men; they are sending their naukar, jaao isko maar ke aao, usko dara ke aao. Yeh kaunsa mardaangi hai?'

Another 555, tea on the lushly landscaped terrace, Karim Lala sticks the blunt edge of a new matchstick into the brown film of cream forming on his hot tea, with a swift swoop swirls it around the stick and flings it into the bin by his side. He debates aloud on whether he should ask for a snack, his man Friday brings him two differently coloured capsules in a transparent pill box. 'Khaana maangta, dawaii deta,' he smiles ruefully that he asks for food and is given medicine. 'Parhezi hai, shakkar hai, but I keep telling my wife and daughters, how can my sugar level decrease if they think they have put me on a diet and I know when I am eating the sweets? Hum ko khaane ka, hum khaayenga, khushi-khushi jaayenga.'

His attention goes to a limp sapling on the terrace-bed, 'Oye,' he yells at his man Friday, 'you all are not even reeding that which requires it. Where is that gardener?' He is informed that the gardener left the job yesterday. 'Tell him I want to see him, send for him, bolo Karim Khan bulaaya.' He slowly gets up from his rocking chair and makes his way to the pained plant, tends to it with gentleness, sighs, 'You pay them so much, yet it has become so difficult to find a decent maali in this city.'

Days can pass like this, with his plants and the newspapers on his terrace, with sneaked cigarettes and sweets; sometimes people visit if they have a problem with a particular Pathan and request Karim Lala to speak to him, he invariably obliges if he remembers who they are; he has his increasing memory lapses punctuated with sharp bursts of lucidity. When he descends the steep steps of his building, he reluctantly attends social functions like the wedding at Radio Club where he did not approve of the food. He prefers to visit his once-kingdom, Dongri, and his Karim Hotel on Jail Road South which his relatives now run; he has no son and this is his regret. 'I would have liked him to have taaleem, education, which I myself have not had and realize its importance now. I tell everyone today, educate your children well, it will be more powerful for their future than your giving them a ghoda in their hand. Leave revolvers in the hands where they belong, the police. And the times have become such that they will have to use it on the gangs in encounters.' He pronounces it as 'counters'.

Elsewhere in Karim Lala's Bombay-watan, police officer Vijay Salaskar readies for yet another encounter. Members of the public refuse to come forward and give evidence against crimes committed in their localities. This lack of evidence coupled with judicial delays results in criminals remaining free, becoming bolder. 'Counter specialist' Salaskar is doing his job, it is just that. 'Earlier I was fascinated with this crack job, not anymore. Now I think it is just work that I am doing for as long as God wishes.'

There is a long overdue ordinance in place, the Maharashtra Control of Organized Crime Act 1999 which stipulates that a criminal booked under it must be produced in court within twenty-four hours and once booked, cannot be released on bail for ninety days; punishment includes death sentence, long imprisonment and fines up to five lakh rupees. To be booked under this ordinance the criminal must have a cognizable offence registered against him in the last ten years. And for this he has to get arrested; there are only 2.61 police personnel for every one thousand of population in the city, the lowest ever in Bombay's history. This includes the police who guard politicians and provide bandobast for visiting VIPs, dharmas and rallies. 'Tikdey shambhar maansa taakun dya' as the political edict normally reaches the police, 'Put a hundred men there', in effect an order to stop protection to 38,314.176 Bombayites for the better part of that day.

Vijay Salaskar is saved bandobast and other tedious duties but he may not be able to save himself from a bullet. 'The future may stop being kind to me in the next few hours,' it occurs to him as he checks with his informers and confirms the trap laid at the servants' quarters near KEM Hospital in the mill area of Parel. 'I could get shot first.' He shakes himself out of it, re-focusses'.

'Wait for two more days,' he tells his man on the mobile, 'if he has to escape let him but do not let him know that a trap has been laid or else he will blacklist the shelter and not allow our target to reach there.'

The next morning at 7.30 a.m., his cell phone buzzes. The target is coming to the servants' quarters today, time unknown. Salaskar and his policemen reach the spot quietly. It is an uneasy wait, no movement—apart from the milling crowds—for two hours. At 11 a.m., two persons arrive on a sleek new motorcycle, the pillion rider is Zahoor Makhanda, Chota Shakeel's manager, wanted for several murders, the man who helped gangster Feroze Konkani escape from J.J. Hospital last year. In the next few minutes the job is done. Salaskar heads for Nagpada police station to complete this case's paperwork. One more down, even the gangsters have lost track of how many more to go.

But of what use are ordinances and guns on what once used to be every one's watan, when the enemy is within. At this very moment it is making its presence felt at the Azad Maidan. The central venue has been deliberately chosen to send out their militant message in India's financial capital, five thousand youth wearing saffron have been brought in from various parts of Maharashtra and are intently listening to speaker after speaker invoke religious pride. 'Ayodhya sirf jhanki hai, Mathura Kashi baaki hain.' 'We have shown them we mean business, now it is time to prove our numerical superiority.' 'We have to ensure their submission because it is their international conspiracy to weaken Hindu India.' 'The Christians convert our people through their missionaries.' 'The Muslims' early morning azaan actually has instructions for them on what to do to us during each day.' The youth applaud.

One of the two elderly gentlemen who have been watching the proceedings from the side remarks to the other, 'This Bajrang Dal is not to.be taken seriously; they won't really do anything.' It's what many had said of the Shiv Sena during its inception.

Meanwhile martial images of mythology are being invoked to prove that the gods, indeed, believe in ethnic cleansing. The youth cheer.

It is merely the run up to India's and Maharashtra's future elections, just that distant clap of thunder over a near-dead city.